NOBLE
CHASE

NOBLE CHASE

A Novel

Michael Rudolph

Ballantine Books / New York

Copyright © 2016 by Michael Rudolph

All rights reserved.

Published in the United States by Ballantine Books, an imprint of Random House, a division of Penguin Random House LLC, New York.

BALLANTINE and the HOUSE colophon are registered trademarks of Penguin Random House LLC.

ISBN 978-1-101-88437-9
ebook ISBN 978-1-101-88438-6

Printed in the United States of America on acid-free paper

randomhousebooks.com

9 8 7 6 5 4 3 2 1

First Edition

Title-page images: copyright © iStock.com / © DigiClicks

Book design by Victoria Wong

3 1350 00351 2870

This publication is dedicated to my wife, Elizabeth, a nine-letter word meaning "Love of My Life." For thirty-five years, she has shared the fun, the excitement, and the terror of sailing with me, both figuratively and literally.

NOBLE CHASE

Prologue

The airwaves crackled with static, so he adjusted the squelch on the VHF radio. Then his scalp started to itch, so he lifted up the back of his hairpiece to scratch the offending spot. She was irritated by the gesture but stood by silently. Finally, he picked up the microphone and sent out the first distress call. "Mayday, Mayday, Mayday. This is *Satin Lady*," he went on, panic building in his voice, and then he repeated, "Mayday, Mayday, Mayday." Channel 16 went instantly quiet. It was an unnatural silence.

The Coast Guard constantly monitored channel 16 and was the first to respond. "*Satin Lady, Satin Lady*," he heard the radio operator say, "this is the United States Coast Guard station on St. Thomas. Give us your position and the nature of your emergency. Over."

He did not reply.

"*Satin Lady* . . . this is the United States Coast Guard. I repeat. Do you copy? Over."

He put the mike to his mouth again. "Yes, Coast Guard. We've hit a reef that's put a big hole in us. We're sinking. We need help!" This time he released the transmit button.

"Okay, *Satin Lady*. We copy. Give us your position. Over."

"I don't know our current position. . . . Water is filling the cabin." His transmission was becoming fragmented.

The anonymous radio operator heard the panic and tried to be reassuring. "*Satin Lady,* stay calm now. Can you give us the time and place of your last known location and your speed since then?"

"We left Fajardo yesterday. Our original heading was 315 degrees northwest. Last night we were seventy or seventy-five miles north of San Juan. We're in a fifty-two-foot sportfisherman with a big tuna tower and a dark blue hull." He kept depressing and then releasing the transmit button on the microphone, sometimes right in the middle of a sentence.

"That's good information, *Satin Lady,* but your voice keeps breaking up. We'll get help to you soon. Is anyone injured? Over."

"I have a woman with me. She hurt herself when we bounced off that reef. She's bleeding badly from the head. The life raft is floating away. It must have come untied. I think we're going down. Help us."

"Do you have an EPIRB on board? It'll help us get a radio fix on you." The young Coast Guard radio operator pronounced the familiar acronym with a thick Spanish accent that made it barely intelligible.

"Do I have a what? I don't understand you."

"An EPIRB. Do you have an emergency position indicator? It looks like a small handheld radio. Over."

"I don't know where it is. We only chartered this boat a few days ago."

"Okay, then, *Satin Lady*. Don't stop to look for it now. First give us a long count to ten. We're trying to locate your position."

"One, two, three . . ." Then silence before it was completed.

"Hang in there, *Satin Lady,* we're on our way. Stand by the radio if you can." The Coast Guard operator looked over at the watch officer, a petty officer second class who had been monitoring the entire transmission, got his permission, and immediately notified Base San Juan. They initiated a general alert.

There was no further communication from *Satin Lady*.

Base San Juan immediately dispatched its closest patrol boat to the scene. The night was clear, the moon full, and visibility good, but nothing was sighted.

The next morning, a sailboat cruising to St. Thomas located a patch of debris floating well outside the search area. They retrieved a partially inflated life raft with the name *Satin Lady* stenciled in blue letters, some bloodstained clothing, and a fouled mess of nylon fishing line still attached to a splintered fiberglass fishing rod. When they docked at Charlotte Amalie later that afternoon, they turned the articles over to the Coast Guard.

Chapter One

The couple walked toward their table, following the circuitous path taken by the maître d'. The dinner crowd at Le Bernardin was its typical group of affluent regulars, yet their cumulative attention was drawn magnetically to the newcomers. Beth looked straight ahead, enjoying the attention. She couldn't tell if C.K. noticed the stares, but if he did, he ignored them.

Beth accentuated her height with a strong athletic stride equally comfortable in a courtroom or on the playing fields of Central Park. On a shelf back in her office, she prominently displayed a coveted Golden Glove Award won in the Metropolitan Lawyers Softball League.

She had inherited blond hair and pale blue eyes from her northern Italian father, intellect and persistence from her Hungarian mother. Her taupe woolen suit was a conservative statement she reserved for clients.

Chun Keun Leung was Taiwan Chinese and wealthy. He was only slightly taller than Beth and had straight black hair with a touch of gray at the temples. He wore a navy chalk-stripe suit and walked with the confidence of one in authority. He was accustomed to being the center of attention.

Some of the diners glanced skeptically at their own dinner

dates and knew with prurient certainty what the attractive woman was doing to satisfy the Asian gentleman. It was all malicious conjecture, of course. The truth was less satisfying than their imagination. The couple was there on business. An attorney out with her client. In fact, they had just met.

The maître d' presented them with the evening's elaborate menu before leaving their table. Their first real conversation of the evening was a discussion of what to order. Beth smiled and nodded to mask her difficulty in understanding her client's accented English.

Minutes later, the waiter approached the table, took their orders, and left. He was followed shortly by the wine steward, who listened to Leung's order and then complimented him on his expert selection. Leung ignored the compliment.

To Beth, everything about the meal was the embodiment of the image she had of life as a lawyer: Supreme Court victories and dinners in four-star restaurants to celebrate them. The perks of winning a $105 million judgment were infinitely better than the exhaustion of losing one. Losers invent excuses. Winners get bonuses. Her initial reluctance to meet Leung for the first time at a dinner instead of in her office disappeared with the weight of his praise and a glass of Taittinger Comtes.

After the flurry of waiters descended and left, C.K. raised his glass for a toast. "A fine champagne is the only drink appropriate for the acknowledgment of a fine achievement." Beth smiled as he continued. "And so, to the distinguished attorney who obtained that remarkable eight-figure judgment against Jasco for us. Here's to a job well done." He drank and put down his glass.

"That's very kind of you. I appreciate it." Beth smiled broadly and took a sip from her bugle-stemmed glass. She had listened to the toast with only half an ear, yet something in it struck a discordant note. She replayed the toast in her mind, then attributed it to her difficulty with his accent. She took another sip of the champagne and the concern disappeared.

"Oh, before I forget," C.K. said, "could you arrange to have the Jasco files shipped to us in Taiwan?"

"Of course. They take up most of two file cabinets."

"I can imagine."

"Are you sure you want it all? We can scan it for you instead."

"No, send the actual files. We make a habit of retaining closed files in our home office."

"Not a problem. We can always use the storage space. I'll have my assistant take care of it."

"I'd appreciate that. Do you have any other Paramount files in your office?"

"Not as far as I know," she responded. "Jasco was the only one we were handling."

"Would you check just to be certain?" The absence of any inflection in his voice made it more of an order than a question.

"Of course. I'll circulate a memo to all the other attorneys." It was easier for her to do it than explain to him why it wasn't necessary.

"I would appreciate that. If anything else should turn up, have your assistant call my office."

"Are you looking for anything in particular?" Her receptors had been dulled by the adulation and blurred by his accented English.

"No, not at all, but my conservative father is fanatical about the preservation of paper records. He feels that no matter how old it is, you'll need it desperately the day after you discard it." He dismissed her question with the knowing shrug of children sharing the foibles of their parents.

"I understand," she acknowledged. "I'll have my assistant call one way or the other."

"Thank you."

"You know, it was quite a surprise when you called from Taiwan last week to set up this date. We all thought Leonard Sloane owned Paramount Equities."

"We create that impression on purpose. My brothers and I let our local people run their operations with as little interference as possible from Taiwan."

"What's the advantage of that?"

"It's cheaper. More efficient. But I suppose we really do it to avoid paying too high a price for regional prejudice. There's always one price for foreigners and one for the locals."

"How do you maintain control, then?"

"We control the checkbook. Every business of ours employs a family member who signs every check, and we always use a branch of Fidelity Bank."

"How come?"

"Because they're headquartered in Taiwan and I sit on their board of directors." He smiled and lifted his wineglass as he spoke, in an effortless gesture that exposed a magnificent sapphire-and-diamond cuff link and a solid gold Rolex watch encrusted with diamonds.

"Where else do you have operations?" she asked, thinking how nice it would be to get a big chunk of that business into the law firm. She made no effort to break off the eye contact he had encouraged.

"We're pretty much worldwide now, mostly real estate. We own and operate properties in Asia and Europe, of course, the United States, the Middle East, not so much in Africa."

"It must keep you running around."

"It does. Are you the name partner in Wilcox, Swahn and Giles?"

"No, that's my stepfather, Max Swahn. He retired as senior partner a few years ago. Clifford Giles runs the firm now."

"Does your stepfather practice law anymore?"

"He and my mother live on a sailboat down in the Caribbean, but he can't resist getting involved. He's working with me now on an article I'm writing about the Jasco case. The *NYU Law Review* wants to publish it."

"I'd like to read it when you're done."

"I'll be happy to send you a copy." Leung didn't know about her intensely competitive nature, and she wasn't going to give him any of that insight. He didn't know that winning was expected of her and that acknowledgment was her Achilles' heel.

"I'll also forward it on to our international trade association in Taipei. I'm sure they'll want to circulate it among the members."

"Terrific. The case had merit. I was just the catalyst," she continued modestly.

"Don't diminish your role. We dislike paying legal fees as much as anyone, but your firm's fifteen percent was well earned." He leaned to one side as the waiter placed their desserts on the table.

"Thank you," Beth said automatically for what seemed the hundredth time during the meal. She didn't correct Leung about their contingency fee—5 percent, not 15 percent—but her antennae were up. This was one mistake too many. "Did Leonard ever send you a copy of the court's decision?" she asked, concern displacing complacency.

"No, I don't think so."

"I'll make sure a copy is emailed to you tomorrow."

"It's too bad that Leonard isn't around to invest the Jasco money in more real estate for us. He was excellent at locating distressed properties."

"Hearing about his death last month was a shock," Beth replied. "Drowning at sea is a terrifying way to die."

"When I get finished interviewing the candidates for his job, I'll send my choice over to meet you. I also want you to know that your firm will continue to receive our legal work."

"I appreciate that," she said.

"There is one thing you can do for us now."

"What's that?" she asked. (Anything, C.K., she thought, just make it billable.)

"My brother Martin and I both graduated from Wesleyan University up in Connecticut. We want to set up a scholarship fund there in honor of Leonard Sloane."

"What a generous idea! That's very thoughtful of you."

"We would like your firm to handle the details."

"We'd be glad to."

"That's the main reason I wanted to meet you at dinner, so we could discuss the endowment without being interrupted."

"We can do it for you. How much of an endowment are you considering?"

"Well, the Jasco verdict was so unexpected, we thought we would take five percent of it."

"I'm sure Wesleyan will be thrilled." And, she thought, so will Clifford when he hears about the flow of new business we'll be getting from the Leungs.

"They already are. I called them this morning, gave them your name, and told them they'd have the 1.75 million in their hands by November first. Can you handle it by then?"

"That gives us two full weeks. Sure, no problem." Again, she took no issue with his error. Obviously, the endowment should have matched their fee, but nothing would be gained by calling his attention to it here in the restaurant. She needed to get more information first. "If you'll give me the name of your accountant," she suggested, "I'll contact him for the financial details."

"I'll leave his name and phone number with your assistant first thing tomorrow morning."

"Good," Beth responded, feeling increasingly uneasy. "We'll get started on it right away," she continued, now wishing the evening would come to an end.

"Excellent," he said. "Even after deducting your fees and the endowment, we still end up with twenty-eight million."

Beth's stomach contracted again involuntarily in reaction to his comment, and she felt the mother of all headaches begin to pound in her head. This man was her client. She had a legal obligation to say something to him, and she had to say it now to avoid misleading him by her silence.

Her face must have betrayed some distress, because C.K. suddenly looked at her quizzically. "Were you going to say something?"

"It was nothing. Would you excuse me for a second while I go to the ladies' room?" She pushed the chair back from the table, knocking her napkin off her lap onto the floor. She didn't bother to pick it up as she got up and made what she hoped was a graceful retreat. As she passed a mirror, she noticed that C.K. had gone back to his dessert.

Beth went into the ladies' room, wet a cotton towel that the matron handed her, and put it on the back of her neck. The matron, a kind, grandmotherly type, solicitously handed her tissues, mouthwash, and advice about overindulgence.

"Jesus, I look awful," she said out loud to the mirror. How could C.K. not know the size of the judgment? she asked herself as she stared at the miserable reflection. If he thinks it was only for $35 million, then what about the $70 million in punitive damages? He must know about them too, right? "Right!" she assured her unconvinced mirror image.

Beth left the ladies' room and pulled out her cellphone. First she tried Clifford's home phone and then his cell, but was intercepted on both by his voicemail. She hung up without leaving a message.

She reassembled her shattered composure, took a deep breath, and went back out to finish what remained of the dinner. "You know, C.K., your math is off a bit," she announced without any preamble as she sat back down at the table, wondering if that wasn't the understatement of the year.

"What do you mean?"

"We collected a hundred and five million from Jasco." She looked closely at his face for a reaction. "Our contingency fee was five percent, not fifteen percent, so even after we deducted it, you still netted close to a hundred million."

"I beg your pardon." C.K. looked straight at her, his face impassive, his eyes fixed. He didn't blink. In a movement of exquisite deliberation, he slowly took another bite of his cake, chewed, swallowed, and put the fork down.

"I said you netted nearly a hundred million." The pounding in her head got louder.

"That's a little confusing. Leonard reported we collected thirty-five million and that your fee was fifteen percent. He wired us a little less than thirty million."

"Well, I don't know what Leonard said to you, or what he wired you, but our fee was five percent, and the gross collection was one hundred and five million. It was all wired into Paramount's account here, but it was your Chase Bank account, not Fidelity."

"Well, I'm certain it's just a bookkeeping error in our New York office. I told you things were a little bit disorganized because of Leonard's death. The money must still be in the bank here. I'll look into it tomorrow."

"Good. Let me know what you find out." Beth was impressed. Seventy million dollars unaccounted for and Leung treats it like a three-dollar bank charge. That's one cool dude, she thought, and no doubt a bad guy to mess with.

When they left the restaurant, Leung's stretch limousine was outside waiting for him. Beth declined without hesitation when C.K. took her arm and asked her if she would like to go over to the Plaza Hotel for a nightcap. He neglected to mention he was staying there, but she already knew that. There was no mistaking the look that accompanied his invitation. Beth parried with a big blond smile and let C.K. handle the pregnant pause.

Safely ensconced back in her apartment, she immediately dialed Clifford again, but with the same result. She tried the marine radio operator down in Tortola on the chance that Max might still be awake and have the radio on, but that was also a dead end. Ditto for his cellphone.

She was too keyed up to sleep, so she turned on her laptop to review the electronic Jasco file. She read it and then reread it, desperately searching for warning signs she might have missed. She only knew that if there was a lapse, it must have happened during that hectic week last August when she was preparing the Jasco settlement documents.

Chapter Two

ic transit gloria. Max's favorite expression burned through Beth's mind the next morning. Aspirin and coffee failed to alleviate her condition. Anxiety increased when she got out of the shower and realized that she had just missed Clifford's return call. Working out at her brown belt karate class didn't help, and neither did the cool October air on her walk to the office. Beth would have preferred to die quietly and with a semblance of dignity in the privacy of her own apartment, but that wasn't going to happen. She had to face the aftermath of last night's discovery. Dinner with C.K. had turned into a Greek tragedy, chorus and all.

The early morning sun tormented her by streaming through the office window, careening off the glass covering her Columbia Law School diploma, bouncing onto her laminated Certificate of Admission, and then piercing through her eyes straight into her skull. She repeatedly caught herself staring unconsciously at the framed photograph of Max and her mother on her desk, the two of them smiling ecstatically at her from the cockpit of *Red Sky*.

She needed to speak to Clifford. She also needed to speak to Max. What would Max have done differently to prevent this debacle? Nothing, she prayed. She wished she had asked him for help instead of going it alone when Clifford insisted that everyone in corporate was too busy. Over and over she asked herself the same question: Had she screwed up?

The Paramount file was spread all over her desk and the conference table. No matter how she twisted around, she couldn't get comfortable. If it wasn't the sun, it was the telephone ringing or the intercom buzzing. This was most definitely not her day.

She examined the paper file for nearly three hours while waiting for Clifford to come back from court. She wanted to be ready for the questions he would surely ask. She checked each document. The answers weren't there, or at least if they were, she couldn't find them.

Paramount Equities had purchased a newly constructed condominium complex in Dallas from Jasco National Bank in 2004, right in the middle of the subprime mortgage loan frenzy that nearly destroyed the banking industry. Jasco had financed the construction of the complex and was then forced to foreclose when the builder went bankrupt.

When Jasco promised Paramount that they would obtain qualified buyers for the units in the complex, and would finance those purchasers with 95 percent loans, the deal fit right into the distressed-property paradigm that Paramount had been using successfully for several years. They had no trouble raising enough money to buy the property.

Within eighteen months, Jasco provided Paramount with buyers for the units, financed the purchases, and then sold the whole basket of mortgages to a teachers' pension fund. The investment quickly went south for all of the participants. Instead of pocketing huge profits, Paramount lost most of its money when the mortgages on the units went into default. It turned out that Jasco's chief loan officer had been conspiring with a group of real estate brokers to create buyers using grossly

inflated false financial statements and bogus property apprais-
als. It was no satisfaction that Jasco's loan officer went to jail
together with four of the real estate brokers.

Paramount sued Jasco for fraud and lost when a jury decided that Jasco was not liable for the criminal acts of its loan
officer. Paramount immediately fired their president and hired
their outside accountant, Leonard Sloane, to be the new president. Sloane's first act as president was to hire Clifford for the
appeal. He paid an advance retainer up front and agreed to an
additional 5 percent contingency fee if they were successful.

Clifford let Beth handle the whole appeal, so all the corre-
spondence in the file was between her and Sloane. She reviewed
the banking resolutions and the settlement resolutions she had
prepared when she won the appeal, particularly anything that
related to using Paramount's account at Chase instead of Fidelity. Sloane had signed all the docs in his office and had them
countersigned or witnessed by other people there. She couldn't
read their names then; she couldn't read them now. She remembered Sloane complaining that he had no notary public over
there, so Beth's legal assistant, Carmen, had even notarized the
signatures.

The insistent buzz of the intercom broke through her intense concentration. "Beth," she heard her name spoken with
the soft southern drawl of Clifford's secretary, "Mr. Giles just
came back."

"Can he see me, Constance?"

"He says he's got an early lunch date and another meeting
starting at two. Can y'all wait until he gets back from lunch at
one thirty?" The question carried the slightly superior tone that
only a senior partner's secretary could affect.

"No, tell him it's very important." Getting in to see Clifford
Giles was a negotiation in itself.

"Okay, just a moment."

The intercom went silent. Beth just waited and stared as the red hold light flashed hypnotically and flashed and flashed and flashed.

"Beth?" the intercom finally spoke again.

"Yes, Constance . . . I'm still here."

"He says okay. But try and make it a short one."

"I'm on my way." She collected the Paramount file and walked down the hall to Clifford's corner office. His door was closed, but as Constance nodded her head toward it, Beth knocked and walked in. The tall, properly gaunt, silver-haired Giles was seated behind his desk, a page out of *Gentlemen's Quarterly,* impeccably dressed in a three-piece suit, vest correctly buttoned, with an ancient unlit Dunhill pipe clenched firmly in his teeth.

"Elisabeth. Come in. I'm so far behind schedule today. I never should have taken that long weekend."

"I know you're jammed, but I wanted to grab you before you went out to lunch."

"The court calendar took forever this morning. The defendant's attorney never showed up, so Judge Blackstrop adjourned the damn thing. A total waste of time." A heavy pipe smoker for many years, he puffed vigorously away on the unlit pipe until suddenly the involuntary heaving of his chest alerted her to the approach of one of his coughing spasms. Clifford reached for his ever-present handkerchief, while Beth pretended not to notice his discomfort. "Hey, you don't look so all-fired great this morning. Do you feel okay?" he asked.

"I'm a little under the weather today," she replied.

"Better take care of yourself."

"I will. It must be the wine and French food I had with C. K. Leung last night."

"How did it go?"

"We have a problem with the Paramount case."

"How so?"

"I don't think Sloane ever sent the punitive damage money to Taiwan."

"What do you mean?"

"All I know is that until last night, C.K. thought we only collected thirty-five million."

Clifford's thoughtful expression didn't change as he calmly looked at his watch, picked up the phone, and rang his secretary on the intercom.

"Yes, Mr. Giles."

"Constance. Do me a favor, will you?" His voice betrayed no concern. "Call up Harry Vicardi at Case Investments. Tell him something's come up and I need to cancel our lunch date. Reschedule it for next week."

"Yes, Mr. Giles."

"And ask Frank Epstein to come into my office if he's free."

"Yes, Mr. Giles."

Seeing that she now had his full attention, Beth shifted around slightly in her chair and began to give him a detailed account of everything she had done on the Paramount case since her victory in the New York Court of Appeals.

Chapter Three

On board *Red Sky*, Max Swahn awoke at six. He got out of the queen-size bunk in the aft cabin and kissed Andi on the forehead in response to her peaceful yawn. He ignored the ravenous expression on Marylebone's face and went up on deck. Not dissuaded, the big gray Persian followed him up the ladder, meowing piteously until Max dutifully scratched him behind the ears.

The morning dawned across the still waters of Savannah Bay, first announcing itself as a dark red glow on the horizon, backlighting the few clouds remaining in the sky. Impelled by the urge to record yet another magnificent sunrise for posterity, Max went back down into the cabin and quickly returned with a camera from his collection, a classic Leica IIIf in nearly mint condition. He set up his ever-present tripod and fired happily away as the day's emerging colors traveled along the light spectrum before bursting into a crisp, brilliant white sunrise across the bay.

He then released the swim ladder over the transom and jumped into the water, swimming his twenty laps around *Red Sky*. Another sailboat had come into the bay during the night, anchoring some distance away.

After drying himself off, Max went below into the galley to

make coffee. As the smell of the fresh brew permeated the boat, he heard Andi stirring in the aft cabin. In a minute, she came up behind him in the galley and jammed her body against his. "Good morning, Maximilian," she said in a voice still heavy with sleep. He felt her pressing against his back and decided that the coffee could wait. Andi, despite the clear evidence of Max's interest, wanted coffee first. She poured coffee for both of them and then climbed up out of the cabin to enjoy her coffee in the cockpit. Max followed her up, sitting on the other side of the cockpit to drink his.

"What do you want to do today?" she asked between sips.

"I really ought to go up the mast and fix that spinnaker halyard. That is, if you're in a mood to winch me up in the bosun's chair."

"Let me know when you're ready to go up."

"I also promised Beth I'd work on our law review article. Maybe I'll give her a call on Skype later."

"Good. She's proud of that case."

"She has a right to be. Clifford's finally stopped needling me for hiring her."

"I know. Now he's taking credit for it."

"She's earned a place for herself in the firm. . . . And on her own merit too."

"You need to tell that to Beth. She thrives on your approval."

"I know she does."

"She needs reassurance from you."

"She can take care of herself."

"It's hard for me to believe sometimes."

"Look, she's brilliant like me, she's practically a black belt in karate, and she learned about firearms from that FBI guy she dated, so don't be so protective." Coming from Max, it sounded more like a demand than a suggestion.

She was quiet, trying hard to suppress the feeling that her motherhood had just been invalidated. "Did they hear anything new about Len Sloane and Erica Crossland?"

"Beats me. What made you think of them?"

"When you mentioned the law review article, I guess."

"She's dead, Andi. They both drowned. Let it go."

"I'm still pissed she hit on you when we flew up for the office Christmas party last year."

"She was drunk because Chase Bank passed her over for promotion. I thought you'd get a kick out of the way I handled it considering we had just met Sloane and her."

"Do you love me?"

"Yes, I love you."

"Then can I have another cup of coffee?"

"Right."

They talked over their coffee for a while longer. Finally, Max got up and went below into the cabin. He rinsed out his cup, then tuned the VHF radio to channel 16.

The early morning chatter coming over the radio was routine. He checked the weather channel as a matter of habit, but the report was pretty much like always, "sunny, warm, and chance of a shower or two in the late afternoon." He then went back up topside. Andi had just finished her morning swim and was drying herself off with one of the big navy-blue bath towels that had been a retirement gift from Max's ex-wife. The name *Red Sky* was embroidered in red script.

"Might as well handle that broken halyard now," he suggested.

"I'm ready if you are."

He got the bosun's chair out of the port locker in the cockpit and took it over to one of the several wire halyards running up the mast. The halyards were used to raise and lower the various sails being used on *Red Sky,* except that in this case they would be used to raise and lower him.

"You look thrilled, Max."

"Let's get it over with." Having Andi winch him up the sixty-foot mast suspended in a bosun's chair was not one of his favorite experiences. She was half his weight, but heights terrified her. In any event, the bay was calm today and the boat was sitting quietly in the water. The mast wouldn't be shaking. He would be shaking.

He attached the bosun's chair to the snap shackle on one of the halyards and handed the other end over to Andi. She wrapped the halyard around one of the winches a few times, but before she could start hoisting him away, a voice from the VHF radio in the cabin interceded. "This is Tortola Radio calling *Red Sky,*" the radio squawked. "Tortola Radio calling *Red Sky.*" The call was repeated three times.

"Saved by the bell," he muttered, quickly and gratefully unhooking himself from the halyard. He went below, followed by Andi on the ladder right behind him, lifted the microphone from the radio, and depressed the transmit button. "Tortola Radio, Tortola Radio, this is *Red Sky.* Over." He released the button.

"*Red Sky,* this is Tortola Radio, we have a call for you from New York. Turn to channel twenty-seven and stand by."

Max reached up and switched channels in time to hear the operator say, "New York, this is Tortola Radio, we have *Red Sky* for you, go ahead, please."

"Hello, Dad." Beth's voice sounded strangely remote.

"Hi, love. How come you used Tortola Radio?"

"Your cell wasn't ringing. You must be in a dead zone for a change. How's Mom?"

"She's standing right here beside me, naturally, waiting to

grab the mike out of my hands. Is everybody okay? You sound preoccupied."

"Everybody's fine, Dad. I had lunch last Saturday with Shari and Lynn. They're both fine. Craig is fine. Grandma is fine. But Clifford and I need to talk to you about something. Can you get to a landline and give us a call later today? Over."

Max heard the concern in her voice and knew that she wouldn't be sending him to a landline about some routine matter. Anyhow, his curiosity would not be satisfied until he could get to a telephone. "We can sail over to Road Town on Tortola and be there by two o'clock or so this afternoon. Suppose I call you guys around three?"

"Fine, Dad. . . . Sorry I can't really talk now. Give my love to Mom. I'll speak to you later and explain everything then. Bye now." The abrupt click at the other end indicated that she had hung up the phone. Max stared at the radio, half expecting the conversation to continue.

"Don't you just love these little anxiety creators?" Andi said.

He nodded in agreement. "Tortola Radio," he then said as he keyed the mike. "Tortola Radio, this is *Red Sky*, Whiskey Alpha Yankee 4 2 7 6. We're finished with our call, thanks. This is *Red Sky* out."

"Okay, *Red Sky*. This is the Tortola Radio Marine operator. Have a nice day and thank you for using Tortola Marine."

He put the microphone back on the radio and looked at his wife. "As soon as we're ready, let's raise the anchor."

"What do you think is the matter?"

"I don't know."

"Well, what do you think? You must have some idea." She was worried.

"I have no idea what it's all about," Max kept answering her repeated speculations. "You heard the exact same words over the radio I did. When we get to a phone over on Tortola, we'll know all the answers. Now, c'mon, let's get moving."

"Okay," she said, "I'll do last night's dishes while you make the bed and shave." She moved over to the galley as she talked.

"Right. There's a nice breeze out there today, so we'll sail over to Road Town and tie up at one of the marinas over by Wickham's Cay."

"Good idea," she replied, turning on the faucet and causing the electric pump to groan into action.

"Easy on the hot water. I need it more than those dishes."

"Don't worry. There's plenty."

Inside an hour, they were ready to go. Andi started up the diesel while Max winched up the anchor. It broke out of the sand and came up easily. In short order, they were motoring out of Savannah Bay. As Andi pointed *Red Sky* into the wind, Max raised the main and unfurled the genoa. When Andi turned off the engine, Max took over the steering, peering through his bifocal sunglasses while standing at the wheel. He took off his canvas tennis hat and tossed it smartly down through the hatch into the cabin below. Marylebone sniffed it briefly and then resumed his nap.

Red Sky was on a port tack, being pushed along at 8 knots by the warm, silent wind. Her wake was unbroken as she sailed in a northeasterly direction along the Sir Francis Drake Channel toward Road Town.

He enjoyed the wind blowing through his curly salt-and-pepper hair. His dark blue T-shirt covered the slight paunch that his appetite had created. His six-foot-two-inch frame had flourished as he discovered that even the most remote islands in the Caribbean sold junk food. "We might as well tack now," he said to Andi. "It'll save us time."

"Where's Marylebone?" she asked, and in response the cat's gray dust mop of a tail moved almost imperceptibly in the cabin below, just enough to indicate his presence. "I see him, he's okay," she said in answer to her own question, and then reached over to release the genoa sheet. "Go ahead and tack, Admiral. Me and the kitty are ready!"

"Calling that fat cat a 'kitty' is perjurious."

"Sssh, he's sensitive."

Chapter Four

The sun beating down on the dock was high and hot. Max tried his cellphone first, but, as usual, there was no signal. Then he walked over to the freestanding telephone booth next to the marina office and stood by the phone, a life-size statue dripping perspiration, waiting for an operator to place his call to New York.

When the call finally went through, the receptionist in the office didn't recognize his voice, asked him twice to repeat his name, once to spell it, and then finally put him on hold while announcing the call. Just great, he thought. My office, my partner, my daughter, and after two years of absence, some new receptionist puts me through the third degree. *Sic transit gloria.* He finally heard the call being rung through into Beth's office.

It was Clifford, however, who picked up the phone and spoke first. "Hi, Maximilian. I'm in the office with Beth and we have you on the squawk box. How are you and Alexandra?"

"She's shopping for food and I'm baking my brains out in this marina. Otherwise, we're both fine. Beth, how are you?"

"I'm okay, Dad," she said. "I have a long story to tell you, can you hear us?"

"Go ahead."

"It's about that Paramount-Jasco case. Remember I told you I was going to have dinner with C. K. Leung?"

"Of course I remember."

"I had that dinner with him last night."

"Good," he responded somewhat tersely, waiting for her to pass on to more relevant information.

"The first thing he told me was how pleased he was with the Jasco verdict. He assured me that we'd continue to get his legal work no matter who the new president was."

"Did the Coast Guard find Len or Erica?"

"Just the DNA identification from the blood on their clothing."

"Got it." He was anxious to have her get to the point. The other shoe, he thought, was waiting somewhere to be dropped.

"So," Beth went on, "all through dinner, C.K. is carrying on about how great a job I did."

"Sounds like the dinner was a testimonial."

"Right. And then during dessert, C.K. mentions to me that he and his brothers have decided to donate five percent of the Jasco recovery to set up a scholarship in Len's memory. That's when I realized we had a problem."

"How so?"

"He also tells me that the five percent contribution equals 1.75 million dollars. . . ."

"Are they also going to contribute five percent of the punitives?"

"That's the problem!" she blurted out. "Until I told him about it at dinner, C.K. didn't know that Paramount collected the extra seventy million. All he knew about was the thirty-five mil!"

"Max, the bottom line isn't very complicated," Clifford interjected. "Leonard Sloane never told the Leungs about the punitive damages and never sent them the money. He used Erica to set up a secret account in Paramount's name at Chase Bank and got the whole hundred and five million wired into that account. Then he wired thirty-five million to the Leungs in Taiwan, less our fees, naturally."

"And the other seventy million?" Max asked, already anticipating the answer.

"Gone," Clifford replied. "Erica handled the entire transaction from her office at Chase, and then erased any record of it from her computer."

"That was convenient."

"All Chase can figure out is that the seventy million was wired out the same day it hit the account, just before Labor Day, and that was six days before Sloane transferred the thirty-five million to Taiwan."

"Gave himself a real head start. Any chance C.K. knew about this?" Max asked.

"I'm convinced he had no idea, Dad, and I was too shell-shocked to question him at dinner. I only wanted to finish the meal and get away from the table so that I could talk to you and Clifford about it."

"Well, you did the right thing. Where's Leung now?" Max asked.

"He's flying back to Taiwan today," Clifford answered.

"What's our malpractice exposure?"

"I have a couple of the associates working on it," Clifford said. "We haven't called our insurance carrier yet."

"Good, we need some answers first."

"Exactly."

"Look, guys, maybe I'll fly up to the city tonight so we can discuss it face-to-face tomorrow morning. I'll call you back in a couple of hours."

"Okay, Max," Clifford said. "Get back to us as soon as you can."

"Goodbye, Dad," Beth whispered. "Sorry to lay this on you."

"Don't sweat it, kid, and don't waste your energy worrying. We'll figure out something." She was new to this kind of problem, and both the lawyer and the father in him tried to reassure her. "Goodbye, you two."

His mind was already racing through a hundred possible scenarios as he hung up the phone. As he walked back to the boat, the permutations increased. By the time he got back to *Red Sky,* his logic had narrowed them down again. Andi wasn't back yet. He found some old Maalox tablets and chewed a couple. When his wife got back to their slip an hour later, he thought he had sorted the conversation out enough to discuss it with her.

Andi saw his angry expression as she handed him the groceries and climbed on board. Unable to wait for her to even put the food away, he started to pour out the whole telephone call. "I just cannot believe how badly Beth got suckered in by that bastard." The more Max talked about it, the angrier he became. He stalked around the main cabin while Andi unpacked in the galley.

"Will you stop rambling and tell me what it all means?" Andi felt her own upset growing in direct proportion to his. It was clear her daughter was in trouble.

"She was too damn excited about winning the decision and too green to realize she was being scammed."

"What did she do wrong other than win a judgment for a hundred and five million?"

"It's real simple. The reason Sloane was able to get Jasco to wire the money into his phony Paramount bank account is because Beth never picked up on any of the warning signs."

"But she had no reason to see them. Sloane was able to set

it up because the Leungs trusted him. They're the ones who should have kept an eye on him. Beth was just the lawyer on the job." She was a protective mother defending a child from attack.

"Of course, of course. Len counted on Leung's absentee ownership to make the damn thing fly, but if Beth had been more careful, it could have been prevented, or at least it wouldn't have been so easy for him to pull off."

"Well, what could she have done? Nobody even knew Leung existed until after Len and Erica drowned. And where was Clifford during all of this?" Andi, never a pushover in any argument, was actively engaged in Beth's defense.

"I know, I know."

"So I'll ask you again: What should she have done? Leung didn't even know who his attorneys were until he saw the paid bill from Clifford."

"Sloane was no dummy. Look, the point is Beth should have checked out his authority before letting Jasco wire the funds into Chase. She didn't get one lousy little piece of verification from anyone else at Paramount to establish Sloane's authority to do anything, let alone open up an account at Chase. She took his word for everything. When he told her he didn't know where their corporate minute books were kept, that was the end of the due diligence as far as she was concerned."

"She trusted her client."

"She actually had a copy of their old banking resolution from Fidelity National Bank in the file. It required two signatures for all transactions. That alone should have warned her to be extra careful. She even let Sloane con her into notarizing the signature of some nonexistent officer at Paramount who supposedly countersigned the Chase banking resolution."

"Come on, Max. Even I can see that's just a lot of administrative nonsense. Len couldn't have pulled it off if Clifford had reviewed the paperwork."

"Maybe so, but he did pull it off."

"Does all that add up to malpractice?"

"That's what Clifford is having researched now. You might as well also know that Beth signed an opinion letter to Jasco's attorneys assuring them that the wire into Chase was completely authorized." He saw Andi's expression crumple at this, but he was still too angry to feel very supportive.

"If it's malpractice, won't your insurance cover the loss?"

"After we eat the hundred-thousand deductible, and then only if the malpractice wasn't intentional. You can be sure Leung will stick in a claim that it was, and that's not covered."

"But it was an accident. Beth didn't do it on purpose."

"It doesn't matter. There's no payoff for mistakes, accidental or intentional. And, by the way," he added ironically, "how do you think it's going to look to a jury when it comes out that Sloane personally paid Beth a twenty-five-thousand-dollar bonus?"

"Clifford told her to keep it!" she fought back in defense of her daughter. "Satisfied clients are allowed to give presents to their lawyers."

"Sure. Flowers, a case of wine, maybe even a watch, but Sloane's personal check should have been deposited in the firm account, not in Beth's. I can just see Leung's attorney arguing that it proves Beth was in on the entire scam."

"That's pure hindsight."

"Trials are all about hindsight."

"Then don't expect Beth to be omniscient."

"The thing that's got me so absolutely furious is that I got taken the same damn way when I first started practicing law thirty-five years ago, only that time the client actually filed a written complaint with the bar association."

"I didn't know. You never said anything to me about that."

"Yes, and before the bar association held a hearing and found me innocent, I had been fired from my job and my father nearly died from a heart attack. It took cardiologists three weeks to save his life." Max heaved with emotion at the memories.

"Oh, Max, I'm so sorry. That must have been terrible." She was distraught by their confrontation. His last disclosure brought her to tears.

"And that's why this is killing me, that Sloane should pull this off and then die, leaving Beth holding the bag." He shook his head sadly. "Her only sin is inexperience or overzealousness." He spoke regretfully now, blaming himself for her failure.

"So what now? Do you think we should go up to New York?"

"I told them I'd call back. I think maybe we should."

"You know what, better that Beth never had that damn dinner with Leung. He'd have never found out otherwise."

"Beth was right to be straight with him. We could never take a chance that Leung might find out himself one day."

"But then you could simply deny knowing anything about it. Paramount won a hundred and five million and Paramount collected a hundred and five million. What happened to the money afterwards wasn't Beth's problem."

"It's more pragmatism than anything else. Suppose there was a criminal conspiracy indictment because we failed to disclose."

"Why don't you call the Beef Island airport while I pack and see what's flying over to San Juan this afternoon? It'll be easy for us to catch a flight there for New York."

"Good idea." He was much subdued and exhausted by his rage. So was Andi.

Chapter Five

Beth could feel the adrenaline flowing and had to remind herself this was not an adversarial proceeding. "Stay cool!" she muttered one last time as she entered Clifford's office. She quickly scanned the expressions. Her stepfather on the couch. Clifford at his desk. Frank Epstein, over by the window, the buffer, sticking to the middle of the road like he always did.

New clients entering Clifford's office for the first time were confronted by him behind the desk, ringed by a couch and three overstuffed red leather chairs, surrounded by dark walnut paneling, and basking in smiles from framed photographs of him shaking hands with four Republican presidents. They knew immediately that they were in a secure place, being guided by competent and conservative counsel.

Beth bent down, kissed Max on his tanned cheek, and sat on the chair that he and Frank had left between them. The three men in Clifford's office each gave Beth a supportive look as they shifted into business gear. Thank God, she thought. Compared with last night's confrontation with Max, today would be easy. The pent-up frustration Max had accumulated during the flight up north had been vented on her with a fury she hadn't anticipated.

"Beth, I asked Frank to join us," Clifford opened the meeting. "His boys have been researching our little malpractice question." The mere use of the word *malpractice* was enough to make her skin crawl. "Why don't you bring us up-to-date on what we know as of this morning?"

"I spoke to Chase Bank again a few minutes ago."

"What did they have to say?"

"It's clear that Erica used her computer at Chase to set up a worldwide string of Paramount bank accounts controlled by Sloane. Chase has located three of them so far, but the money was long gone from each, in and out in hours. They're still working on it."

"Well, if we have to . . . ," Clifford said. "One of the best bank investigators in the business is a good friend of mine."

"You mean that Israeli guy Rheinhartz?" Max asked.

"Except he lives in Zurich now."

"Maybe you should give him a call."

Clifford nodded and then continued, "What did your research turn up, Frank? Do we have a malpractice problem?"

"It's pretty much a question of fact . . . ," he began.

"Like we tell our clients, huh?" Max commented dryly.

"Exactly. Beth had the right to rely on Sloane's authority unless she knew or should have known about some restriction. Like a lot of things, it all boils down to her due diligence and whether she was careful enough."

"That bonus check she deposited into her personal account won't help on that issue," Clifford said.

"I deposited that check on your specific instructions!" Beth charged in.

"I'm not saying you did it on your own," Clifford replied.

"The bastard was setting me up!"

"Clifford, you and Frank both knew that Beth was in over her head when she handled the closing documentation. She asked both of you for help."

"Oh, come on, Max," Clifford said. "Beth got caught on something that any novice should have avoided."

"Listen, she tried, but you were all too busy to provide oversight. That fee may have dulled Beth's caution, but it should have piqued yours." Max spoke calmly, but his voice was uncompromising. There was no question of his priorities.

"Yes, but she's the one that got nailed and it places us all on the spot. There's no need to personalize it."

"Then let's cut out this 'we' and 'she' crap. This is our joint problem." Max was an old hand at arguing with Clifford, no quarter given or asked. To hear them go at it, one would never suspect these were two lifelong friends. Beth had never heard it before. She was hard-pressed to sit there and listen to it, glued to her chair by the force of their vehemence.

"Come on, relax, you two." Frank was an imperturbable veteran of these encounters. "And I didn't mean to imply any fault either, Max. No one's pointing the finger at Beth."

"Frank, are the individual partners personally liable even though we're organized as an LLC?" Max asked.

"Without question. Section 1205 of the Limited Liability Company Law makes that clear. All partners are liable. I can go into more detail if you want."

"Not necessary," Clifford interrupted. "Save it for the brief. So, what are we going to tell Leung?" His question was largely academic. Both the code of ethics and their insurance policy demanded full disclosure.

"I don't see any choice," Beth offered. "Complete disclosure is our best protection. If we don't tell him something and he finds out on his own, then we have real trouble. It could be a whole lot more than malpractice. The downside risk is too great."

"Yes, I agree."

"We could be guilty of concealing a conspiracy."

"If there was a conspiracy, Beth."

"Oh, there was a conspiracy, Frank. Erica and Sloane had been planning it for a long time. One of the bank accounts Chase located in Providence was set up a year before we were even retained." She accidentally dropped her pen on the floor and mentally kicked herself for the clumsiness as she bent over to pick it up.

"How're you holding up to all this, Beth?" Frank's concern was genuine. "I remember the first time a client threatened me with a malpractice suit. It was only a ruse to avoid paying a fee, but the threat can be traumatic."

"Oh, I'm fine today. Yesterday wasn't so great, though," she admitted. "It's tough to learn that clients like Sloane can't be trusted."

"Yes, it's sobering to learn why so much of our time is devoted to protecting ourselves from our own clients."

"I guess covering your rear end is a fact of life, Clifford. It comes with the license to practice law. You all had to learn to do it. I learn quickly."

"You will." Max nodded reassuringly. "And your skin will get thicker."

"When are we going to call Leung?" Frank asked, looking at his wristwatch. "It's almost eleven p.m. in Taiwan, too late to reach him today. We'll have to try him tomorrow."

"No. I have his home number," Beth responded. "We might as well get him on the phone right now. Let's get it over with."

"It's your dime." Clifford moved his phone over toward her.

"I have a tape recorder with me if you want to use it." Frank took the tiny device out of his pocket and put it on Clifford's desk.

"I don't think that's such a good idea," Beth volunteered.

"It's one more thing we'd have to produce for discovery by the other side if there's ever a lawsuit. It could prove embarrassing."

"She's right." Max offered his support. "And unless we tell Leung about it, it's an invasion of privacy."

"I'd hate to think we're reduced to taping conversations we have with our clients," Clifford said.

"And what we tell him today won't be an issue anyhow," Beth continued. "After we finish the call, I'll email him a confirmatory letter with all the details. I'll circulate a draft to you before I send it."

"Good idea." Clifford joined her support group. "Anybody want some more coffee first?" Without waiting for their response, he called Constance on the intercom and asked her to bring in a fresh carafe.

"I've got a thousand things to do, Clifford. You don't need me to hang around for the phone call, do you?" Frank asked.

"No. No reason. Thanks. Listen, Max and I are going to have an early lunch over at the Harvard Club. Join us around noon?"

"Sorry, I can't make it," he said, getting up from his chair. "I already have a date." He walked out of the office, closing the door quietly behind him.

"How about you?" Clifford asked Beth.

"Thanks, but you'd better excuse me also," she said, knowing full well that Clifford wanted lunch alone with Max. Beth took the piece of paper with C.K.'s number out of her folder and reached over to the phone on Clifford's desk. After dialing the lengthy international number, she pressed the speakerphone button and sat back in her chair.

The speaker amplified the ringing throughout the silent office. The three lawyers stared at the phone, listening intently. In Taiwan, C. K. Leung answered on his private line.

"Mr. Leung?" Clifford asked. "This is Clifford Giles calling from Wilcox, Swahn and Giles in New York. How are you?"

"I am fine, thank you." His voice had a hollow sound as he continued. "I am sorry that we did not have the chance to meet when I was in New York earlier this week."

"Beth is here with me now. We have you on the speaker." He did not mention Max's presence.

"Well, hello there, Beth. How are you?"

"I'm fine, thanks, C.K." She shifted uncomfortably in the leather armchair next to Clifford's desk. "Sorry to bother you at home so late in the evening."

"Not at all. These days I always seem to be on the phone until ten or eleven o'clock. Business is a twenty-four-hour affair now. Have you sent back our files yet?"

"As a matter of fact, they're being packed up already. They'll probably go out this week."

"Good. Please take care of it for me."

"I will. Now, if you have some time, Clifford and I want to discuss the Jasco judgment with you. . . ."

"Of course."

Beth described the details of the embezzlement to Leung as accurately as she could. She told him only what she had learned and very little of what she concluded. He offered no comment as she spoke, he created no dialogue. Beth chose her words carefully to avoid ambiguity, following her own frequent advice to litigating clients: Always speak as if your conversation is being recorded. The occasional electronic beep she heard from Leung's end of the line confirmed the wisdom of her advice.

"Is the loss covered by your E and O insurance?" Leung interrupted her to ask at one point. Beth had anticipated the question but still felt her heart drop to the floor when she finally heard it asked.

"That's not really the issue," she responded with as much conviction as she could muster. "We've had the whole professional liability question thoroughly researched and our conclusion is that we acted properly."

"I have no doubts about the performance of your firm. You can hardly be faulted for winning. The issue is what happened after you won."

"Sloane was the president of Paramount," Beth continued confidently. "He was acting with both apparent authority and the actual authority you had given him." Max nodded with approval as he heard the assurance growing in Beth's voice.

"Of course." C.K.'s response conveyed nothing.

"I have to tell you something else for the record, C.K.," Clifford now interjected himself. "When it comes to the question of any potential liability that this firm may have, we're really in no position to give you an opinion because of the obvious conflict of interest. I suggest you consult with another law firm for any answers in that area. We would, of course, cooperate fully and completely."

"I understand." Again Leung was totally noncommittal.

"Have you reported this theft to the police yet?"

"We are still discussing that. Take no action at your end."

Beth started to say something, but Max, sensing her need to apologize, silenced her with a finger to his lips. He and Clifford did not want her to extend the conversation any longer than was absolutely essential to complete the disclosure to the client. They certainly didn't want her to start communicating any of her feelings of guilt to Leung over the phone.

When Clifford and Beth had finished talking to him, Leung

thanked them politely. He then hung up the phone and turned to the small book he kept by one of the several other phones sitting on the large desk. He found and dialed the number of the bank investigator in Zurich recommended by Fidelity Bank. When Dieter Rheinhartz answered at the other end, it was in German. Leung identified himself in English and arranged for a meeting in three days. He then placed a conference call to his brother Andrew in Seoul and his brother Martin in San Francisco.

The expected return call from Taiwan came in two days later, but it was not C. K. Leung on the phone. Constance announced on the intercom that there was a Mr. T. C. Chen on the phone from Taiwan, asking for Beth. "He says that he's an attorney representing the Leung family and that he knows Beth from college."

"Switch it over to Clifford's office, please."

Clifford and Max shot questioning looks at her as she entered, but she shrugged, indicating her lack of name recognition. "Put him through, Constance," Beth said as Clifford reached for the speakerphone button.

"Hello, Mr. Chen. This is Elisabeth Swahn."

"Tsing Chia Chen here," the youthful Chinese voice responded, hesitating when her lack of recognition became evident through the amplified phone. "Excuse me . . . ," he proceeded, "but weren't you friends with Brian Rhoden at Columbia?"

"I still am, but your name . . . I don't recall it."

"I rowed on the eight-man junior varsity crew with Brian. It wasn't that long ago, was it?"

"Brian did crew at Columbia, but—"

"Hey, wait a moment," he interjected. "My nickname in college was 'Charlie.' Does that help?"

"Of course. Now I remember." She didn't, but it seemed the diplomatic approach and she would check with Brian later. Her ex-fiancé never forgot a name. "How are you?"

"Fine. I returned to Taipei after graduating from Michigan Law School and have been practicing here ever since. I see from Martindale-Hubbell that you stayed on at Columbia."

"Yes. I went to Columbia Law. Does your firm represent C. K. Leung?"

"Yes, we do. He asked me to call you about that little problem with Paramount Equities. I thought I might use our old friendship to try to work things out with as little inconvenience as possible."

"Well, what do you have in mind?" Enough of that good-old-boy routine, she thought.

"Well, Mr. Leung first asked me to assure you that he is absolutely certain that neither you nor your firm had any intentional involvement in assisting the deceased Mr. Sloane. On the other hand, the Leung family has sustained a considerable loss and Mr. Leung feels that perhaps your firm was not as careful as it should have been."

"What do you suggest, Mr. Chen?"

"I do not suggest anything, Beth. But my client suggests that the whole matter could be resolved quickly and fairly if your firm were to return the fee it made on the case."

"Anything else?" There was no animosity in her question, merely a request for confirmation. She looked across at Max staring intently at the phone, hoping to get a better sense of Chen's real position, while Clifford feigned disinterest by reading some papers on his desk.

"No, and in exchange, he would release you and your firm from all claims, which would, of course, relieve you from the risk of an intentional-wrong claim. We all know that such a claim would be outside the coverage of your malpractice insurance and that the assets of all of your partners would be personally liable for the entire missing seventy million dollars, with the added possibility of punitive damages on top of that."

"If we settle, are you in a position to send us documentation establishing C.K.'s authority to speak for Paramount?"

"I will pass that request back on to Mr. Leung."

"When would C.K. like an answer?"

"Mr. Leung has instructed us to withhold the institution of suit for sixty days. If he receives the reimbursement within that period of time, that will be the end of it."

"Your position seems quite clear. Let me have your firm's address and phone number. If we need to contact C.K., should it be through you?"

"Of course."

"I understand. Thank you for calling."

"Oh, and one more thing. Mr. Leung asked me to remind you to send out his files—"

Beth hung up the phone and looked at Clifford. "What is his preoccupation with those damn files?" She asked the question out loud, not expecting an answer.

"Maybe there's something in the files he's concerned about," Max said.

"I don't know, Dad."

"Something important enough to make him want to settle a potential seventy million claim against us for five and a quarter million?"

"Why is he being so kind?"

"He mentioned those files to me at dinner, then over the phone two days ago, and through that T. C. Chen guy just now."

"Look, let's not worry about that," Clifford said. "Send him the files, but be sure to sanitize them first and copy anything that looks relevant to the due diligence question."

"What about the retainer?"

"I have no intention of returning our fee to him."

"I agree," Beth offered. "It's extortion."

"Exactly. I don't trust this C. K. Leung. He strikes me as an unctuous sort of chap."

"But he's not the bad guy," Max said. "He got screwed by Sloane."

"Maybe so, but we're not going to stand by while he finds the money on his own and then tries to recover twice by making a fraudulent claim for reimbursement against our insurance company or his."

"You're right there. Paramount must carry insurance against employees' thefts."

"Do you think we should send him the files if we're not going to settle, though?" Beth asked. "Maybe there's some leverage here that we don't know about."

"You may be right about that," Clifford replied.

"And if we may go to the mattresses," Beth continued, "let's also make C.K. prove he owns Paramount before we turn over anything to him. I'm finished assuming anybody's legit."

"Good point, but a client does have a right to his files. Okay, let's hold the files until you get the proof you want from C.K., and then send them to him."

"I will," Beth said. "But are you going to turn this thing over to the insurance company?"

"Yes. I'm not too concerned about our intentional tort liability."

"Suppose the insurance company decides it was intentional and they refuse coverage?"

"It's more of a theory than a reality, Beth. My inclination is to turn the whole thing over to the carrier, pay the hundred-thousand deductible, and simply let them handle the matter. It will be cheaper for us in the long run."

"I understand," she replied.

Clifford sat quietly for another moment before getting out of his chair and walking over to Beth. "Will you excuse us, Beth? This now becomes a matter for me to discuss privately with your stepfather."

"Of course, but I intend to pay for the deductible myself."

"No, you won't," Max said. "If we can't get the insurance company to waive the deductible, I'll cover it."

"That's very paternalistic of you, old chum, but I wish to point out that if any other associate in the firm ever screwed up this way, you would have been the first one to fire him right on the spot, no trial, no hearing, no explanation. The issue here isn't the hundred thousand but the reputation of the firm."

"I'll resign," Beth offered.

"Oh, don't be childish," Clifford said irritably. "No one's firing you or asking for your resignation."

"We should try to locate the money ourselves. What about that investigator you mentioned two days ago?"

"I spoke to Dieter last night. He told me he's already been retained by C.K. He's meeting with them in Taiwan tomorrow."

"That doesn't surprise me, given his reputation," Max said. "Can you get him to keep us in the loop?"

"He understands we have a serious interest in the case."

"How well do you know him?" Beth asked.

"Let's just say I'm glad C.K. has retained him."

"Maybe we should hire our own guy also. Do you want me to find out who HSBC uses for its investigations?" She knew she was becoming emotional but no longer cared. The damn money had to be found and returned to C.K. The conflict she had caused between Max and Clifford only added to the weight of the personal responsibility she already felt.

"Forget it. We're not spending half our fee for a private investigator. The firm will pay the hundred-thousand deductible if it's necessary and go on to the next case. Set up an appointment with our insurance company."

"That bastard stole seventy million and used me to pull it off!" Her face turned red with the force of her explosion, but Clifford wasn't impressed.

"And he drowned. There's no personal satisfaction available in this for you. Let it drop."

"Clifford is right," Max interrupted.

"C.K. said he'd wait for sixty days. We have a two-month window of opportunity to recover the money ourselves. There's more to it than satisfaction."

"Look, I want you to let it drop. Max, do you agree with me on this?"

"Absolutely."

"Well, fine, then. So why don't you prepare the letter you are going to send to Leung and let your stepfather and me trade old war stories for a while."

She felt thoroughly chastised by his patronizing rebuke but had the good sense to recognize the time for a graceful retreat. She smiled, uncrossed her legs, got up out of the chair, and left Clifford's office. Only her mother would have understood the glint in her eyes and the set of her jaw.

Beth looked up as Max stuck his head into her office. "Are you and Clifford finished?"

"Yeah. Your mother and I are having dinner with him tonight."

"I can't make it. I have a softball game to play."

"You're not invited. Are you ready to go to lunch?"

"Sure. Just let me grab my jacket. Is Mom going to meet us at the restaurant?"

"If she wants to get fed. By the way . . ." He looked admiringly around her office. "Your new furniture is beautiful."

"It's tainted with Sloane money. I feel like returning it to the store."

"Totally understood. Just contact the insurance company and let them handle things from here on in."

"I'll do that, but I'm going to find the money."

"Listen to me. You don't have any say around this place. Clifford makes the rules."

"I have sixty days."

"Let the insurance company handle it."

"All they know how to do is delay, stall, and settle. I want to clear my name."

"No one has said anything about *our* name."

"I have. That bastard used me. Even though he's dead, I can still track down the money and return it to C.K."

"You don't know anything about banking protocols."

"No, but Brian'll help and he wrote most of them. He runs the whole wire department now over at HSBC."

"Clifford won't let you do it."

"I'll do it in my spare time. He gets no say in that."

"Nonsense!"

"Then I'll quit or I'll take a leave of absence. One way or another, I'm going to see this thing through. I caused this problem and I'm going to solve it."

"Put on your jacket. We'll talk about it on the way over to the restaurant."

Chapter Six

Andrew Leung, the only brother educated in Taiwan, spoke first in Mandarin. "We should not be doing this, I keep telling you. We have to get someone else."

C.K. looked at him sternly across the conference room table. "Listen to me, Andrew, the matter is settled. Rheinhartz has been in the waiting room for almost an hour, so let's get him in."

Andrew wasn't satisfied. "But, Chun Keun," he continued to protest, "the man is a Jew and ex-Mossad. If it should come out, our Arab partners will blacklist us."

"They will do far worse if they find out we've lost their bank access codes."

"Let's get on with the meeting," Martin said. "I want to hear what this Rheinhartz has to say."

"But we should focus our efforts on finding a copy of the bank codes. We need to access our bank accounts."

"Our computer experts discovered that Sloane made two backup copies before erasing the hard drive," Martin said. "Everything possible is being done to locate them."

"Stay on it. Maybe something will turn up when I get the Jasco files from the lawyers. What about Sloane's personal checking accounts?" C.K. asked.

"We still don't have those," Martin answered. "There weren't any of his personal papers around the office."

"And his condo?"

"I didn't have a chance to check it out before you called me back to Taipei. I'm having it searched now. Eddie Huang should call within the next hour or two."

"Do you want to ask this Jew to work on the codes also, or just on the theft?" Andrew asked.

"Let us see how the meeting goes." Not commenting on his brother's last remark, C.K. got up from his chair and opened the door to usher Dieter Rheinhartz into the conference room. Speaking now in English for the first time, he introduced Rheinhartz to his two brothers and quietly pushed a button under the table to begin recording the conference.

Rheinhartz, a rather fat, sixty-three-year-old Israeli expat living in Zurich, sat at the foot of the table. He was irritated by having been ignored in the waiting room. He managed to look slovenly despite his custom-tailored dark blue suit, but his reputation as a bank investigator was based on results, not on appearances. His services were constantly in demand and did not come cheaply.

A servant knocked and entered the room with an ornate sterling silver tea service and offered green tea to those seated around the table. She was followed by another servant carrying a tray of small individual pastries. Only Rheinhartz took pastry. The Leungs stared disapprovingly at the relish with which he ate.

"I want to thank you for taking the time to come to Taiwan, Herr Rheinhartz," C.K. said. "I know you have a very busy schedule, and my brothers and I are very appreciative."

"Well, as you know, Mr. Leung," Rheinhartz responded in

English heavily laced with his Israeli accent, "that is why I never take on more than three or four matters at a time. My reputation is based on results."

"And we appreciate your undertaking this matter for us." Martin spoke from his seat on the only windowed side of the table.

"The president of Fidelity Bank personally asked me to help, so I am glad to be of service," Rheinhartz replied. He felt the start of a painful ache in his left arm, a constant reminder of his near fatal beating by brutal Chinese youths during his teenage years in Singapore when his father had moved their family there. He rubbed it vigorously in an automatic reaction, a gesture that C.K. noticed.

"Is something the matter?" he asked.

"I have a minor circulation problem. Old age, I guess."

"You should see a Chinese doctor before you leave Taiwan. Acupuncture will cure that," C.K. offered. "It's better than Western medicine. If you wish, I'll be happy to give you the name of my personal physician here in Taipei."

"Perhaps I will try him if I have time. Thank you for your concern."

"Mr. Rheinhartz, what do you have to report?" Martin demanded. C.K had abruptly summoned him from San Francisco because of the Sloane matter, and he was anxious to get back.

"Quite a bit, in fact," Rheinhartz replied.

"Please go ahead," C.K. said, tempering his brother's more abrasive personality.

"We've traced the funds from Chase Bank in New York, where they were deposited by Jasco on September third, to the Algemene Bank in The Hague, then to the Schweizerische Bankgesellschaft in Zurich."

"That's an excellent start, Herr Rheinhartz," C.K. said. As

he spoke, the muffled sound of a ringing phone filtered through the room. His attention was diverted to one of the cabinet doors across the room. Simultaneously, a small red light began flashing over it. "That must be Eddie for you on the private line," he said in Mandarin, and Martin walked over to the cabinet. He spoke softly into the phone for less than a minute.

"What did he find?" C.K. asked him, still in Mandarin.

"Two personal checking accounts of Sloane's, one in New York and one in Providence, Rhode Island."

"Why Providence?"

"Eddie is checking further."

"Good."

"Eddie wants to know about notifying the police."

"Tell him under no circumstances!" C.K. said. "We can't afford to have the authorities asking questions about our Arab investors."

"Do you want him to find out if the lady lawyer knows anything about the bank codes?"

"I do not think she knows anything. She was too upset when she told me about the missing money."

"She does not deserve your sympathy, C.K."

"It is not about sympathy. Leave her alone until we see how things develop."

Rheinhartz carefully ignored the conversation. The Leungs were unaware of his fluency in Mandarin. It was during his years in Singapore that he developed knowledge of the major Chinese dialects. He couldn't speak them well, but he understood them, a useful talent when dealing with Chinese shielding their private conversations.

C.K. finally looked back at Rheinhartz and resumed the conversation in English. "I am sorry to have interrupted you, Herr Rheinhartz. Please continue."

"I obtained the complete files at each of the banks, aliases, forgeries, and all. I have copies here for you." He handed the documents across the table to C.K.

"I am very impressed," C.K. said as he briefly thumbed through the papers. "You have accomplished a great deal in a few short days."

"*Danke,* but I am afraid that is where the trail has ended for the time being."

"What do you mean?" Andrew asked.

"The money was withdrawn on September sixth in cash from the Union Bank in Zurich," Rheinhartz said.

"What kind of currency?" C.K. asked out of mild curiosity.

"Swiss francs," Rheinhartz answered immediately. "I have the exact breakdown of the denominations if you wish."

"That will not be necessary," C.K. said, impressed that Rheinhartz was offering those details. "But does that mean they eventually changed the money into gold or maybe bearer bonds?"

"*Ach nein,* no," Rheinhartz said reassuringly. "It only means that the search becomes more difficult. The money must have been redeposited in a bank. We will pick up the trail in another day or so."

"But suppose it's been stashed somewhere?" Martin asked.

"Stashed?"

"Hidden."

"Oh, yes. I understand, but I'm certain it was redeposited and withdrawn several more times," Rheinhartz said. "Sloane and his accomplice had plenty of time to make arrangements."

"But they did not anticipate dying," C.K. said.

"If they are dead," Andrew added impatiently.

"We have the DNA results," C.K. said, and then asked,

"Herr Rheinhartz, I am sure that you would like to get back to Zurich. Do you have anything else to report?"

"We will keep working on the matter and let you know as soon as we learn something."

"Fine. I suggest you plan to come back to Taipei during the first week of November to bring us up-to-date."

"As you wish."

"Good." C.K. took a leather attaché case out from under the table and handed it to Rheinhartz. "Here is the retainer you requested."

"In British pounds?"

"Just as you requested. Five hundred thousand pounds."

"Thank you." Rheinhartz opened the case and briefly checked its contents. Satisfied, he lifted himself out of the chair, brushed the crumbs off his suit jacket, and extended a hand to each of the Leung brothers. Martin and C.K. both stood up to shake hands with him. Andrew ignored the gesture and remained seated as he took a toothpick out of his pocket and began working on a recalcitrant piece of food. When Rheinhartz left the conference room, Andrew got up to close the door behind him. The thud of the massive oak door slamming shut expressed his continued dissatisfaction.

Chapter Seven

Beth awoke under protest to face the dark, damp, and generally dreary Sunday morning. Max and Andi had returned to the Caribbean last Tuesday, right after the law firm turned C.K.'s malpractice claim over to their insurance company. Since then, Beth had worked hard to convince herself that the Sloane matter was dead, literally and figuratively.

By ten thirty a.m., she was back from her regular karate class and decided to go over to the office for a few hours of work before ending up at Brian's to watch the Giants play in Dallas. Although she and Brian Rhoden were no longer engaged, they still shared joint custody of their season tickets out at MetLife Stadium and remained close friends.

She checked her mailbox on the way out and found a fat piece of mail from Max nestled among the bills and circulars from yesterday's delivery. She put it in her pocket to read at the office. In view of the rain, she took a cab.

The taxi got her to the office in short order. As it pulled over to the Park Avenue curb, the door was opened for her by two Asian men standing in front of the building waiting for a cab. One of the men had a burn scar where his right eyebrow should have been. As they brushed by her, getting into the cab, her sense of smell was assaulted by the odor of their stale cigarette smoke.

She walked through the revolving door into her building and over to the entry log on the clipboard at the front desk. She noticed that no one else from the firm was signed in, so their floor would be empty. The youthful security guard sitting at the front desk had his head buried in an engineering textbook and barely grunted in response to her greeting, not bothering to look up at her as she signed in.

The law firm occupied the entire twenty-ninth floor. Her elevator stopped on the floor and the doors opened. There was no mistaking the same odor of stale cigarette smoke. Beth instantly became concerned and stepped out quickly. She unlocked the glass entrance doors that triggered both the sonic and infrared alarm systems. Once in, she entered her security code and relocked the outer doors, turned on the hallway lights for the front part of the suite, and walked into her own office.

When she noticed that the door to her credenza was partially open, she called down to the security desk in the main lobby. The security guard assured her that she was the only one on their floor today and that the closest anyone else had been was a real estate broker about an hour ago showing some clients the vacant thirtieth floor. Before hanging up, she asked him to buzz her before letting anyone else up to her floor. Then she plugged her iPod into a speaker, put her feet up on the desk, and opened the envelope from Max, savoring the rarity of a handwritten letter.

There was nothing in the first few pages of the letter to indicate it was any different from the regular travelogues she loved to get from him. Then she saw that Max had enclosed a clipping torn out of an island newspaper. It was a notice placed there by the Gold Coast Charter Company on Guadeloupe, offering a reward for the recovery of a stolen sailboat called *Sindicator*. Max wrote that it was probably coincidence, but he remembered that Sloane had a ketch down in the Caribbean named *Sindicator*.

It wasn't until she read his letter a second time that she felt the repressed anger percolating to the surface. There must be a way to find the truth. A chance to clear her name and erase her guilt. Why would Sloane charter a fishing boat in Puerto Rico if he had a perfectly fine sailboat in Guadeloupe? And why would a thief steal the sailboat? Good questions, just no answers. Forget all her good intentions; she either needed to find solutions to problems or add more excuses to the pile she already had. She had trusted a thief, been wronged, and now she had to make it right.

There were too many coincidences and sleazy characters entering her life lately. First Sloane, then C.K., and now that Scarface down at the cab, all giving her cause for suspicion and anger.

She wanted Max's help. There's no way he was satisfied any more than she was. She turned on her computer and started a letter to him. After telling him that she wasn't buying all this coincidence, she added that there was more to it than just the sinking of *Satin Lady*. She asked him to check the whole thing out, maybe sail over to San Juan to visit Blue Lagoon Charters and the Coast Guard. Get the details about the charter and subsequent sinking. Talk to Gold Coast Charter, too.

She sent the email to Max and got online to do some research. The occasional ring of the office telephone was ignored. Anybody who wanted her on a Sunday would know her private number. Her attention was distracted momentarily by the whirring sound of elevator cables groaning into action. Sometimes it sounded like the elevator was stopping on her floor, but the alarm remained silent.

Her first searches on Google were into the newspaper and

magazine webpages. She checked for news items back over the last year but came up with a large goose egg except for one small article appearing in a San Juan newspaper almost two months ago that gave a brief description of the *Satin Lady* accident.

Beth then moved over to the Orion NYCORP database, where she located and printed out copies of Paramount's incorporation documents filed with the New York Secretary of State.

She then tried to get into USCORP, looking for copies of their federal tax returns, but was repeatedly denied access. After a half hour of frustrated attempts, she gave up and decided to handle the problem the way she always handled difficult access problems: she picked up the phone and dialed Brian.

"It's two p.m. already," he answered impatiently. "Where are you?"

"The game's at four p.m., and 'hello' to you too."

"Can you pick up some salsa and salted cashews on the way over? I have chips and beer."

"Brian, I need you to help me get copies of some federal tax returns online."

"So much for foreplay. What's your problem?"

"You know the problem. I can't get into the account without the access code."

"So you want me to hack it for you, right?"

"Isn't that why HSBC made you its director of technology?"

"Hang on. I'll dial up and send you a link with a session code."

"Thanks, Brye." She clicked on the link as soon as he emailed it to her, identified the session code at the bottom of the page, and gave it to Brian over the phone. In less than a minute, her cursor developed a mind of its own and she knew he had taken control of her computer from his apartment.

"What's the name of the database?" he asked, and she told him.

"What's the name of the corporation?" he asked, and she told him.

"You want to print it or save?" They both laughed at his expression of confidence.

"See you in a little bit." Beth hung up the phone while Brian did his techie magic.

She had Paramount's U.S. tax returns in no time flat and was intrigued to find that a company called Lenco Importing was listed as the only shareholder of Paramount. Lenco was described as the owner of all the shares. There was no mention of C. K. Leung, but that didn't really surprise her. She had expected his foreign ownership to be well hidden behind a string of U.S. companies to avoid any alien withholding taxes. She would have to check out Lenco to see where that would lead.

Most of the access codes for the credit and insurance industries had been available for years on blogs frequented by hackers. She and Brian had used them in college when it was a game. Now she was going to use them for real. She wanted to know everything about Sloane and Erica, from their height and weight to their insurance and hospital records, and from their credit history down to the amount of the last check they had written to Con Edison. It was all available.

She worked slowly and meticulously for another hour, following each trail until it ended. She cut it close but still made it to Brian's in time for the Giants–Cowboys kickoff.

Chapter Eight

Max stopped off at the Road Town public library to check his email in their Wi-Fi lounge while he waited for Andi to finish her recertification course in offshore emergency medicine at Peebles Hospital. He met her at one p.m. at an open-air restaurant down by the water. They went over to a table and sat down to enjoy the harbor view. A ferry, with only a few passengers this time of year, was just pulling into the dock, loaded mostly with island freight.

"How was the OEM course?" he asked her.

"I learned some new defib techniques for that defibrillator we *should* have on board."

"I know you want one. How much is it?"

"A couple of thousand, but we'll get a discount on our liability insurance to help cover the cost."

"Let's wait until we start getting in some charter deposits."

"That's what I figured, but I did buy us a new suture kit to replace the old one. We needed some fresh injectables anyhow."

"You're the medic."

"Oh, and I'm supposed to practice my technique this week. They lent me a hypodermic syringe. I can use your arm or buy a few oranges."

"My choice or yours?"

"Let's order lunch. . . ."

There was no menu, only a chalkboard to indicate what the owner, a buxom West Indian who called herself "Sister Margaret," was in the mood to prepare that day. It was the off-season, and she greeted them like long-lost relatives. Maggie took their lunch orders and then went back to the kitchen area, separated from the dining terrace only by a counter. The smells of her cooking merged over the grill and crossed from the kitchen onto the terrace, permeating air already hot and humid from the midday sun.

Max opened up the Tortola newspaper to see if the reward notice for *Sindicator* was still there. It was.

"Andi," he said, "did I ever tell you that Len Sloane owned a sailboat down in Guadeloupe?"

"Maybe. I don't remember. Why?"

"Take a look at this ad in the paper. I sent the same ad to Beth last week." He took off his glasses as he passed the newspaper across the table.

Andi took the newspaper out of his hands. Looking at the ad did nothing to refresh her recollection. "It still doesn't bring anything to mind. What makes you think he had a boat by that name?"

"When I met him at the Christmas party last year, he was trying to impress me, so he told me about this big sailboat he had bought down in the Caribbean."

"So what's that got to do with anything else?"

"Well, what I remember most is liking the name he mentioned to me. He had named the boat *Sindicator*. You know the good memory I have for boat names."

"So what about it?"

"Beth wrote me about it on Sunday. She's a little curious

that a boat with that name was stolen at about the same time that Len and Erica drowned."

"One thing has nothing to do with the other."

"It may. It may not. Suppose the stolen boat was Len's?"

"And suppose it wasn't?"

"Look, I know you don't like to talk about it, but just suppose it was his boat. That would be some coincidence, wouldn't it?"

"You shouldn't have sent the ad to Beth in the first place. Boats get stolen down in the Caribbean all the time, usually by smugglers who sink them after one run."

"Right, and there must be a number of boats around with the name *Sindicator,* but suppose this particular one was Sloane's?"

"What are you getting at?" Andi didn't enjoy thinking about the Paramount matter.

"Nothing." Max totally changed pace. "I just think Beth is right. It is interesting. Right, Maggie?" He addressed that question to Sister Margaret, who had started unloading a tray of food at their table. She obviously had no idea what they were talking about, but that had never bothered her.

"Whatever you say, Mr. Swahn, I'm sure is right." Maggie finished unloading and left the two of them to eat.

Max anointed his hamburger and fries with ketchup and proceeded to eat. Andi started on her salad. There was the usual amount of picking and sharing between them.

"The silence is deafening," she said. "What's going on in that mind of yours?"

"Want some more of my french fries?"

"I'm not talking about your french fries."

"Want another bite of my hamburger?" He passed it over to her, but she shook her head in refusal.

"I'm talking about Sloane."

"Beth asked me to call Gold Coast. I'm going to call them after we finish with lunch."

"Why?" She was losing her appetite rapidly.

"Because Beth and I want to know if it's the same boat."

"Sloane's dead. The matter's dead. . . . Please, Max."

"What's one little phone call? It'll take me a second."

"You know, Max, I love you, but sometimes you're a pain in the butt."

"Yes, dear. Got a couple of quarters?" He got up from his chair as Andi opened her pocketbook.

"I really wish you wouldn't do this." She was already resigned, however.

Max took a final mouthful of his drink and went over to the pay phone by the counter. After three attempts at calling Guadeloupe, he was connected with Gold Coast Charter. The agent at the other end answered with a heavy island accent.

As soon as Max explained to him that he was interested in the reward advertisement, the agent was eager to tell all that he knew. He said they had been running the ad for about a month. After a few minutes of conversation, Max thanked him and hung up the phone. He felt Andi's eyes boring into his back, so he turned around quickly and returned to the table.

"So?" she asked as he sat down across from her.

"This is going to knock your socks off."

"I can't wait."

"The stolen boat wasn't owned by Sloane."

"See, I told you so," she said, feeling relieved.

"The boat was owned by Paramount Equities," he said triumphantly.

"No way." The feeling of relief quickly passed.

"Way!"

"Holy shit!"

"You know what I think?" he asked.

"No, but you're about to tell me, right?"

"Right. If the weather's nice tomorrow, let's sail over to Puerto Rico. We can spend a few days there. Do some shopping. See a movie."

"Why?" Her antennae were up.

"Beth asked me to talk to the guy who chartered the fishing boat to Len and Erica. She also wants me to talk to the Coast Guard. Come on, it'll give us something to do."

"We have plenty to do. Our own charter season is almost here."

"Oh, I forgot to tell you one other thing. . . ."

"How would you like me to stick a hypodermic needle up your north forty?"

"Wait until I tell Beth this one. It seems that a couple of Chinese were on Guadeloupe to see the guy from Gold Coast Charter last week. They were asking about the same boat."

"You think it was Leung?"

"Had to be."

"What's the matter, Max? Things too dull around here?"

Chapter Nine

Women of all sizes were in a feeding frenzy as they hunted voraciously through the racks in Bloomie's lingerie department. Beth walked over to the nightgowns and started checking the racks, a mindless exercise that allowed her to concentrate on Sloane's son. She had discovered Bob Talcourt's existence Sunday when she accessed a database containing Sloane's insurance records and found him named as a beneficiary on a life insurance policy. Tracking him down to the small radio station outside of Providence where he worked as an engineer hadn't been too much of a problem. Now, she wanted to meet him. She was absorbed in thought and didn't notice Amy come over.

"Jesus, where the hell are you?" Amy asked. "You look like you're a million miles away from here. Do you know you have a size eighteen flannel nightie in your hands? It'd fit you and me together."

"I was thinking about that Paramount case."

"I thought the bad guys drowned."

"That's what I thought, but I got an email from my dad this afternoon. Len Sloane may still be alive."

"Oh, great! What makes him think he's still alive?"

"Something he found out in Puerto Rico yesterday. If Sloane is alive, I want to personally cut his balls off. I owe him."

"I know the hell he's put you through," Amy said sympathetically, "but what can you really do? He drowned."

"I found out he had a son. Uses his mother's maiden name. The guy dropped out of MIT, of all places, to join the Peace Corps, and now works for some radio station in Rhode Island."

"He sounds interesting."

"I know, doesn't he? Now the problem is the best way to approach the guy. Got any brilliant ideas?"

"No, but I'll tell you what. When we get over to your place, we'll nuke a few frozen dinners and discuss strategy over a bottle of Beaujolais."

"You're on. Did you pay for the bras already?"

"Yeah, while you were daydreaming here among the nightgowns. I'm all set."

"Let's go, then."

It was only a short walk over to Beth's apartment on Sixty-third Street. Once inside the apartment, they took off their coats, opened a bottle of wine, and sat down to enjoy a glass while waiting for their dinners to cook. "This new couch is so beautiful," Amy said. "And the mirrors make the room look huge."

"Thanks. I love the way it's shaping up." Beth had moved in after breaking up with Brian and spending weeks trooping around Manhattan, looking for a one-bedroom apartment she liked and could afford. This one came complete with high ceilings and wainscoting plus views of the East River.

"The place looks like a home at last."

"And not like a dorm, you mean."

"Well, it did, you know."

"I owe it all to winning that Paramount case." She kicked her sneakers off and stretched herself out on the oversize club chair.

"So anyhow, what are you going to do about meeting that guy?" Amy asked, turning on the television set.

"I don't know. I'll think of something."

"How about the direct approach?"

"What's that?"

"Follow him after work. Find out where he goes at night. Meet him there and get him to pick you up. Men are suckers for that."

"Oh, great idea. Really great. Talk about looking for Mr. Goodbar."

The bell on the microwave went off, interrupting the conversation, and Beth went into the kitchen to take out the two meals. She put them on plates and carried them into the living room, where she handed one to Amy sitting on the chair and sat on the couch with the other.

"Where does he live?" Amy asked.

"I don't know yet."

"Why not try telephone information for the area?"

"Don't you think I tried that first?"

"How about calling the personnel office at the radio station where he works and giving them some bullshit story like you're calling from a doctor's office about some major medical benefits. They must get calls like that all the time."

"It's too small an outfit. They don't have a personnel office."

"Then why don't you take a trip out there. Go to the station. Tell him you're there about his father's life insurance. That'll get his attention."

"You're not suggesting I tell him the truth, are you?"

"No, of course not. That's ridiculous."

"So what do I do?" Beth asked.

"I'm all thought out and the wine is finished. Come on, I'll help you clean up and then I'm going home." Amy got out of her chair and collected the few dishes. Beth picked up the glasses and followed her to the dishwasher.

"You know what?" Beth said.

"What?"

"I'm making this whole thing too complicated. I could never pull off one of these phony approaches. It's just not my style."

"Got a better idea?"

"Yes. Keep it as close to the truth as possible. I'm going to go pay a condolence call. What could be more natural and plausible? His father's lawyer coming to pay her respects."

"And traveling all the way to Providence, Rhode Island, just because a client died?"

"I'll tell him I had a deposition to take in town. . . . As a matter of fact, I really could set one up," Beth said.

"How come?"

"We do have a lawsuit up in Providence. Instead of dragging a witness to New York, I'll go there. It's easy!"

"What then?" Amy asked.

"If Talcourt doesn't know anything and believes his father is dead, nothing. I made a trip out to Rhode Island for nothing. Big deal."

"Do you think he's going to tell you if he does know something? Break down in tears and confess to it all?"

"Of course not. But you know what? If I get the feeling that he does know something about his father being alive, I'll find a way to get it out of him. This means too much to me."

"Wait a minute. You're talking funny."

"What do you mean?"

"Beth, we've been friends since junior high. This isn't some loss at a softball game you want to avenge. You're scaring me."

"There's nothing to worry about. All I want to do is meet the son. How can I get into trouble with that?"

"Let me count the ways. . . ."

"You sound just like my mother and my boss."

"Two people I've always admired."

Chapter Ten

Beth opened up the attaché case and put the Henshaw folder inside. Max had bought her the brown leather case when she passed the New York State bar exam three years ago. She carried it around like a badge of honor and treasured each new scratch as a scar earned in battle.

Just when Carmen buzzed to let her know that the car for LaGuardia would be downstairs in fifteen minutes, Clifford's secretary stuck her head into the office. "Beth," she said, "Mr. Giles would like to see y'all before y'all leave."

"Sure, Constance," she replied. "Tell him I'll be right there."

As Beth entered Clifford's office, she saw him sitting behind his desk, puffing away on a cold pipe, head buried in concentration among piles of papers. "You wanted to see me?" Beth asked.

Giles picked up his head at the question. He coughed several times and then cleared his throat. "Yes, just for a second. I was looking at the office calendar. Why are you going to Providence today?"

"We have a deposition scheduled there for two this afternoon in the Henshaw case." She stood in front of his desk, not bothering to sit down for what she hoped would be a brief conversation.

"I can see that, but why? It's a small trademark infringement case and the client doesn't like to pay for this kind of travel. Aren't we entitled to depose the witness here at our office?"

"Yes, but the attorney for the witness told me his client was too sick to travel here and I didn't want to postpone the deposition for another month. Discovery in this case has to be completed very soon and I don't want to ask Judge Van Platten for an extension of time. You know how sticky he can get."

"But you had a valid excuse here," Clifford said, suddenly experiencing another spell of coughing, this time needing to use his handkerchief.

"I'm sorry, but I thought it was the best way to handle it." She tried to end the discussion quickly by making it her judgment call, but could see that he was far from satisfied with her answer. She probably wouldn't have been satisfied either if she were sitting on his side of the desk.

"Well, it's too late to do anything about it now. Why did you set it up for two p.m.? What are you going to do if you can't finish today?"

"Don't worry, I'll finish. The lawyer said his client is more alert in the afternoon and he promised he'd let me continue today until I finished."

"Better take a toothbrush. You know what those kinds of promises are worth. Call me if you're going to stay over."

"Right. I'd better run. My car's probably downstairs already." Beth turned to leave the office.

"Good luck."

"Thanks. I'll speak to you later." She turned to leave. "Do you want me to leave you some cough drops? They're right here in my bag."

"No thanks. I'll be fine." Clifford had already returned his attention to the file on his desk as Beth left the room. He made a note on his diary to bring up the matter of unnecessary travel at the next firm meeting.

Beth walked out of Clifford's office and into her own. She put on her camel-hair coat, grabbed her attaché case and the shoulder bag containing her clean underwear and extra makeup. She stopped by Carmen's desk on her way out to the elevator.

"I'm going. See you tomorrow."

"Okay, Beth. Have a good trip."

"Try to finish the Leipzig brief before you go home tonight."

"I'll give it a shot."

"Thanks."

Her car was waiting out front when she got downstairs. The plane to Providence boarded early and took off on time with less than half of its seats occupied. Beth used the hour flight time to review the Henshaw case for the deposition. It didn't take long. Clifford was right. It wasn't a complicated matter.

She felt guilty for scheduling the deposition in Providence instead of New York and guilty for having lied about it to Clifford. She was, however, finally on the way to her confrontation with Sloane's son. The anticipation dominated her thoughts. The Henshaw deposition was only the rationalization and the excuse.

She put her file away and let her thoughts drift back again to Talcourt. In her mind, she went over the questions she would ask him. She mentally anticipated his answers and went on to new questions.

She had thought about calling him first but had discarded the idea, afraid that any advance notice would give him time to think up excuses for not seeing her. She did, however, call the radio station anonymously to make sure he'd be there. They said he finished his shift every evening at six p.m. Fine, she thought, that would give her plenty of time to finish the Henshaw deposition and get over to the station.

The plane landed on schedule at T. F. Green Airport and Beth went to the Avis desk to pick up the car Carmen had reserved for her. She drove out of the airport onto I-95 and was downtown in Larry Coopersmith's office on South Main Street by one forty-five p.m.

The witness in the Henshaw case was an elderly retired businessman whose recollection of the disputed four-year-old events was faulty. Both he and his attorney were being cooperative, so Beth saw no need to work him over unnecessarily with a rough cross-examination. By four forty p.m., she had run out of questions and closed the deposition. The stenographer promised her a transcript within ten days.

She walked over to her car, noted the expired meter and the ticket stuck behind the wiper blade. She took the ticket off and stuffed it in her coat pocket. Then she opened the car door, started it up, and in a minute was on her way north toward Talcourt.

Chapter Eleven

Beth drove up to North Providence, found the radio station, and parked her car on the side street across from it. WFEX-FM was a five-thousand-watt station playing soft rock for its audience in the Providence area.

Upon entering the building, Beth found herself in an office furnished with four closely packed metal desks loaded with the day's accumulation of empty coffee cups, but no people. Bright fluorescent lights were on the ceiling. One side wall was decorated with calendars and old album covers. The other side wall had the shelving that contained the station's library of CDs. The back wall had a large glass picture window and a door that opened into the first-floor broadcasting studio.

Beth walked over to the picture window and looked through it into the studio. She saw a muscular man sitting alone in the studio working at a console, his black hair in dreadlocks, full beard, with a diamond stud in his right ear. He was wearing jeans, sneakers, and a paint-stained sweatshirt from a Mount Pleasant High School. When he saw Beth, he smiled broadly and with his hand motioned her toward the studio door.

She walked over to the door, opened it up, and stuck her head inside. "Can you tell me where Robert Talcourt is?"

"Upstairs in studio two recording some advertisements. Is he expecting you?"

Beth was surprised by the quiet, articulate voice. It was in direct contrast to the imposing physical picture the man presented.

"Not really. Can I go up there?" she asked.

"You can, but you'd probably trip and break your neck on the unlighted stairs. Why don't you let me have your name and I'll call him."

"Beth, Elisabeth Swahn."

"Will Bobby know you, Beth?"

"Maybe. Tell him I was his father's attorney. I'm in town on business and dropped in to say hello."

"Okay, just a second." He picked up a phone and dialed a two-digit number. "Bobby? It's Justin," he said into the phone before dropping into a Jamaican Creole patois. Beth heard what he said, but that was about it. She couldn't understand a word.

After a few seconds of listening, he laughed and hung up the phone. "He says he'll be down in a few minutes and that I shouldn't try too much of my Rasta nightclub routine on you. He's just finishing up now. Why don't you find yourself a clean spot out there to sit while you wait. And my name's Justin."

"Thanks, Justin," Beth said.

"I admit, the place does kind of look like a disaster hit it at the end of a day."

"That is something of an understatement," she replied as she looked around the office. She heard his laughter even as the door to the soundproof studio closed behind her. She looked around, found a swivel chair next to one of the desks, and sat down.

In a few minutes, Beth heard the thudding of footsteps bouncing down stairs. Must be an old wooden stairway, she thought, an old and very creaky wooden stairway, in fact, out in the hallway. When Bob Talcourt came into the room, she was amazed first and foremost by his height. This guy must be more than six five, and he's slender, she thought. And he's young looking, almost a baby face. Not at all like I imagined. He's also got nice eyes behind those horn-rimmed glasses, and all those great brown curls rolling down the back of his neck.

"You want to see me?" As he entered the room, he spoke to her in a monotone reserved for uncategorized strangers. "I'm sorry, but I didn't catch your name when Justin mentioned it." He was dressed casually, wearing khakis, black western-style boots, and a dark green V-neck sweater that scooped low enough to expose a few hairs on his chest.

"My name is Beth . . . Elisabeth Piccolo-Swahn. My firm represented your dad in a case earlier this year." She was trying to sound as cordial as possible.

"Well, hello, Beth. My father and I were not very close to each other. What can I do for you?" It was a man's voice, not at all boyish like his face.

"I was in Providence for a meeting today and thought I'd stop in to pay my condolences. We were all very upset when we learned about your father's death."

"Well, thank you. I appreciate that. And I didn't mean to sound so abrupt," he added. "It's just that my father died two months ago and I didn't expect to meet anyone in Providence today who knew anything about it. How did you find me?"

"When your father retained us last year, he filled out our information sheet and listed you as next of kin. I never noticed it until I was going through the file last week getting it ready for storage." First lies out, Beth thought to herself. How many will it take?

"That's more than just interesting. I never thought he con-sidered me his next of kin." He shoved aside some coffee cups and sat on the edge of the desk across from Beth.

"What makes you say that?"

"After he divorced my mother, he never bothered to visit or bring me to his place. I tried to start up the relationship when I came back to the States two years ago, but I never got very far."

"Where were you?" She already knew . . . from Google.

"I was in Zaire with the Peace Corps trying to build and operate radio stations for the natives. It seemed like a good idea at the time, but it never got off the ground."

"Did you come back to Providence after that?"

"When my fiancée invited me back to attend her wedding to some other guy, I decided it was time to return to the States."

"What a thrill that must have been."

"Well, it's no matter. Anyhow, I'm being rude. The coffee here is hot, although highly contaminated with I don't know what. Can I get you a cup?"

"Thanks, I'd like that."

"How do you take it?"

"Milk, Sweet'N Low if you have it."

"No problem. Let me see if I can find a clean cup around here."

"You know, I had a great deal of respect for your father. When he died, I had no one to even send a card to." I wonder if lying becomes easier, she thought. I feel like the mystery guest on *To Tell the Truth*.

"Hey, listen, I didn't even hear about it myself until a week after it happened."

"Are you serious? How did you hear?"

"His secretary got a call from some guy down in San Juan who had chartered the boat to my father. He wanted to know where his boat was. Diane didn't know who to call, so she finally called me and I called the Coast Guard. I heard about the accident from them."

"That must have been a shock," Beth said, focusing her attention on his facial expressions, looking there to figure out where truth ended and fiction began.

"Well, the Coast Guard didn't really have much to say. Just that there had been an accident with my father and his lady friend reported lost. They even mailed me an old red polo shirt they said was his. I don't even know if it is his . . . it could belong to anybody for all I know."

"How awful." She was moved by his distress. "You don't even know, then, if he's really dead." She shifted back to her search for information, trying to provoke him into extending the conversation.

"Of course he's dead."

"But you don't have any real proof."

"He ran the boat up on a reef. They sank. He died. How much proof do I need?"

"Did he have any life insurance?" She already knew about a Metropolitan Life policy from the computer printout in her file.

"I found one policy. He must have taken it out as part of his divorce settlement with my mother. But when I called the insurance company, they wanted some proof of his death."

"Makes sense. What company?" Beth asked. "Some are better than others."

"Metropolitan Life."

"Do you have a lawyer working on it?"

"No."

"How much was involved?" She was skeptical about his disavowal.

"The policy was for three hundred and fifty thousand dollars. Why do you ask?"

"I was just thinking about why you'd want to let it go by without fighting for it." Take it easy now, Beth, she thought, don't push him too hard. You just met, and this isn't a courtroom.

"There's more to life than money."

"Of course there is, but money is one of the essential parts."

"You want to help me collect?"

"Someone should. Was there a will?" Good, she thought, let him think I'm hustling for business.

"I'm not sure I want to push it."

"Did you know you were the beneficiary of his life insurance?"

"No, but I guess he didn't really have anyone else. Except maybe his girlfriend, Erica."

"I never met her."

"My dad never had much of a family. An older brother out on the coast died years ago. I was his only child. The only reason he had any memorial service at all was because my mother had her minister here in town say a few words."

"Does your mother live in Rhode Island?"

"Yes. She married a local doctor a couple of years ago. They're living up in Warwick. I guess she felt like receiving absolution when she heard about my father's death. She made a donation to the church so they'd hold a service."

"That was very kind of her, no matter what you think."

"How do you know what I think?" Bob asked. His voice suddenly took on a defensive cant.

"It comes through clearly from the way you talk."

"I try not to show the anger."

"You're not good at hiding it."

"Hey, look, my father deserted me when I was eleven."

"Everybody's got their own life to live."

"That's a crock!" he erupted emotionally, clenching his right hand into a fist for emphasis. "That's easy to say and not so easy to accept." His face flushed.

Beth stood her ground, refusing to blink at his display, but inwardly she was moved by its intensity and connected to its cause. "I can imagine how you feel," she said softly. "I lost my father when I was a lot younger than you were." Boy, she thought, he sure sounded real that time.

"I'm sorry. I have some buttons that are pretty easy to push. Dumping on you isn't fair."

"That's all right, perhaps I should go." Beth looked at her watch and saw that an hour had passed. "I have a plane to catch. Thanks for your time." She started to get up, uncertain if she wanted to spend any more time with this man.

"Don't be silly. I'm glad you came. Come on. Let's go and have a drink." His ebullience returned as quickly as he had blown it.

"No, I mean it. It's getting late."

"Please, Beth. I'm not usually so antisocial. And I'm also embarrassed because at twenty-five, I can't forgive my dead father for leaving my mother, and what's worse, I dump it all on somebody I just met."

"Well, it's got to be real quick."

"Great. Just let me call Justin in the studio for a second." Bob reached over for the microphone on the desk and picked it up. "Justin?"

"Yes, Bobby?"

"If Marcie calls, tell her I'll be a little late."

"Should I tell her why?" Justin asked.

"Be a good boy now. Just give her my message."

"No problem. See you tomorrow."

"Right. Good night." Bob turned, put down the micro-phone, and motioned Beth toward the door. "Come on," he said to her. "I'll take you over to Barclay's. It's right down the block." He followed her out the door into the street. The early evening wind hit them with a refreshing gust of cold air.

"Who's Marcie?" Beth asked, buttoning her coat as she walked on the sidewalk with him. (Your wife?)

"My stepsister. I share a house with her and her husband. She worries about me a lot."

"The way Justin was teasing you, I thought the relationship was different." (Sometimes, it's good to be wrong.)

When Bob held the door open for her at Barclay's, she gave him one point for ordinary courtesy. When he pulled out a chair for her at the table and carefully slid it under her as she sat down, it reminded her of Max out with Andi, a definite positive. But when he actually stood up for her as she returned from the la-dies' room, she knew then that whatever else Sloane's son might turn out to be, he was certainly a gentleman in the classic tradi-tion.

"So is this where you radio guys hang?" she asked him.

"Yeah, it's the closest place with the best burgers and the latest hours."

"Do you live near here?"

"A few blocks away."

"Where was your father's place?"

"He rented a place on the other side of town. I had to sign some papers when he sold our house because I was on the deed with him."

"How come?"

"My mother insisted on it because she didn't trust him."

"Makes sense."

"And I know he must have taken back a mortgage from the buyers because after the sale, I deposited a monthly check from them into a joint account I had with him. The checks stopped this year."

"Maybe they defaulted."

"Who cares."

"You really ought to check it out. Might be worthwhile for you."

"Are you volunteering?"

"It's not a big deal."

"Is that a yes or a no?"

"It's a yes."

"What'll it cost me?"

"Just pay for the beers."

"It's a deal."

"When did he leave Providence?"

"He got a condo in New York about two years ago when he went to work for Paramount."

"So tell me about yourself. Seeing anyone?" (Ping! Ball's in your court.)

I've been seeing a professor from Brown on and off, more off than on."

"How come?"

"She's totally focused on getting tenure and I guess I'm looking for a little more commitment. How about you?"

"I broke up with the guy I was supposed to marry last year and moved into my own apartment. Then I dated an FBI agent I knew from law school for a while, but he got relocated to San Diego last summer, so nothing's going on lately."

"Do you have any brothers or sisters?"

"I'm an only child. My real father died in an accident when

I was five, so my mother raised me alone until she married my stepdad. He has two daughters and a son that I'm very close to."

"That's great. I'm close to Marcie too, and I play basketball on the same team as her husband."

"I guess you could say we have stuff in common."

"I guess. . . ."

She was back out at Green Airport in time to return the rental and catch the eight thirty flight back to New York. By ten fifteen, she was back in her apartment, reviewing and making notes on what she had learned.

Chapter Twelve

"Beth?"

"Yes, Carmen."

"There's a call for you. Robert Talcourt? Sounds like he's trying to sell you something."

"I doubt that."

"Want me to get rid of him?"

"No. Put him through." The opportunity to talk to him again interested her on several levels.

The intercom beeped again and the green LED started flashing. Although alone, Beth self-consciously straightened her blouse, ran her fingers through her hair, and took a deep breath before picking up the phone. She decided to keep the conversation at arm's length until she knew what he was calling about. "Elisabeth Piccolo-Swahn here," she announced formally, although this time the hyphenated version sounded a little pompous to her ears.

"Beth? It's Bob Talcourt. Leonard Sloane's son."

"Bob. Oh, hi!" she said, as if in belated recognition. "How're you doing?"

"Fine. I'm in the city today, and I thought I'd give you a call."

"What brings you here?"

"I had an interview this morning for a DJ spot."

"Hope it went well."

"So do I. Listen, I've been thinking about some of the things you said when you were in Providence Monday, you know, about my father's estate and his insurance. I picked up a box of papers from his condo after he died. I thought maybe if you had some time today, we could get together for a few minutes and talk. Maybe you could look over some of the papers for me."

"My day's kind of jammed, Bob. I have a major hearing on for tomorrow." She instinctively applied one of Clifford's elementary rules for getting new clients. They must perceive their attorneys to be very busy and successful.

"I didn't expect to be coming to New York either, but the station didn't call me until late last night. If you're too busy, we can make it some other time."

"Hang on a second. Let me take a look." She started scrolling through the office diary, hoping to find a window when Clifford would be out of the office. A conference with Sloane's son was not something she wanted to share with him. Anyway, what did Bob want to see her for? She was the one trying to investigate him. If he was involved with his father's scheme, what was he calling her about? And if he wasn't involved, what was he calling her about? Well, she thought, only one way to find out, and she hit the flashing light on the phone.

"Bob? You still there?" she asked.

"I'm still here," he replied.

"How about three this afternoon? I can squeeze a little and shift things around."

"I was kind of hoping you were free for lunch."

"Lunch is impossible. I can't make it," she answered. She didn't want to meet him outside the office, and she also wanted some time to get ready for him.

"Or for drinks after work."

"Thanks, but I'm probably going to be stuck around here until late. Why don't you come over to the office around three and we can talk then."

"Fine. I'll see you then. What's your address?"

"We're at Ninety-seven Park Avenue. The twenty-ninth floor."

"What's the cross street?"

"Fortieth."

"See you at three. Bye, now." And he hung up the phone.

Beth looked at her wristwatch. It wasn't much past ten. The day was going to be all anticipation and no concentration if she didn't keep busy. Too much time left for conjecture and assumptions. Why didn't I just agree to see him for lunch? she berated herself. Because, fundamentally, I'm suspicious of his motives, that's why. What can I find out from him about the Paramount case? Does he know anything?

She got up from her blue leather swivel chair, went over to her credenza, and unlocked the bottom drawer where she kept her personal possessions. She took out the file on Sloane she'd accumulated and began to review it. Right on top was the insurance printout that had alerted her to Robert Talcourt's existence.

She also had the printout of a personal financial statement Len had given when he'd used Paramount's name to buy the sailboat in Guadeloupe. It looked like the local seller down there had taken back a purchase money mortgage for 80 percent of the yacht's selling price and had then immediately assigned it over to the Royal Bank of Scotland. The bank, however, had preapproved the credit based upon Len's guaranty. Why had Sloane's personal guaranty been necessary at all? Paramount's profitable corporate statement should have been enough. Maybe Frank Epstein could help. She picked up her phone and dialed his intercom number.

"What is it now?" he barked into the intercom.

"Have I caught you at a bad time, Frank?" she asked timidly.

"Oh, sorry, Beth," he apologized instantly. "I thought it was Estelle again." His tone improved immediately when he recognized Beth's voice. Being Max's stepdaughter helped her get inside the firm's door, but once there, she had worked long and hard to prove herself. It had not been easy to gain acceptance from the less-privileged eyes that were constantly looking for signs of nepotism.

"The bookkeeper bothering you?"

"Every damn office problem gets dumped in my lap. Being managing partner is eating up all my time. Estelle is afraid to order a paper clip without clearing it with me."

"Got a second? I need some help."

"Sure. What's up?" Frank was always generous with his time. He enjoyed a reputation for accessibility when other attorneys needed advice. In short, a lawyer's lawyer.

"Suppose an individual wants to buy a boat in the name of a corporation he owns, or at least controls, and the corporation has very substantial assets and a strong financial statement. Why would a bank still insist on a personal guaranty from the individual?"

"Offhand, I can think of a number of reasons. The corporation's assets may not be liquid enough. It may be cash poor even though it owns a lot of things. Land, for example. It's not always easy to dispose of. A bank doesn't want to have to work too hard to collect if there's a default. It may be hard to foreclose on a boat mortgage if you can't find the boat."

"That makes sense."

"More often, however, the bank may just be concerned that

the corporation is acting ultra vires. Buying a boat may not be authorized by its corporate charter or bylaws. The bank wants to be sure it has some individual it can look to in case some minority stockholder or director starts screaming."

"I see."

"Other times . . . ," he said as he warmed up to the subject, "a bank will insist that the loan be made to a corporation because it intends to charge an excessive rate of interest and wants to avoid the usury laws."

"Right. Because corporations aren't protected by usury laws."

"Exactly. Then the bank gets the individual who's the real party in interest to guarantee the loan so they can indirectly charge him the usurious rate."

"So they effectively get the individual to waive his protection from usury."

"You got it. Offshore banks typically do it as a matter of course. Naming the corporation as the borrower is strictly a subterfuge. The individual guarantor is the real party on the hook."

"Thanks a lot." She hung up the phone and returned to the file in front of her. Something else in the financial statement had attracted her attention. Paramount Equities was described as a Netherlands Antilles corporation and not as a New York corporation. Possibly just an error. Maybe there was more than one Paramount Equities Corporation, or maybe the New York corporation had simply qualified to do business down in the Netherlands Antilles. If it was a different corporation, who were its owners? Did C. K. Leung own it? This was something that Carmen could start checking out for her this afternoon. She hit the intercom button.

"Yes, Beth," Carmen answered.

"Could you come in?"

"*Beth!*" she protested. "It's lunchtime! You promised."

"It'll just take a second," Beth reassured her.

Carmen's desk was only eight feet away from Beth's office. She entered the office with her dark metallic-green trench coat already half on.

"There's something I want you to do for me."

"It's almost twelve and I'm supposed to meet Claudette on the corner. Can't it wait until I get back?"

"Of course. I want you to speak to Frank Epstein's secretary and find out the name of the corporate agent he uses for his international searches. Call them up and ask them to make a search for a Paramount Equities Corporation organized down in the Netherlands Antilles. If they find anything, I want copies of the corporate charter, bylaws, and anything else that might be on file."

"Who do I bill it to?"

"Bill it to Paramount."

"I thought we closed that file out."

"We did."

"Then how can I bill it to them? Estelle will have a heart attack."

"Bill it to them. I'll take care of Estelle."

"What are we doing for Paramount now? I thought they were finished since Mr. Sloane drowned. Did we get a new case from them?"

"On second thought, you're right. Bill it to me." (And stop asking so many damn questions.)

"See you after lunch. Do you want the door open or closed?"

"Open, please."

After Carmen left, Beth made some notes to follow up on and one or two others to speak to Max about when she called him later on. Only during frequent coffee breaks did she allow her thoughts to return to the three p.m. meeting coming up with Bob Talcourt. Resistance leads to persistence. I play league softball with two hundred alpha males and I'm totally relaxed. I work with them in business, I'm fine. Yet when I have the slightest interest in a new guy, it's a fight to focus on anything else.

She knew this afternoon was going to be more than a business meeting for her, despite what Bob had said over the phone. He was tall, casually assured, smart. He had a strong chin and a cute butt. But first and foremost, he was Sloane's son.

Chapter Thirteen

When Beth completed the affidavits she needed for court the next day, she went to the bathroom and checked her makeup and hair. Then she looked at her watch and straightened up the papers on her desk. She looked at her watch again. It was three thirteen p.m. this time.

"He's here." Carmen was finally on the intercom, announcing Bob's arrival.

"Who's here?" Beth playing it cool.

"You know . . . Mr. Talcourt," she answered, before dropping into a stage whisper. "That's some tall hombre! *Muy hermoso.* Do you want me to bring him in?"

"No, have him wait a minute. I'm finishing up something now. . . . Anyhow, he's late."

"Okay. Just say when."

Fifteen minutes later: "When."

"Do you want me to bring my book in and take notes?" It was more of a salacious request than a question from her middle-aged legal assistant.

"Carmen! Behave yourself. You've got a husband who adores you, and three kids nearly as old as Bob Talcourt."

"Not for me. For you."

"Just bring him in, will you."

"You're twenty-seven years old," she admonished Beth. "There's more to life than this office."

"Carmen, bring Mr. Talcourt in. *Please!*" The insistence in her voice got through because the intercom fell quiet and it didn't take long before Carmen was showing Bob into her office. This time he was wearing a broad smile, jeans, and a tan suede sport jacket with contrasting leather elbow patches over a yellow button-down shirt with a maroon striped tie.

Beth took a few seconds to enjoy the sight before she stood up and walked out from behind her desk to greet him. She looked at him closely, held his smile with her own, and extended her right hand, gripping his hand firmly. As the pause approached pregnant, they broke eye contact. Beth went back behind her desk and sat down in her chair. Bob looked around the office and then sat on the couch across from her desk, crossing his legs casually to reveal the same well-worn pair of leather boots he'd had on up in Providence.

She spoke first. "Can we get you something to drink? Coffee or soda?"

"Your assistant already asked me. I think she's bringing me in a Coke. By the way . . . ," he added, "those photographs on your back wall are outstanding. Did you take them?"

"No, my stepfather did. Photography is his hobby."

"That one with the fog shroud draped over the sailboats in the harbor is pure tranquillity. He's a good shooter."

"Thanks. I think so too," she said, and then continued: "You know, your call surprised me."

"Why?"

"I didn't expect to hear from you again."

"I had to be in New York on real short notice today. I'm up

for a job at WKYN and they wanted me to bring in some of my tapes."

"That's terrific. Good luck."

"Thanks, but that's not why I wanted to see you."

"What's up?"

"Remember we were talking about my father's insurance policy?"

"Sure. You told me you hadn't made any claim on it."

"I think maybe I'd like to try."

"You don't need a lawyer for that. You just need to send in the policy and a copy of the death certificate." Then she belatedly recognized the problem. "I see. You don't have a death certificate."

"No policy either."

"I thought you told me you had the policy? How did you know there was one?"

"After you left, I checked what I had found in my father's condo. It wasn't a policy, only some premium notices."

"Proof of death is going to be the big problem. You are going to need an attorney for that."

"That's not what the investigator from Metropolitan Life said when he stopped by the day before yesterday."

"Oh, you already made a claim?" she asked, certain that she had caught him in a lie.

"No."

"Then how come somebody stopped by?" She was skeptical.

"Come to think of it, I don't know. Somehow they knew about my father's accident and wanted to know when I was going to make a claim for the insurance proceeds."

"Seems a little strange. An insurance company going out of their way to invite a claim." It would make me suspicious, she thought, watching closely for his reaction.

"I didn't think much about it at the time. He asked me a lot of questions. Tried to find out what I knew about my father's death and I told him I didn't know anything. I really don't." It was obvious he saw nothing unusual in the visit.

"What was the man's name? Did he leave you a card or anything?"

"No, and I didn't think to ask. Kind of fat with a heavy European accent. I remember he grabbed a powdered sugar doughnut off my desk as he was leaving the studio and managed to get most of it on his charcoal-gray suit."

"It shouldn't be hard getting his name from MetLife," she said, "but you should be careful when unexpected strangers start asking you unexpected questions."

"I know, I know. The truth is I don't have the temperament to work my way through this bureaucratic maze. Can you practice law in Rhode Island?" The look she saw him deliver across the desk was an intriguing mixture of little-boy pique and big-boy charm. That's some interesting combination, she thought.

"Practicing law in Rhode Island isn't the problem," she answered. "MetLife has its main offices right here in New York. We can sue them here if we have to."

"So will you do it for me? You're the only lawyer I know."

"Litigation is expensive in New York. It would be cheaper if a Providence firm handled it for you."

"What does your firm charge?"

"Well, they bill three hundred and sixty-five dollars an hour for my time, but I'm not a partner in the firm. Some senior partners charge over seven hundred."

"I'd be tapped before I left your office the first day. Is there any way you could take your fee out of the recovery?"

"We don't generally take cases on a contingency, especially one this small. We'd also need some kind of advance retainer."

"Well, do I have a case?"

"You'd have to prove the fact of your father's death, and I'd have to do some research on what's required. The problem is if we need to go all the way to trial. It's a big risk for us if we're handling it on a contingency."

"And an impossible expense for me if I pay for it on an hourly basis."

"Exactly."

"Well, could you check it out with your boss and let me know?"

"Sure, I'll speak to Clifford about it when I see him tomorrow."

"Thanks. You know, when we met in Providence, I didn't want my father's insurance money. I didn't know him and figured I didn't have the right to it."

"And now?"

"I've decided it isn't a morality issue. If he had nobody besides me, I might as well get the money. Call it compensation for my abandonment. And besides, if I get this job in New York, I can use it to buy myself an apartment."

"You can't buy an apartment in New York for three hundred and fifty thousand dollars."

"I don't need anything big. And it doesn't have to be in a fancy neighborhood. Chelsea or Tribeca would be fine."

"They're both neat areas, but you're going to have to look hard to find anything at that price."

"I'll worry about it after I get the job. There are a million jocks from out of town all trying for the same gig."

"Well, I hope you get it."

"Thanks."

She smiled, thinking how genuine he seemed. Perfect sitting on a horse or in front of your fireplace. "Well, listen," she said, looking at her watch, "it's four fifteen and I have court tomorrow. I'm going to throw you out."

"I'm sorry. I forgot about the time."

"It's just that I have a lot to do. I didn't mean to sound so abrupt."

"Don't be silly. I know you're busy. But how about a drink later or, even better, how about dinner? I'm staying in the city tonight."

"No, I'm sorry, really," she said, her resistance wilting. "And I'm not trying to be coy, but I do have to work late tonight."

"I'm nothing if not persistent. There's a new Indian place I want to try. Café Jaipur on Seventy-fourth and Second."

"I really can't." She was weakening. This time her negative response didn't even convince her.

"Think of it as an attorney-client business dinner. I'll deduct it as a business expense. When do you figure you'll be finished here?"

"Probably around eight or eight thirty," Beth answered, deciding that enough was enough already. It was starting to sound childish. What she really wanted to do was meet this man for dinner. That shouldn't be so hard for her. It was only a meal.

"Terrific. Suppose I call you here at eight. No commitment, no obligation. If you feel like it, we'll go out. Okay?"

"Okay," she said, "I'll tell you what. Give me a call at seven and I'll see how I'm doing."

"Great. Speak to you later." He got up to leave.

"Hey, before you go, didn't you say something about finding some papers of your father's?"

"I left them at the hotel. I'll bring them to the restaurant."

"No problem. Here's my private number," she said, handing him a business card.

Bob took the card from her and put it in his pocket as he walked out of her office. After he left, Beth started to write, but it was mindless doodling designed to hide the vacant expression on her face. Her conflicting emotions were free to crash headlong into one another, turning the day into a real-life soap opera. What was she doing going out for dinner with Sloane's son? A rhetorical question if there ever was one. Could he be as innocent as he looked, or was he just a good actor? If Clifford would only let her handle the insurance claim, it would be the perfect opportunity to find out.

Beth couldn't tell Clifford that the client was Sloane's son and that the claim involved his life insurance policy. Clifford was not about to let her get involved with an offshoot of the same matter that was probably going to result in a malpractice suit by Leung. She had earned Clifford's trust and was now about to abuse it big-time by concealing relevant information.

She decided to do some research on insurance law immediately so tomorrow she could sell Clifford on the case. He believed in an hour's pay for an hour's work. Contingency litigation had to offer the prospect of a big recovery to justify the risk. Too bad it wasn't a $1 million policy.

She was looking forward to dinner with Bob.

When the cab dropped her off at Seventy-fourth and Second, Beth saw plenty of restaurants on the block, but no Café Jaipur. She checked on her cellphone and found that Bob had given her the wrong address. Café Jaipur was at Seventy-sixth and Third. Close enough to walk to, which she did. Bob was waiting outside for her with a handshake and a grin on his face somewhere between apologetic and sheepish.

As soon as they sat down, Bob reached into his shoulder

bag and handed her a large envelope. "Before I forget again, here's that package of papers I mentioned."

"Thanks."

"It was in a box I found in his condo with my name on it. The rest of the stuff was just family junk. Camp pictures, birthday and Christmas cards I sent him, nothing important, so I left it home."

"It must have been important to him if he saved it."

"I suppose."

"Does your father own the condo?"

"I checked, but he rented it."

"Who's the landlord?"

"Some outfit called Paramount."

"Paramount?" She hoped she didn't sound too interested.

"Yeah. Some of their bills are in the package you have."

"I'll take a look at it all tomorrow after I get the okay from my boss." She wasn't about to share any information about Paramount with him.

"Sounds good. The only thing I took out of it was some New Zealand money I found tucked inside an expired passport of his."

"When did he go there?"

"I have zero idea."

"You know what, send me the passport. You can never tell what might prove important."

"I'll mail it tomorrow."

"I would so love to sail to New Zealand."

"You sail?"

"I never miss a chance. My parents live on a sailboat down in the Caribbean."

"I tried to learn to sail in camp one year. Spent most of the time in the water trying to right the boat."

He laughed and she laughed, but she was really thinking how nice it would be to sail into a sunset with him. I hope he's not one of the bad guys. What a drag that would be.

Indian food had never been a favorite of hers, but she enjoyed sharing the vegetable pakora and chicken jalfrezi with Bob. She even found enough room left over at the end to share a delicious cottage cheese confection called ras malai for dessert.

I like being with him, she thought during the meal. That unpretentious personality of his is special. He acts natural and he's not afraid to laugh at himself. Even down to the cute way he described how he finally stumbled onto Café Jaipur himself after the cab dropped him off on Seventy-fourth Street.

They lingered over coffee, extending the dinner by mutual consent. She was sorry when it ended, but at the same time she wanted to get back to her apartment to look over the papers Bob had given her.

Back in her apartment after dinner, she got into bed, put on her iPod, and pulled up the red plaid comforter that Brian had given her two years ago during the waning days of their relationship. Since then she'd had her share of frogs and princes, but no commitments. Oh well, she thought, celibacy wasn't too bad if you didn't make a cause célèbre out of it.

After unwrapping a Klondike bar, she opened Bob's envelope and began to examine its contents. She nibbled on the ice cream bar as she went along, making notes of the things she wanted to check at the office tomorrow. There was one set of papers stapled together that looked like incomplete applications to several different offshore insurance companies, million-dollar proposals, too. She hadn't seen them mentioned in the insurance printout she had. So why only a $350,000 policy with MetLife?

She was nodding and focusing when a CD fell out of the envelope and onto the bed next to her. She picked it up and grinned at the name *proCKtoscope* printed on the label. Someone has a sense of humor, she thought. Wonder what's on it. She vowed to check in the morning and dropped the CD off the bed next to the file already on the floor.

Chapter Fourteen

Arriving back from court the next morning, Beth hit the office running, threw her attaché case on the couch, hung up her trench coat, and dialed Frank Epstein's number on the intercom.

"Frank, what do you know about insurance law?"

"Well, I'm probably not the world's greatest living expert, but I can tell a term policy from a whole life policy if that helps."

"Got a minute for me? I'll come to your office."

"Okay."

She unlocked the bottom drawer of her credenza, got the Sloane file, and added the papers she had gotten from Bob Talcourt. She kept out the insurance applications, made copies after blocking out Sloane's name, and handed them to Frank as she entered his office.

"When did we get an insurance case in the office?" Frank asked as he looked over the proposals.

"We didn't exactly. I picked it up last night."

"Did you speak to Clifford about it?"

"Not yet," she answered.

"Clifford doesn't like insurance cases. Be careful, will you, Beth, with that Paramount case still hanging over our head."

"I'm trying to develop some business for the firm."

"It must be a wealthy client."

"He's dead."

"Well then, it must be a wealthy beneficiary. These proposals are all for several million dollars or more. Do you have the actual policies?"

"I don't know if they were ever issued."

"They're all offshore insurance companies, too. Look at these . . . Netherlands Antilles, Panama, Cayman Islands."

"That's one of the things I wanted to ask you about. Why would somebody want life insurance from an offshore carrier when there are so many companies in the United States?"

"Cheaper rates, maybe, or less stringent physical examinations. I've also seen where some of these offshore companies are willing to take greater risks than the U.S. companies."

"Such as?"

"Well, remember the old rule requiring the owner of a life insurance policy to have an insurable interest in the life of the insured?"

"Sure. That's to prevent insurance policies from becoming lotteries. You have to be a relative of the insured or have some valid business interest."

"Exactly. Like key man insurance among business partners. Well, some of these foreign insurance companies have been known to be careless with that requirement from time to time."

"One of these proposals alone is for five million dollars. How would you find out if a policy had ever been issued?"

"I don't know, Beth. That's out of my bailiwick. You understand those online resources. Maybe you can learn something from them."

"I tried, but nothing came up."

"I'm sorry I couldn't offer you more." He handed the papers back to Beth, who got up out of her chair.

"Thanks. Please don't mention it to Clifford. I want to do some more research first."

"Okay. Don't forget to check for conflicts with other clients."

"I will."

She walked back to her office and checked her voicemail. Bob Talcourt had called. She made a fresh cup of coffee before sitting down to return his call. As she dialed his number, anticipating the sound of his voice made her feel good.

"Bob?" she asked as the phone was picked up.

"Hi, Beth. How did court go this morning?"

"Who knows. They're so backed up it can take months before you get a decision."

"I enjoyed dinner last night."

"So did I. Did you hear anything from WKYN yet?"

"That's why I called. I'm still in the running."

"That's great. What happened?"

"They want to hear some more of my tapes. That's usually a good sign. I'm going back to Providence now to pick them up."

"Why don't you just have somebody send them here for you? Federal Express would be here by tomorrow morning."

"I thought of that, but they're locked up in a file cabinet in my apartment, and anyhow, there's some transmission problem I have to handle back at the station tonight."

"I hope you get the job." She meant it.

"Thanks. Now that I'll be back in New York tomorrow, I thought we could have dinner Saturday night."

She resisted: "I don't think so, Bob. I don't have any information yet for you about your case. I just got back from court and haven't had two seconds to talk to my boss about it."

"So what. I want to meet you for dinner without any business reason."

"It's not a good idea." (No, what it is, is insane!)

"Why?"

"If I'm going to represent you in a lawsuit, I need to be objective."

"I just want to have dinner. That's hardly a commitment."

"What time and where?" she finally asked after a brief pause, intended more for effect than anything else.

"I don't know. Let's make it seven thirty. I have no idea where. Why don't I call you when I get back into town tomorrow. We can talk about it then."

"Sounds good. Speak to you then." As she hung up the phone, her mind took over with the inevitable round of questions about Sloane's death and the missing Jasco money. She completed the rationalization process with the thought that dinner with Bob would be a good chance to learn more about what he knew.

She still had to speak to Clifford but postponed the confrontation long enough to go into her bag for the CD she had found among Sloane's papers. She turned on her computer and inserted it into one of the drives. She tried everything but couldn't bring up anything. She finally decided to call Brian for help after she spoke to Clifford. Brian would know how to open it up.

Beth got up from her desk and walked down the hall to Clifford's office. His door was closed, and since Constance wasn't at her desk, she just knocked on his door and walked in.

Clifford was on the phone. He nodded to her when she walked in and, with his hand, motioned her to sit down. Beth could tell from the affectionate tone of his voice that it was a personal call.

While waiting for him to finish, she focused her attention on the papers she had carried in. The sun, streaming in from the window through the venetian blinds, slanted obliquely across his desk, partly shrouding his face in streaks of contrasting shadow and light, withdrawing his physical presence from the room. The effect was ghostlike, causing Beth to wonder about his pallor.

In the three years that she had worked for Clifford, he had offered little insight into himself. His personal life had remained just that. He was her affectionate mentor, but never without his impeccable reserve. Although he was Max's closest friend and had been his law partner for more than thirty years, that kind of intimacy was not extended to her. She only knew him to be a brilliant, oak-solid attorney and a very private person.

Clifford hung up the phone and turned his attention to Beth. "Any word from the malpractice carrier?"

"No. I'll call them again as soon as I get back to my office." Without any preamble, she then began to tell him about the Talcourt insurance case, embellishing it to make it seem as attractive as possible. She studiously avoided mentioning Sloane's name.

When she finished her careful presentation, it looked like Clifford was thoughtfully considering the matter of their retention. She could see that he wasn't particularly thrilled with the idea.

"Beth . . . ," he finally started, "it's a bad case for us to get involved with."

She sat in the chair, listening silently as he continued. "The liability is unclear and there's not enough of a potential recovery to make a contingency fee worthwhile." He was only confirming what she had suspected he would say.

"But I can settle it quickly. Hopefully the insurance company will fold as soon as we serve a summons and complaint. I told Mr. Talcourt that if we couldn't settle it with the carrier, we would want the right to withdraw or discontinue before trial."

"Nonsense! You're daydreaming!" Clifford said sharply, emphasizing it with a fit of dry coughing. "You know perfectly well the court isn't going to let us out of a case on the eve of trial. The time spent on depositions alone could eat up the whole fee if we're lucky enough to get a recovery in the first place. No, I think you should pass on this one."

"Clifford," she pressed on, "Talcourt can be a good source of business. I'm not going to need to take any depositions. I can get us to the settlement stage with five or ten hours' work, maximum."

"Cases like this are a dime a dozen."

"But you keep telling the associates how important it is to develop business for the firm, and here's a potential client with his finger in the entire radio communications business. It could lead to big matters."

"I encourage associates to develop their own sources of business, but your stepfather and I didn't build this firm with small contingency cases like this one. The economics of it are all wrong."

"Clifford, let me take this one. I'll keep a close watch on the hours and it won't affect my regular billings."

"It's such a small case, Beth. Why are you so anxious to handle it? Is there anything else I should know?"

"No, I told you all I know," she said, trying conscientiously, but with minimal success, to maintain eye contact with him. Did he know the name *Talcourt*? Had he connected the name with Sloane? "I just think that this is a client who will amount to something and turn into a good long-range source of business."

"I'll tell you what. Run it through the office dockets to make sure we don't have any conflict of interest with existing clients, and if it comes up clean, get a five-thousand-dollar retainer up front against a twenty-five percent contingency and run with it for a few hours of work. Your judgment is usually good. I'll go with it."

"Thanks, Clifford." This time she couldn't meet his eyes. There was a very real conflict of interest with the potential Paramount malpractice case.

"But I also want you to let me know immediately if the hours get out of hand, and that means anything more than four or five hours."

"I will," she said, concentrating now on any part of his face except his eyes. "Are you feeling okay?" she asked reflexively, suddenly aware that his face had retained its unhealthy color even now that the sun had moved on.

"Fine. Why?" he responded with a shrug.

"Nothing. You just look a little thin."

"I've been trying to shake a cold," he said without concern. Clifford's attention was already on something else because she saw him take a little red address book out of his vest pocket and thumb through the pages.

"What time is it in Zurich?" she heard him mumbling almost to himself as he found the page he was looking for. "Ah, forget it. It's not important," he went on, still mumbling and apparently still alone in a conversation with himself as he watched her walk out of his office, closing the door behind her.

He was careful, though, not to begin dialing the long telephone number until she had left. As he waited for the number to ring, he stared at the notes he had made on a memo pad while Beth was talking. He kept underlining Talcourt's name until the phone was picked up at the other end.

Beth walked back to her office, feeling painfully guilty about abusing Clifford's trust in her. She sought justification, figuring that as long as she turned out the hours, Clifford couldn't complain. So much for integrity.

"Brian?"

"Who else would be in my house at six thirty picking up my phone?"

"I didn't want to call you at the bank. I got a problem."

"Sorry. I have a date tonight and still have to shower."

"But it's important. I need to open a CD that might be connected to the missing seventy million."

"Figuring out a password should be child's play for you."

"I figured out the password without a problem, but all I keep getting is a blur of numbers scrolling across my screen and I can't stop them or make sense out of what they are."

"Okay, let me open up my computer. Watch for the email."

"Thanks, Brye."

In very short order, Brian took over control of her computer and began the process of examining Sloane's CD. Propelled by his expertise, the cursor flew around the screen as windows opened and closed faster than her eyes could follow them. Finally, the screen froze to reveal thousands of numbers unseparated by any spaces except for an occasional Chinese character.

"Beth, I don't understand Chinese, but I'm pretty sure this is a massive series of 128-bit encrypted bank access codes. Very sophisticated stuff."

"So how do I figure it out?"

"I see sequences like this all day long at the bank. As a matter of fact, I drafted these protocols when I first went to work there. If you're not the sender or the intended recipient, it's just meaningless gibberish."

"Oh, great! Enjoy your date."

Chapter Fifteen

When Bob offered to pick her up at her apartment on Saturday night, she accepted. No problem so far. Then, impulsively, she suggested he come up first for a drink. He couldn't
accept fast enough. At that point, there was no way for it to
qualify as a business date any longer.

Now here it was, nearly eight o'clock, she wasn't ready and
had a feeling that Bob would be the prompt type. She gave the
apartment a final check, made sure the bathroom was reason-
ably neat after her shower, and closed the bedroom door, relieved she had cleaned the apartment in the morning.

She took the sour cream and the bottle of Pinot Grigio out
of the refrigerator and added a package of freeze-dried onion
soup mix to the sour cream. After peeling the price sticker off
the wine bottle, she put the onion dip and the wine out on the
black enamel glass-topped cocktail table she had bought with
part of the Jasco bonus.

She had finished lighting the candles when she heard the
house phone ring. The doorman told her that Bob was downstairs and asked if it was okay to send him up. She searched for
Clapton on her iPod and put on "Wonderful Tonight" just as
the doorbell rang.

When Bob came into the apartment, he smiled warmly,
handed her a bouquet of pink carnations, and shook her hand.

Then he said how much he liked Clapton. With that, all her reservation, lawyerlike or otherwise, flew out the window and her natural exuberance took over. It continued to rise when she came out of the kitchen with a corkscrew for the wine, only to find him sitting in the middle of the couch with a contrite look on his face and a big blob of onion dip on his finger.

"Oh, shit!" she said under her breath. "I forgot to put out the chips."

"It wasn't a problem," he said, licking his finger clean, "I started without them."

"Hang on a second. I have some in the kitchen."

"Perfect. I'll uncork the wine in the meantime."

She handed him the corkscrew and went back into the kitchen. When she returned with the chips, he was pouring wine into the two glasses she had left on the table. She took the glass of wine he handed her. "I hope you like it, otherwise I have some vodka and some tequila in one of the cabinets."

"No, thanks. This is fine," he said, and then added, "Cheers," before taking a sip of the wine.

"And to the job offer you want."

"Amen to that." He took another sip while looking around the living room. "I like your apartment."

"Thanks. I finally put some effort into it this summer."

"It's beautiful."

"I used a bonus I got for winning a big real estate fraud case." She looked at him for any reaction to her oblique reference to the appeal she had won for his father. If he caught the jab, he didn't show it. She sat on the couch. "How's it going with WKYN?"

"I don't know really. I only dropped off the tapes yesterday. I probably won't hear from them for a few days, at least."

"The competition's rough, isn't it?"

"Of course it is, but that's what makes working in New York the big time. The pressure to achieve here is incredible."

"Yes, but you know what, so are the rewards. I enjoy the competition."

"And the money?" His eyes appraised the Chagall lithograph on her wall along with the nineteenth-century primitives.

"It's one of the best ways to judge how well you're playing the game. On the other hand, living in New York costs an arm and a leg, so it kind of offsets the bigger salaries we get paid here."

"I can see you like being a lawyer."

"I love it, and sometimes I even get to think I'm good at it."

"You're lucky. Liking what you do best. What turns you on the most?" he asked.

She thought about it for a minute, ignoring the innocent double entendre. "The trial work," she finally answered. "It's intellectually stimulating and it gives me the competition I used to get from athletics."

"An ex-jock. And a Republican, no doubt."

"Ex nothing." She grinned while striking a pose and protested: "A tomboy, if you please, and a Republican, except on the abortion issue. Socially more of a liberal, though. And what about you? What makes you tick?"

"Originally, I saw myself as a pro basketball player with an engineering degree to use afterwards. Then in college, I realized I wasn't good enough to make it in the NBA."

"How tall are you, six four, six five?"

"Six five, a little more, but MIT isn't actually the proving ground for aspiring athletes."

"So what happened?"

"After my junior year, I decided a degree in electrical engineering wasn't for me either. I wanted a career in radio and I wanted to do something useful for the third-world nations. That's why I volunteered to go to Zaire with the Peace Corps. I wanted to do good things and save the world."

"How was the Peace Corps?"

"I enjoyed it, but it was an excuse to avoid getting on with my life. Like extending my childhood."

"But you didn't think so then, when it counted. And anyhow, what's so wrong with postponing the need to face the world for a while?"

"I think now I was reacting to the way my father was before he ran out on us. He was consumed by the urge to make money at any cost and yet was always complaining that we never had enough. It controlled his whole life."

"Maybe he was overwhelmed by having a family to support," she suggested.

"So are a lot of guys."

"He reacted differently," she said, not actually trying to be supportive of Sloane, but it had that effect on Bob anyway. She could see his temperature rising.

"But he always blamed everyone else for his failures."

"It's hard for some people to accept responsibility. I'm used to hearing clients blame the cruel world for their problems."

"And I suppose they just pick themselves up, like he did, and walk away from their family?"

"Some do it physically, others do it emotionally."

"The result's the same too. He left us when I was eleven and I felt like I had been discarded."

"Then he went ahead and died on you." She was goading deliberately, testing. She wanted to know.

"And the son of a bitch didn't even call to say goodbye!" he erupted, and Beth saw his pain was deep. She was moved by its intensity and felt bad for having provoked him.

"Now I'm the one who feels awful." She was genuinely sorry, more so because of her motivation. "I didn't know your father that well."

"No. I'm the one who's sorry for getting carried away. I also laid it on you up in Providence. I hate whiners. It's old news and he's gone anyhow." The emotion of the moment had passed. Despite his youthful sensitivity, he wasn't one to dwell on self-pity.

"We both have a lot of unwashed laundry. Both our fathers deserted us by dying. Only yours deserted you twice."

"I guess you could say that. Anyhow, it's history and I'm here with you now and that makes me feel good."

"I'm glad. Me too."

"And that perfume you're wearing is delicious." He leaned over toward her, gently caressing her long blond hair with his fingers while emphasizing the extent of his pleasure with a deep inhalation of her scent.

Her reaction to his touch changed their relationship forever. She had no idea what to say or where to take it. Clichés fought for control over her intellect. The touch of his hand on the back of her neck sent a shiver of pure ecstasy vibrating throughout her body, causing her to arch the nape of her neck to extend the sensation. She felt her mind go blank.

Finally, intellect rebooted, and her head resumed control over her body. It was too soon for this to happen. She separated from him and stood up.

"Whiskey Tango Foxtrot!" she exclaimed, breathing hard. It was more of a gasp for air than a comment on society, but it did break the spell of the moment, and they both ended up laughing hysterically.

She reached over to the cocktail table and filled their glasses with the last of the wine.

"Just in time. I'm starving," he said. "Let's go eat."

"Good idea," she said.

Beth double-locked her apartment door as they left, and together they walked silently on the plush brown carpeting down the long hall to the bank of elevators that serviced her floor. While they were waiting for an elevator, he turned to her and, without any hesitation, touched her cheek and gave her a gentle kiss. No probing. Just his lips lingering softly on hers. And he tasted delicious.

Chapter Sixteen

Beth was in her office reviewing the final draft of the Talcourt life insurance complaint. She signed the attorney's verification at the end and handed it to Carmen. "Give it to one of the file room clerks to serve on MetLife tomorrow morning. Call up MetLife and ask them where he should go."

"Madison Avenue and Twenty-fifth Street. The first floor."

"You checked already?"

"What do you think?" she answered triumphantly as she turned to walk out of Beth's office.

"Terrific. Good job. Take an extra minute or two for lunch today. You've earned it."

"Minute or two nothing. L and T's having a sale on men's clothing this week, so I'm going over there to pick out a birthday present for my husband. If I get sidetracked at the jewelry counter, I may be a little late."

"Enjoy yourself."

"Mr. Giles stopped by when you were in the back conference room. He said to tell you that if you don't get your October billing in to the bookkeeper by tomorrow, you're not going to get paid Friday."

"It's all done."

"Oh, and Tim Flaherty from our malpractice carrier called you."

"Call him back for me now."

"Coming right up." Carmen made the call and transferred it through to Beth in her office.

"Hi, Tim," she said when she picked up the phone. "Anything new in our case?"

"This guy Charlie Chen from Taiwan has called me three times in the last two days trying to settle it."

"Same number?"

"Yup—5.25 million."

"He's out of his mind."

"Listen, Beth, when you consider the huge malpractice award possible after a trial, it might pay for your firm to consider a settlement no matter how small the risk of losing."

"What kind of figure are you talking about?"

"Our risk assessment people have authorized me to offer Leung two million dollars just based upon our estimated cost of bringing the case to trial."

"Do they think we have any liability?"

"Not really, but we all know that the weakest case has some nuisance value."

"I know that, Tim. Let me talk it over with my bosses and I'll get back to you."

"Take your time. We can't settle the case without your approval anyhow."

After she finished talking to Tim, she opened up the diary on her laptop, counted off twenty days, and made an entry on December 8 to remind her when the MetLife answer would be due. She didn't care if their attorneys requested extra time, as long as they let her examine the MetLife file on Leonard Sloane, his life and his death.

She stared at the open diary, her thoughts wandering for a change to her relationship with Bob, never forgetting that it rested on an undisclosed foundation—her effort to find the Jasco money, her number one priority. If that created an impenetrable obstacle to some future relationship between her and Bob, so be it. There were more important things in her life right now. She would have to keep her needs and feelings in sync with her goals.

Chapter Seventeen

Dieter Rheinhartz spent the morning at Chase Bank searching for a fresh lead. He had asked for the meeting when the Jasco money trail disappeared into a morass of red tape and privacy laws in Zurich. For two hours, the bank's security officers repeatedly assured him they had every intention of being cooperative, but their actions sought only to cover their corporate rear end. As far as they were concerned, Chase had followed regulations. They were in the clear and weren't going to provide Rheinhartz with any information that might expose them to liability as Erica Crossland's employer.

On his way out of the meeting, he was approached in the hallway by Jim Connally, Chase's vice president in charge of security.

"Sorry we couldn't be of more help, Dieter."

"I hoped that Chase would be more interested in recovering the money."

"We are, but our legal department is more concerned about our potential liability to Leung."

"Has he started suit?"

"I can't really discuss that. Come on, though, I'll walk you down to the elevator."

"By the way, congratulations on your promotion to VP security."

"You helped me get that. You know, I never really had a chance to thank you for that lead you gave me in London last year. It saved our international division a bundle."

"Glad I could help, Jim. Fraud prevention makes banking safer for everyone."

"I agree. By the way, did you have any luck tracking the Jasco money to the Rhode Island Hospital Trust in Providence?"

The question was asked just as the elevator doors closed, and everything about it surprised Rheinhartz. In the first place, he hadn't been to that bank at all; and in the second place, it hadn't been mentioned in any of the documents he had inspected. The more he thought about it, the more he became convinced that it was Jim's way of giving him some information without violating instructions from Chase's legal department.

In any event, it was the only new lead he had, and tomorrow was an open day on his schedule. If he went right up to Providence, he might get there early enough to visit the Hospital Trust today. It would also give him another opportunity to visit Talcourt.

The Metro-North train made it to Stamford in time for him to connect with the Amtrak train for Providence. He called up the chief of security at the Rhode Island Hospital Trust and arranged to meet with him between four and five p.m. By the time Amtrak pulled into New Haven, Rheinhartz was dropping in and out of a light sleep frequently interrupted by the pain in his left arm.

When he arrived at the bank, the chief of security asked a data-processing clerk to check for any Leonard Sloane accounts, and they were able to locate one. Before he left the bank, Rheinhartz successfully identified two possible transfers from that account to banks down in Caracas.

With photocopies of the account tucked away, Rheinhartz took a cab over to WFEX-FM on the chance Talcourt would be there, but he learned Bob wasn't due until that evening. He left a message for him with Justin and went back out to the Hotel Providence on Mathewson, where he was staying for the night.

Tomorrow morning, he'd take a limousine up to Boston and catch a flight from there to Caracas. The dates and amounts of the transfers were close enough to make investigation worthwhile.

After checking in at the hotel, he asked the desk clerk for a place to have dinner and was given an assortment of menus from nearby restaurants to look at. He ended up at a restaurant over on Cushing Street. When the taxi dropped him back at the hotel after dinner, he went up to his room, carefully hung up his suit in the closet and sat down at the small round table by the telephone.

He first called the radio station, asking for Talcourt, but it was Talcourt who answered the phone.

"Mr. Talcourt, this is Fritz Ehrenwald." It was the name he remembered using. "We met when I came to see you about your father's insurance policy."

"You're the guy from MetLife."

"Actually, I am an independent claims adjuster. Mr. Talcourt, I wonder if I could see you tomorrow morning about your claim."

"There's no point in doing that. I've turned the matter over to a lawyer in New York."

"Would you mind telling me who he is?"

"It's a she. Beth Swahn at Wilcox, Swahn and Giles. If you give me your number, I'll pass it along to her."

"No, that won't be necessary," he said abruptly. "Sorry to have troubled you."

Rheinhartz hung up the phone and reached into his leather bag for his cellphone to call C. K. Leung in Taipei.

"Good morning," Leung said as he picked up the phone.

"Mr. Leung? This is Dieter Rheinhartz."

"Yes, Herr Rheinhartz."

"I am in Providence, Rhode Island. I have some information for you."

"What have you learned?"

"It is likely that a wire transfer of your money went from the Rhode Island Hospital Trust here in Providence to one of two banks in Caracas."

"Why Providence?"

"I do not know that yet. It might have something to do with the fact that Sloane has a son here."

"That's very interesting. When will you be leaving for Venezuela?" Leung was confident that Rheinhartz was going. He only wanted to know when.

"I'll go to Boston tomorrow morning and fly to Caracas from there."

"Call me when you have something to report. The matter is becoming quite urgent."

"I have instructed my people to give it full time and effort. And one other thing."

"Yes?"

"I found out that Sloane's son has started suit against Metropolitan Life Insurance Company to collect on a small policy it issued on Sloane's life."

"How does that concern us?"

"His attorney is Elisabeth Swahn at Wilcox, Swahn and

Giles in New York. . . ." This time, Rheinhartz sensed a definite pause in the conversation.

"It doesn't concern us," Leung finally answered. He then hung up.

Rheinhartz still had one call to make. He opened the stocked bar next to the triple dresser, took a glass from the bathroom, and poured a Scotch for himself. Then he called Clifford Giles to bring him up-to-date on his search for the missing funds.

Contrary to his statement to Rheinhartz, Leung was indeed interested in the information about the insurance litigation. "Concerned" would be a better word to describe it. Immediately after hanging up with Rheinhartz, C.K. called Martin in San Francisco and passed on the news.

"I told you so!" his brother exclaimed. "I knew the attorney was in on it."

"I think you may be right."

"If she's working for Sloane's son now, she was in it with Sloane from the beginning and that means she has our bank codes."

"I think you're right about that too."

"I'll call Eddie and catch the red-eye to New York tonight. What about you?"

"I'll be there tomorrow."

"We only have three weeks left, and our Arab partners are going to be very upset if there is any delay in payment."

"I will call the attorney tomorrow and give it one last try."

Chapter Eighteen

When C.K. surprised her with a call the following morning, Beth was ambivalent about taking it. Then she decided that nothing could be gained by ducking him, so she picked up the phone.

C.K., sensing her hesitation, got right to the point: "I'm in New York for a few days and want to resolve the Sloane matter while I'm here."

"I'm in favor of that."

"I also want to talk to you about some new business."

"I'm not sure that's being realistic."

"Please, can we get together for lunch?"

"I was supposed to start a trial today, but it's been adjourned until after Thanksgiving."

"Is the Regency at one p.m. okay for you?"

"Yes. Will anyone be joining us?"

"No, just you and I."

After going through her accumulated email, Beth returned a phone call that had come in late yesterday from the attorney representing MetLife. She agreed to his request for an additional month to answer the Talcourt complaint. In return, he agreed to let her inspect the Sloane file, so she made an appointment to go to his office.

She was looking forward to today's lunch with Leung for the chance to resolve the malpractice claim and perhaps learn what he really wanted. The chance of new business was remote but not impossible. When she told Clifford about the date, he approved the idea, although he wasn't pleased when she mentioned it would take place at C.K.'s hotel. "Be very circumspect and careful," were his parting words to her.

At twelve forty-five p.m., she took a cab to the Regency and entered the lobby through the revolving door. At the front desk, she announced herself to the clerk and asked him to notify Leung of her arrival. While he did, she crossed the white marble floor to the other side of the lobby and sat on a cushioned settee positioned to see the bank of elevators in front of her. The hushed pace of activity was enhanced by the Baroque chamber music being filtered softly through the lobby's sound system.

She stood up a few minutes later when she saw Leung get out of the elevator and walk toward her. He greeted her again with a kiss on the cheek and a handshake.

"I am glad that you could come over," he said to her.

"Good to see you again."

"One slight problem," he then said. "An overseas emergency blew up an hour ago and I'm expecting several important phone calls. I had my secretary arrange our lunch in my suite. I hope you don't mind."

"As a matter of fact, I do mind. You should have called."

"I thought you'd accommodate me since we do have confidential business of our own to discuss. I dislike doing that in a restaurant."

"I understand that, but we do have conference rooms at my office and we have complete privacy there. We handle sensitive matters for clients throughout the world."

At that point, C.K. smiled apologetically and offered to

move the meeting to her office if she felt uncomfortable. Beth took that as a challenge, accepted the imposition, and told him his suite would do for a working lunch. She then called Carmen with the change of plans and told her she'd be back in the office by two thirty.

They got out on C.K.'s floor, and the door to his suite was held open for them by a woman in a pale green silk cheongsam whom C.K. introduced as his "secretary." He then motioned Beth to a couch in the middle of the room, but she chose an upholstered armchair next to one of the room's three windows. It might be melodramatic paranoia, but her back was covered and her view of the room was clear.

Besides the closed bedroom door off to her left, she could see a separate enclosed kitchen off to the right-hand side of the suite. Through the open kitchen door, she noticed a chef preparing food. There was a circular dining table at one end of the sitting room that had been set with four place settings. She, C.K., and maybe his secretary were three, she thought, wondering who and where number four might be.

"I thought you said it was just us at this meeting?" she asked C.K.

"Just one newcomer I hadn't expected, but he is on our side, so no need for concern."

Before sitting down, C.K. turned his back to Beth for a moment while he opened up a zippered tan leather briefcase lying on top of the walnut wet bar and took out a folder. "This is the new matter I mentioned to you yesterday," he said, turning back to face her. He walked over to where she was sitting, handed her the papers, and sat on the couch. "We hope your firm will be able to handle it for us."

Beth looked briefly through the papers and then at C.K. as he started to talk. "As you can see, we are interested in acquiring a company that owns and operates a large chain of upscale motels in the Northeast."

"It looks very interesting," she commented while starting to mentally envision the mammoth size of the transaction and the fees it would generate.

"What you have is the proposed contract of sale the seller delivered here yesterday," he said, indicating the papers in Beth's hands.

"We can handle the legal end for you, provided you are ready to release your Jasco claim against us," she said calmly. "We have excellent people to handle all aspects of the transaction, real estate, corporate, and tax."

"Excellent. Take the contract back to your office and give me an estimate of your legal fees after you've had a chance to review it."

"I'll get back to you first thing next week."

"Excellent."

"I'm sure we can work out a satisfactory arrangement."

"I know we can."

"Now what about the Jasco matter?" Beth asked. "We need to get that out of the way first."

"Good. What can we do about it?"

"You just need to release us. I'm sure you've been advised by your own attorneys that we have no liability."

"Of course. Otherwise we wouldn't be discussing new business."

"I understand that you have been in contact with our insurance company."

"We have, but unfortunately, their reaction time is slow, and we would like to resolve the matter more expeditiously."

"What do you have in mind?"

"I thought that perhaps you might be able to encourage faster action by the insurance company. We would consider a further reduction of our claim in exchange for a decision before I return to Taiwan this weekend."

"How much were you thinking about?" she asked impassively. It was obvious that C.K. was dangling the motel fee as a carrot for her cooperation in getting the malpractice insurer to pay off on his claim.

"I will be very candid with you, Beth. We will accept 2.5 million dollars, provided I have their approval before I leave. That is probably about what it will cost the insurance company to defend our suit. The figure is non-negotiable."

"Well, I think it's high for a baseless claim, but I'll call the insurance company when I get back to the office."

"Now, there is one other thing—" He stopped in midsentence as the bedroom door opened and a heavyset man wearing a rumpled light gray pinstripe suit came out, followed by Leung's secretary.

Beth was not completely surprised to see that someone else besides C.K.'s secretary had been in the bedroom all along. This phantom was apparently going to be number four at the table, although she had been led to believe that number four would arrive from outside the suite. His presence confirmed her impression of Leung. Secrecy and surprise were his modus operandi. Truth was irrelevant unless it suited his convenience.

"Yes? What is it?" she asked C.K., continuing the conversation while waiting to be introduced to the newcomer.

"What happened last summer with Leonard Sloane was not your fault," C.K. said, ignoring the newcomer while shifting tactfully to a subject sensitive to Beth.

"I know that, and I'm glad you know it too." She was reluctant to talk about a confidential matter with C.K. in front of this other man, who was standing patiently by the bedroom doorway, brushing off the lapels of his suit jacket.

"If we thought your firm had been involved in any way, we would have taken appropriate steps to remedy it, and I can assure you that I wouldn't be sitting here with you today discussing this new venture."

"I realize that," Beth said, all the more curious about the other man present in the room with them.

"What happened was not your fault, and what's to be done about it is not your problem either," C.K. continued.

"I'm not exactly sure what you're driving at now." She stood up, irritated about this unidentified stranger still standing quietly in the doorway leading from the bedroom.

"We are doing whatever needs to be done to recover the money," C.K. said.

"We assumed as much last month when you asked only that the fees be returned. By the way, I haven't been introduced to this gentleman yet"—indicating the man in the doorway.

"Forgive my poor manners. This is Dieter Rheinhartz. He is helping us recover the money Sloane stole from us."

"I'm pleased to meet you, Mr. Rheinhartz. I didn't realize you were in the other room," Beth said in a rebuke intended for C.K.

"The pleasure is mine," Dieter said. He sat down heavily on the large couch, within easy reach of the hors d'oeuvres.

"My name is Elisabeth Swahn," she added as the realization struck her that Rheinhartz must be the same man Bob told her had visited him in Providence. He obviously had nothing to do with Bob's insurance claim. He had been working for C.K., which meant C.K. knew all about the lawsuit against MetLife.

"Mr. Rheinhartz was working with my assistant in the

other room," C.K. said. "I apologize for not telling you of his presence before," he added, acknowledging the cause of Beth's anger.

"I was concerned about the attorney-client privilege being waived by the presence of an outsider."

"I appreciate your concern for protecting our confidences. However, we may talk freely in front of Mr. Rheinhartz. We have complete confidence in his discretion."

"Well then, perhaps you'd be willing to clarify the implication behind your repeated emphasis on statements about our not getting involved in the recovery of the money," she said to C.K. calmly but firmly. "Particularly since we haven't been involved in it."

"You have been involved, however," Rheinhartz interjected contentiously, entering into the conversation for the first time. "You are representing Sloane's son in a lawsuit against his father's life insurance company."

"That suit is a matter of record," she said. "I obviously cannot discuss anything with you that involves another client, but I can tell you that the suit has nothing whatsoever to do with any efforts to recover the money Sloane stole. It involves a life insurance policy, nothing more, nothing less. And, Mr. Rheinhartz," she said, moving onto the attack now, "I'd appreciate it if in the future you would avoid having any direct contact with Mr. Talcourt, regardless of what alias you're using at the time."

"I apologize for that, Miss Swahn. I spoke to Mr. Talcourt before I was aware of your representation."

"And you also told him you were from the insurance company, didn't you?" Beth continued.

"Correct me if I am wrong, Beth," C.K. said to her before Rheinhartz had a chance to answer. "Isn't it necessary to prove Sloane is dead in order to recover?"

132 / Michael Rudolph

"Or at least produce enough evidence to create a presumption of death."

"Sloane is dead," C.K. said, "and his body will never be recovered." His tone of voice left no doubt as to the finality of his conclusion.

"Indeed!" Beth agreed, avoiding a hallelujah for emphasis.

"I believe that is Mr. Leung's point," Rheinhartz said. "Your lawsuit will force the insurance company to prove that Sloane is alive."

"That is the idea," Beth said confidently.

"We would prefer not to encourage any investigation of Sloane's death," C.K. said to her. "We have made our own investigation and are satisfied that he and Miss Crossland are dead."

"I'll represent Sloane's son just as I represent every client," Beth responded emphatically. "He's entitled to the best case I can develop, but if you would care to share your findings, perhaps the matter can be expedited." She remained firm against this two-pronged attack launched by C.K. and Rheinhartz.

"I appreciate your dedication, but we are asking you to put an end to this," C.K. said, sidestepping her request.

"Well, then we're in agreement, because we both want to be finished as quickly as possible," she said. "I think we're clear on each other's positions."

"Miss Swahn," Rheinhartz said, shifting to a new facet of the same subject, "why is your stepfather working with you on the insurance case?"

"What's my stepfather got to do with this?" she asked casually, not liking this man very much, to say the least.

"What we find confusing, Beth," C.K. said, "is why he seems to be conducting his own investigation down in the Caribbean."

"I don't know what you mean." She knew exactly what he meant.

"On November third . . . ," Rheinhartz said, now reading authoritatively from a small notebook, "Max Swahn visited Blue Lagoon Charters and the United States Coast Guard in San Juan regarding the disappearance of *Satin Lady*."

"That was two weeks ago. I have no idea if or why he was there." She dismissed the information with a wave of her hand, treating it like so much trivia.

"We know why he was there," C.K. replied. "The point is that there is no need for any further efforts to be made by anyone toward locating Sloane. He is dead and eventually we will recover the money he stole."

"You gentlemen are forgetting one thing," Beth said, controlling her rising anger. "I have a client's interests to protect, even if it's only for three hundred and fifty thousand dollars."

"The insurance claim is of no interest to me," C.K. said dispassionately, his voice as steel gray as his suit, unwilling to entertain any contradiction from Beth.

"Metropolitan Life will eventually pay you something just to get rid of the case," Rheinhartz added. "They will not want to spend any money on an extensive investigation."

"Maybe so," she continued adamantly, "but that doesn't change the fact that Leonard Sloane and his girlfriend used me for their scam. My investigation will end when I am satisfied and not until!" Beth resisted the urge to just stand up and leave. She was not about to be told that her personal honor and professional integrity were less important than C. K. Leung's money and power.

"We understand that this is a matter of honor for you, Beth," C.K. said, now respectful, "but it is a matter of honor for the Leung family also, and you must not interfere with our efforts." He was leaving no room for compromise or doubt as to his position.

"Your efforts to find Sloane or your efforts to recover the seventy million dollars?" she asked, making no effort to mask the sarcasm in her voice.

"The money is our only interest now," C.K. said. "I have told you we are satisfied that Leonard and his woman died in the boat accident."

"But your actions belie your words," she probed.

"Sloane was able to steal seventy million dollars from my family because we placed our trust in him and he abused that trust," C.K. said. "I must emphasize that because Sloane is dead, recovering that money is the only way available for us to restore our honor."

"Then just tell me how you're so sure he's dead?"

"Because we were able to locate *Satin Lady,*" Rheinhartz answered dramatically, provoked by Beth, ignoring the angry glare the disclosure brought to Leung's eyes.

"You salvaged *Satin Lady*?" she asked C.K., hardly controlling her amazement at learning the size of the resources he must have committed to the investigation.

"There was no need to salvage her," C.K. said, continuing what Rheinhartz had started, his eyes, however, still reflecting his displeasure. "We simply located her and had a diver go down to identify the wreck. The water was not particularly deep."

"Were there any bodies on board?" she asked them both.

"None were seen, but we did not expect to find any," Rheinhartz continued. "I would imagine that predators disposed of them within a few days."

"You're probably right," she said to him after some hesitation, calm enough now to try to end the discussion without any more of a breach in the relationship. She turned toward Leung again and said, "Look, C.K., I know that you're an innocent victim here, but both of our families have honor to restore." She saw C.K. nod in agreement while Rheinhartz sat silently in his chair, smiling smugly as she spoke.

"If our relationship is to survive this terrible theft," Beth continued, using courtroom rhetoric to emphasize her sincerity, "you and I cannot fall prey to the deceit and mistrust engendered by the legacy of Leonard Sloane. I do not understand why my investigation will conflict with your efforts at recovery." She paused for effect. "But I will respect your request to the extent that I can."

"It gives me great pleasure to hear you say that, Beth," C.K. said, apparently satisfied with her position. "You have confirmed what I already knew from your victory in the Jasco case. You have a maturity beyond your years."

"Thank you," she replied, still resisting a walkout on these two sharks without another word.

"If you'll excuse me," Rheinhartz said a moment later, "I would like to stay for lunch, but I am late for another appointment." He got up, brushed himself off, and went into the bedroom. He reappeared with his overcoat and shoulder bag, passed by Leung without shaking hands, and went directly over to Beth. Leung turned his back to Rheinhartz and followed his secretary into the bedroom, closing the door behind him.

"Goodbye, Mr. Rheinhartz," Beth said to him as she got up from her chair, the two of them now alone.

"Goodbye, Miss Swahn. I hope you didn't take anything I said personally. I find you a remarkable young lady and an extremely competent attorney," he said with complete sincerity.

"Well, thank you," she said.

"Here is my card," Rheinhartz said quietly, handing her a

business card as he opened the door. "Be careful with these Chinese and call me if I can be of any assistance." He left without further word and shut the door behind him. Beth put the card in the pocket of her suit jacket without looking at it. At the same time, C.K. came back into the room and he and Beth sat down for lunch.

"Beth, there is another matter of some delicacy I need to ask you about. May I assume that our relationship is still attorney-client privileged?"

"Of course."

"Shortly after we learned of Leonard's death," he began, "we learned that vital bank records were missing from our computers. To put it into perspective, without them our entire business is in jeopardy."

"What type of records?"

"It is not necessary at this point to go into detail. Let me just say that they had nothing to do with the Jasco matter and therefore should not concern you."

"I see."

"We know that Leonard intentionally erased the records before he absconded with Erica. What we do not know, however, is whether he made any backup copies before erasing the information. We suspect that he did. We hope that he did. The information is crucial to us."

"As you said, what has that got to do with me?"

"Since Leonard paid you twenty-five thousand dollars personally, we think that he may have also given you a copy of those records. A thumb drive or maybe a CD. If you have it, we must get it back."

"I sent you everything I had." She looked at him calmly, suspecting more than ever that she had what he was looking for so desperately.

"The files you returned were of no help."

"Then I don't know what else I can do. And I'll tell you something else, don't make some absurd connection between the check and any other problems you might have."

"I must emphasize the crucial nature of these records. We need them back immediately."

"I'm afraid I can't be of any help."

She looked at her watch and pushed her chair back from the table. "If you'll excuse me, C.K., it's later than I expected and I have to get back to the office for another appointment. I'm going to pass on the rest of the lunch."

"But Beth . . . ," he started to protest.

She looked at his secretary and continued: "Please get my coat."

"I am sorry you must leave," C.K. said. "If you should locate our missing records, I hope you will contact me at once."

"I do not have any of your records. I trust that I have made myself clear on that issue."

"Yes, you have. Perfectly clear. Thank you for coming over."

Beth picked up her attaché case and shoulder bag, looked C.K. in the eye, Oriental inscrutability to Hungarian tenacity, and walked out of the suite into the waiting elevator. Alone for a minute, she took Dieter's card out of her pocket and saw he had written, "Bank codes are Arab $$," under his address. She put his card back in her pocket before reaching the hotel lobby.

C.K. closed the door to his hotel room, took out his cellphone, and quickly texted his brother Martin, "Renew your efforts more vigorously this time!" Martin, waiting in the lobby with Eddie Huang, nodded to Eddie, who immediately left the hotel by a side entrance. Meanwhile, Beth was in a cab and back at the office before two p.m.

Chapter Nineteen

≡≡≡≡≡≡≡≡≡≡≡≡≡≡≡≡≡≡≡≡≡≡≡≡≡≡

It was Carl's turn to drive to the Giants home game, so Beth sat with Brian in the back, while Amy sat up front with Carl. Getting out of the city through the Lincoln Tunnel had been a breeze, but the late Sunday morning traffic on the southbound Jersey Turnpike out to the Meadowlands was rapidly filling up with carloads of fans heading to MetLife Stadium for the game against San Francisco.

Carl had been playing leapfrog with a dark blue limousine since the tunnel. First it would pass his tan Volvo, then slow down until Carl passed back, and then it repeated the maneuver again. Two New Yorkers locked in infantile vehicular combat to pass the time away. Neither Carl nor his passengers saw anything unusual in that.

"That limo doesn't know what the hell it wants to do," Carl said indignantly to his three passengers. "The driver speeds up, he slows down, he speeds up, he slows down. He has a cellphone glued to his ear and a big GPS screen on the dashboard. What an asshole!"

"Take it easy, will you," Amy protested. "Don't get involved with him."

"He's probably going to the game also," Brian volunteered.

"Its side windows are dark. Can't see who's in it," Carl said as he passed the limo again. "Now he's falling back."

Brian lost interest in the limo and turned to Beth. "Hey, did you have any luck with that CD?" he asked her.

"What CD?" Thinking about Bob for a change, she was disconcerted by the question.

"The one you called me about."

"Oh yeah. The CD."

"What CD?" Amy piped up.

"I told you about it. It was stuck in the papers I got from Bob."

"So were you able to figure out what was on it?" Brian asked.

"Still can't ID the banks." If they were Arab, money laundering might be involved, but she had no intention of making it the subject of a casual conversation on a Sunday drive with her friends. "Thanks for the help, though."

"By the way, how're you doing with Bob?" Amy asked, twisting around in her seat to face Beth. "Spoken to him lately?"

"I'll tell you all about it later," Beth replied.

"Who's Bob?" Carl asked from the front seat. "Some new boyfriend?"

"No, just some new client," Beth answered, trying to disarm a subject she preferred to avoid in front of the boys.

"You didn't tell me you were dating someone," Brian said.

"I'm not *dating* him. He's a client, that's all. I spoke to Amy about some mutual funds for him."

"Don't forget to remind me about that," Amy said, trying to backpedal helpfully. "I did some research on that fund he was thinking of buying."

"Great," Beth said. "I'll speak to you during the halftime show."

"It figures. We never get to hear the good stuff," Carl moaned in protest, but he and Brian quickly got involved in their own conversation about the relative merits of the opposing quarterbacks.

"When's your mom flying in?" Amy asked Beth.

"Thursday . . . Thanksgiving."

"What time?"

"She lands at JFK around noon. We'll probably go right over to my stepsister's house for dinner. Don't forget Mom's taking us to the Met Saturday night."

"How come Max isn't coming?"

"They hit something last week and put a dent in *Red Sky*'s prop. He's staying down to haul her and do some maintenance work."

"Am I going to get a dinner date with her?" Brian asked.

"No. Every time Mom sees us together, she thinks it means something."

"So you stay home," Brian said. "I'll take her out by myself."

"Thanks. Not."

"Well, give her a kiss for me anyhow."

"You know I will." Their breakup had devastated her mother. Beth only remembered the relief and was thankful she'd kept Brian's friendship.

Carl began to work his way over to the right as they approached the stadium exit. He looked over his shoulder and saw the lane jammed with trucks lumbering along at 70 mph without any intention of voluntarily letting him into their midst.

After several abortive attempts, he succeeded in getting into the lane. At the same time, an eighteen-wheeler loaded with steel beams began to pass him on the left. Before completing the maneuver, the huge truck started to drift into Carl's lane, as if determined to defy physics by occupying the exact same spot on the road as the Volvo.

Carl sensed its massive presence, but Amy confirmed it with her startled scream. The driver of the rig was slowly moving it over, pinning the Volvo closer to the soft shoulder. The more Carl moved to his right, the more the eighteen-wheeler closed in on his left. He couldn't slow down because of another truck pressing down on him from the rear, and he couldn't speed up because of a truck in front. His Volvo was boxed in. The frantic sound of his horn was lost in the roar of the huge diesels surrounding him. Beth and Brian stared transfixed at the unfolding scene, fearing the worst, unable to control the outcome.

The driver of the eighteen-wheeler, sitting high up in the cab, was well past the Volvo when his monstrous tires ground into the left side of the car. The sickening noise they made was a cross between chalk screeching across a blackboard and a dull hacksaw blade cutting bone. The tires left thick streaks of black rubber along the entire length of the Volvo. The smell of burning rubber permeated its interior.

Carl fought for control of the car as the full weight of the trailer's load forced them inexorably toward the drainage ditch along the roadside. When the second set of trailer tires made contact, he completely lost control, and reflexively wrapped his right arm around the shrieking Amy. The left front of the Volvo was lifted violently off the road, causing it to swerve to the right.

The Volvo skidded onto the shoulder, bounced in and out of the drainage ditch on two wheels, and twisted around, landing back on all four wheels before hitting a large rock. The eighteen-wheeler continued on its way, license plate obscured by mud, devoid of any logo or markings.

The shaken passengers sat there for a moment, bruised and badly frightened. After checking one another for injuries, they got out of the car and simply stared at the driver's side of the Volvo, streaked graphically with black rubber and deep gouges down to bare metal.

"The bastard never saw us!" Carl said, dialing 911 on his cellphone.

"Are you okay?" Amy asked him.

"I'm fine," he replied. "Anybody see his license plates?"

"I tried, but he was too far away," Beth answered.

"Crazy son of a bitch!"

Cars and trucks on the road continued to speed past. Because of the impenetrable wall of eighteen-wheelers surrounding them, the incident had been hidden from view. After a few moments, Carl and Brian got back into the car to check things out, while Beth and Amy waited outside for the police to arrive.

The dark blue stretch limousine then reappeared. It passed them, slowed down, and suddenly braked, pulling off the road and stopping on the shoulder about fifty yards in front. Seated in the rear, Martin Leung told his driver, Eddie Huang, to go check on the Volvo's passengers.

Eddie got out of the limo and walked over to Beth. His sunglasses failed to hide the scar over his right eye. It jangled her memory, but under the circumstances, she didn't immediately remember why. He asked solicitously if everyone was okay before walking around the Volvo to examine its damage and retrieve a GPS tracker he had hidden under one of its fenders earlier in the city. In the back of the limo, Martin looked out the window and smiled with satisfaction.

As Eddie walked back to the limo, Beth finally made the connection and told Brian where she had seen Scarface before. She took a quick photo of the limo with her cellphone before it pulled back out into stadium traffic. Her life had just been threatened by somebody for something. She was fairly certain that the somebody was C. K. Leung and that the something was the CD she had. Now she needed to do something about it.

The flashing lights behind them finally signaled the arrival of the state police, so they waited until the troopers were finished with them and then limped back to Manhattan. They had all agreed that going to the game was no longer on the table, so they decided to spend the afternoon recovering at Brian's place.

Before the first beers were finished, Beth had obtained the limo's plate number from her photograph and had used Brian's laptop to download a copy of its registration from the New York State DMV webpage. She was not completely surprised to see that the limo was owned by a Lenco Leasing. She was more surprised to see that Leonard Sloane had signed as president.

Chapter Twenty

By four fifty p.m., Beth was finished lawyering for the day. She locked her credenza, called Amy, and arranged to meet her over at the Oyster Bar for drinks at six p.m. She had plans for dinner with Bob, who was on his way in from Providence for another interview tomorrow. The cool, crisp air was a welcome respite. It elevated her spirits, turning the one-block walk over to Grand Central Terminal into a stroll.

She elbowed her way through the bottleneck created by the narrow passageway under perpetual construction from the Park Avenue entrance into the main waiting room of the terminal. The waiting room was packed.

She headed to the ramp leading down to the Oyster Bar on the lower level, following two middle-aged men headed in the same direction. As she approached the entrance to the restaurant, located in a quieter part of the station, the two men suddenly turned around, blocked her way, and then lunged at her.

The one on her left violently shoved her up against the marble wall across from the restaurant door, pinning his body against hers. She reflexively threw out an arm to maintain her balance as he grabbed her attaché case. Then she pivoted, jammed her foot down on his instep, and drove her other knee up into his groin as high and as hard as she could. He dropped her attaché case and doubled over in pain.

The mugger on her right grabbed her bag. She saw his fist arch viciously toward her stomach and instinctively flexed her abdominal muscles to absorb the punch. At the same time, she did her best to gouge out his eyes with her thumbs.

In the face of such unexpected resistance, the two men broke off their assault and ran away in different directions. Beth was seething. Not scared, totally furious. As several commuters came to her aid, she chased after the man with her bag, who was sprinting for the subway entrance. After running a few yards, she stopped, hopelessly handicapped by her high heels. She started to take them off and then thought better of the idea. The muggers were gone anyway, lost in the maze of tunnels connecting the east side subways at Forty-second Street. She stood there alone, gasping for breath.

It was all over in less time than it took to tell about it. The crowd that assembled around her after the mugging cheered her resistance. The Metro-North cops were solicitous. Amy arrived while she was talking to the cops. Beth wanted to go right back to the office to make the phone calls necessitated by the loss of her bag, but Amy insisted that they go into the Oyster Bar for a drink. She could take care of stopping the credit cards and changing the door locks when she got home. A drink would calm her down now.

While they were having their drinks, it was Amy who commented on the bad karma of a trailer truck sideswiping them on Sunday and Beth's mugging today. Beth was clear that karma had nothing to do with any of it. Her office had been searched by Leung's people. Carl's Volvo had been sideswiped and her bag stolen, all by Leung's people.

An hour later, when she got back to her apartment with Amy, the bag was waiting at the concierge desk. The doorman told her that some Oriental-looking guy had left it in the lobby.

Everything was rifled through, but nothing was missing. She notified American Express and MasterCard anyhow. Amy insisted on staying in the apartment with her until a locksmith finished rekeying both locks. Then, and only then, she left.

When Bob called her a little later, she begged off dinner. As soon as she mentioned the word *mugging,* Bob insisted on coming right over, quickly hung up, and was there within fifteen minutes.

Sitting together on the couch, she started telling him about the assault and then segued into the near disaster on the way to the Giants game. The more she described each, the more Bob only wanted to make it all better for her. His own common sense pointed to more than happenstance connecting the sideswiping, the mugging, and then the return of the bag. When he told her so, Beth knew that the time for disclosure had come, so she told him as much as she felt she could about his father's theft.

"I'm amazed that my father could do something like that," he said at one point. "I'm stunned. He was so passive. How come you never said anything to me about it?"

Beth shrugged. "Your father pulled it off because I was a naïve, stupid asshole. When you and I first met, I had to be certain you weren't in on it with him. I didn't know what your relationship was with your father until we got to know each other."

"Our meeting wasn't just a condolence call, then, was it?" he asked quietly.

"It's not easy for me to tell you about this," she said tremulously. "Our relationship didn't exist when we met up in Providence. You could have been a part of the whole scheme." She picked up a tissue from an end table and noisily blew her nose into it.

"And if I was? Weren't you taking a terrible chance?"

"Sure, but it was a chance I had to take."

"You're a tough cookie, aren't you."

"Not so tough. Your father slickered me because I forgot the basic rule: Trust, but verify. I was also on an ego trip over a huge money victory. I'd be very surprised, though, if today there was some nefarious side of your personality you've hidden from me."

"You mean you'd have figured it out already?" His levity relaxed some of the tension.

"You know, I'm a single woman living in New York. It was a calculated risk when I invited you up to my apartment the first time."

"You calculated right."

"It was just a little too soon for me."

"Is that an invitation?" he asked, his libido aroused by the thought.

"It is," she murmured, gently turning his face to hers with her hand.

Chapter Twenty-one

First came the hugging and kissing at the elevator, then Beth carried one of her mother's suitcases into the apartment. Andi shoved the other one in herself and kicked the door shut behind them. "What time does Lynn want us for Thanksgiving dinner?" she asked.

"We'll go over around five p.m. We have plenty of time."

"The place turned out beautifully," Andi said as she sat on the couch and looked around the living room.

"Oh, I'm so glad you like it." Beth walked over to the couch, picked up her mother's outstretched hand, and pressed it to her lips and cheek, mumbling something about their sharing one heart, just as she used to do when she was four. "I've missed you so much since you moved down to the islands."

"We're always together, kid, you and me. Just like we've always been."

"True love forever, huh?"

"True love forever, darling." She pulled Beth's face down to her and kissed her on the forehead before releasing the strong grip on her hand.

"How's Max doing?"

"He's fine. A little bent out of shape because I came up here without him."

"Tell him to read his charts next time," Beth said, "and watch his depth finder."

"It wasn't his fault," Andi said in his defense, smiling as she remembered the experience.

"I figured that, but what happened?"

"We ran into a submerged container last week while taking a charter party over to Christmas Cove for lunch. The husband was at the wheel, blindly following Max's instructions and ignoring what his eyes told him."

"Any real damage?"

"Mostly to Max's ego, but then the prop started vibrating the next day. We hadn't booked any charters because we were coming up here, so he stayed down to get it handled."

Beth went into the kitchen while her mother was taking a shower, grabbed a Diet Coke, and walked back out to the living room. Sitting in the rocker made her aware that her stomach was still tender from the mugging, something she had no intention of mentioning to her mother. She opened up her shoulder bag and dumped out the mail she had picked up from her box in the lobby yesterday.

She put the Christmas catalogs aside for later reading pleasure and tossed the junk mail on the floor for disposal in the trash. For the moment, she also put aside the green envelope that had come directly to her apartment from the Antigua office of the Trans-Caribbean Title Company. She knew that had to be a response to her request for information on Sloane and Paramount.

Her curiosity was aroused, however, by a handwritten express mail envelope addressed to her in a classical European scroll. She ignored its grease stain and the absence of any return address, but was intrigued by the Venezuelan postage. The only thing she found inside was a business card from Dieter Rheinhartz, but when she saw the words *Banco Union, Caracas, Eric Leonard,* and a phone number carefully printed on the back of his card, she immediately grabbed her phone and began dialing.

*"**Hola, eso es** Banco Union, Caracas."*

"This is Elisabeth from Branch 275 of Chase Bank in New York. Do you speak English?"

"Yes, I do. How can I help you?"

"I need to verify some information on a new account at our branch."

"What is the name on the account, please?"

"Eric Leonard."

"What is your badge number?"

"AZ10PS467MM." Beth crossed her fingers as she spouted off a random series of numbers and letters.

"Hold on a minute."

"No problem."

"Yes, Eric Leonard has an account here."

"I'm supposed to verify his address and the age of the account." Beth felt her heart trying to pound its way out of her chest.

"It's been open for over two years with an average monthly balance of four thousand seven hundred and fifty U.S. dollars. The address he gave us is on Antigua."

"Anything else?"

"There was a cash deposit of five hundred thousand in U.S. dollars made just recently. September first, to be exact."

"Do you know what bank it came from?" she asked, almost certain already that it was Sloane. The deposit had been made a week before *Satin Lady* sank and was for the same amount withdrawn from the bank in Switzerland that Erica had used.

"Sorry, I can't give you routing information."

"Is it still on deposit?"

"No, the money was withdrawn on September twenty-fifth."

"Do you know where it went to?" It has to be them! That was more than two weeks after *Satin Lady* sank.

"No. It was taken out in cash, U.S. dollars."

Chapter Twenty-two

On Saturday night, they were out of Beth's apartment by seven fifteen p.m. and in a cab with Amy headed for Lincoln Center. With the trees around the complex sparkling brightly under their year-round net of tiny white lights, the plaza was bathed in crystal brilliance reflecting off the frozen vapor exhaled into the icy air by the arriving crowd.

"How was dinner at Lynn's?" Amy asked.

"Too much good food as usual," Beth replied.

"Did you tell your mother about C. K. Leung?"

"Thanks, big mouth. No, I didn't have a chance to tell her." The icy dagger Beth shot over to Amy made it clear she hadn't told her mother about the Jersey Turnpike or the mugging either.

"How was I supposed to know that?" Amy asked.

"Tell me what?" Andi asked.

"I had lunch with C. K. Leung last week. He offered me a chance to do some work for him. A real estate deal."

"How big?"

"Motels all over the Northeast," Amy volunteered.

"That's big!" Andi said, her voice flat with awe. "I'm amazed. I thought for sure you'd never hear from him again."

"Now tell her the rest," Amy said.

"Remind me to confide in you again, Mata Hari."

"What is the rest?"

"I told him we wouldn't be able to do the work."

"How come?" Andi asked in an even tone of voice.

"There's a conflict of interest with another case I'm handling."

"Right," Amy interjected. "A three-hundred-and-fifty-thousand-dollar insurance case."

"You and Clifford couldn't work your way around it?"

"I didn't tell Clifford, and don't you mention it when you have dinner with him tomorrow night."

"Doesn't he have a right to know?" Andi asked.

"It was my new business. I decided not to bring it into the firm."

"That's a little presumptuous, isn't it?" Andi asked.

"No. It was my call. By the way, Clifford hasn't been looking so well lately. He's been coughing worse than usual, more than his regular smoker's cough. See what you think when you see him."

"I will, but don't change the subject. I have the distinct feeling that the story behind your decision is more interesting than the decision itself."

"I'll give you all the sordid details at dinner. Oh, by the way, squealer"—Beth turned to Amy—"C.K. sent a couple of his men over to the office yesterday with two dozen roses. They even set it up themselves on my credenza in a Waterford crystal vase they brought."

"He must really want you to reconsider," Amy said.

"Or go to bed with him," Andi offered.

"I guess, but there's no chance of new business, and sex was never in the cards. I also got some interesting documents from Antigua today. I'm still carrying the envelope around in my bag."

"What kind of information?"

"Let's go in now and I'll show it to you when we get to our seats."

"Okay," Andi said. "I'm getting cold anyhow."

They entered the Met and gradually asserted themselves through the crowd, absorbing the familiar aroma of old money and new. They slowly went down the grand staircase to the orchestra level, where Andi detoured to the bar for a glass of champagne.

With time to spare, they walked down the aisle to their seats, where Beth resumed the conversation. "I found a company down in the West Indies that does real estate title searches. I asked them to check Guadeloupe and Antigua to see if they could find any records of property owned in the name of Sloane, Crossland, or Paramount."

"Did they find out anything worthwhile?" Andi asked skeptically.

"They sure did. It turns out that a corporation called Paramount Equities owns a house on Antigua. They sent me a copy of the deed."

"Are you sure it's the same Paramount?" Andi still sounded unimpressed.

"Yes, because this particular Paramount filed an official Antiguan motor vehicle registration form two years ago signed by an Elliot Slanger as its authorized officer. I compared the signature with Sloane's handwriting. It's an exact match."

"He and Erica were planning to rip off Leung even then."

"It seems Paramount also owns a fifty-one-foot ketch down on Guadeloupe by the name of *Sindicator*. A bank on Barbados holds the mortgage. I have that documentation too."

"So? Max told you about the sailboat."

"Yes, but all he found out was that it was chartered from Gold Coast Charters on Guadeloupe. Now I know it was registered there by this Paramount Equities. I'll make a copy of the whole report for you to show to Max next week. See what he thinks."

"What I think is that you're in a losing game."

"I don't agree," Beth insisted adamantly.

"Sometimes you're as stubborn as your stepfather."

"What do you expect? I come from his loins," Beth explained, knowing her mother only used the *step* word when one of her two charges misbehaved.

Andi harrumphed and turned her attention to the program on her lap as the Met's crystal chandeliers started their slow cable ascent skyward to the ceiling.

Amy dropped them off in a cab back at the apartment after the opera and dinner. Malden came out of the building, buttoning up his doorman's jacket, and opened the cab door for mother and daughter.

"Hi, Beth," he said, and then, surprised to see Andi, "Well, hello, Mrs. Swahn. It's nice to see you back in New York."

"Thank you, Malden."

"Say, Beth, I got some flowers for you in the package room."

"Flowers? Would you get them for me?" They followed the doorman toward the elevators in the rear of the lobby.

He opened up the locked door to the package room located next to the elevators and brought out the flowers wrapped in bright yellow paper. "Couple of Asian-looking guys dropped them off about an hour ago. They wanted to go up to your apartment, but I told them 'no way.'"

"They're beautiful," Andi said, opening them partially. "Who're they from?"

"I don't know yet. Here, take my bag and the keys. I'll carry the flowers up. Thanks, Malden. See you tomorrow."

"Good night. Nice to see you again, Mrs. Swahn."

"Good night, Malden," Andi said.

"The roses smell delicious," Beth said in the elevator with her arms around the flowers. "The elevator has never smelled so good."

"Which key is it?"

"The same key opens both locks now, top and bottom. The silver one with the double notch."

"Did you set the burglar alarm?" Andi asked as the two women walked from the elevator down the corridor to Beth's apartment.

"I didn't bother. Hurry, open up the door. These flowers are dripping all over my coat."

"Just a minute. Let me unlock it," Andi said as she unsuccessfully tried the two locks, first the top, then the bottom, then in reverse order, and then repeated the process again.

"What's the problem?"

"You didn't have the top lock on," Andi said, finally getting the door open.

"I'm sure I put both locks on."

"No, you didn't."

"Well, so maybe I forgot."

"Here, let me turn on the light so you can put the flowers down."

"Don't forget to double-lock the door," Beth said as she walked into the kitchen and put the flowers on the counter.

"I did already."

"They're from C.K. again," Beth said, reading the card that had been pinned to the flowers. "I'll put them in the cloisonné vase Brian bought me."

"That man makes me nervous."

"Who? Brian?"

"No. C. K. Leung."

"Why? Did you ever meet him?"

"No, but what's that got to do with it?"

"He's extremely attractive and can charm your pants off. That's why."

"Keep your pants on, daughter."

"Yes, Mother," she said obediently.

"Did you take out the garbage today?" Andi asked, sniffing at the air.

"Sure. When we left to go shopping this afternoon. Why?"

"This place smells," Andi responded, testing the air as she walked into the bedroom.

"All I smell is the roses. The apartment smelled fine when we left for the opera."

"Well, it has a sour smell. Where's your room spray?" Andi asked from the bedroom.

"Wait, now I smell it too. . . . The spray's in the bathroom. Try under the sink." Beth's senses went on full alert, scanning the apartment carefully. It was body odor she smelled, a bad body odor. She didn't want to alarm her mother, but something did feel wrong.

Andi came out from the bedroom, her face pale under her year-round tan.

"What's the matter, Mom?" The look in her mother's eyes frightened her.

"I just had a terrible thought. Check your jewelry."

Without another word, Beth quickly opened her top dresser drawer and began rummaging through the lingerie for the antique tortoiseshell powder jar that contained some of her jewelry. "Everything's here." She then walked over to the night table by her bed and turned the hollow-based lamp upside down to let the soft red velvet case fall out. She untied the blue ribbon, opened the flap, and scanned the assorted rings and bracelets. "No, everything's here too. What about your big suitcase in the closet?"

"I didn't have anything valuable in it. What I'm not wearing, I have in my purse."

"Wait a moment," Beth said. She opened the bottom drawer of her bureau and then breathed a big sigh of relief as she pulled out a brown manila envelope. "I just had this paranoiac flash that C.K. had his men steal my Sloane file, but it's here." She started to untie the string that held the file closed.

"We're just imagining it all." Andi laughed nervously.

"Oh Jesus, Mom!" The sudden and serious alarm in Beth's voice exploded throughout the apartment.

"What is it?"

"It's the file. Someone's been in it. Look." She held up the papers. "They're all out of order. I didn't leave it this way."

When Beth saw the horror she had created in her mother's face, her own anger was multiplied by the reflected fear. "I'm calling the cops." She angrily picked up the phone on her night table.

"What good is calling the police?" Andi asked, quickly regaining control over herself. "Leung is in Taiwan, isn't he, and there's nothing missing."

"I want the cops to have a record of it. That son of a bitch is not going to get away with this." Beth paced nervously, circling back and forth between the night table and the bedroom door, shifting the phone from ear to ear, her freedom of motion restricted by the length of the telephone cord that connected her to the jack on the wall.

"Hang up the phone and start thinking," Andi said firmly.

"I don't know what you're into, but I do know that it's dangerous and I don't think you know how nasty it is, either."

"I do know, and let me tell you I don't care how much money
or power C.K. has. It doesn't give him the right to invade my
home and scare the shit out of you and me."

"Of course not, but it's insane to let Leung know you recognize him as the enemy just because you're mad. Calling the police in a fit of temper may turn out to be dumb."

Beth slowly put the phone back on the hook. "It would
probably be a waste of time to report it anyway," she said with
resignation.

"Why couldn't you and Max let the whole thing drop when
you had the chance?" Uncontrolled tears of frustration started
forming in Andi's eyes. She got up suddenly from the bed and
walked into the living room, sitting down on the couch.

All of Beth's anger vanished, instantly replaced with concern when she saw how consumed with fear and fury her own
mother had become. She followed her into the living room and
sat on the couch next to her, holding her hand, while she received a lecture on the dangers of ego-driven revenge. It was a
disjointed monologue that ended only when Andi brought her
own emotions under control.

"Would you feel more comfortable if we went to a hotel for
the night?"

"No, I'm okay now. First I want to kill your friend C. K.
Leung, and then I want to call Max," Andi said.

"It's too late. We'll call him tomorrow."

"You two are going to stop this game."

"We'll talk about it tomorrow."

"Wrong, and stop patronizing me, Elisabeth. We'll talk
about it now!"

"All right, but let me make us a couple of brandies first."

"Excellent idea," Andi said, her color returning.

"At least he didn't get to see the letter from Venezuela or those documents I got from Antigua. They're all safe in my pocketbook. He also doesn't know that I have his CD."

"Yeah, boy, are we lucky!" Andi said sarcastically, and then asked as an afterthought, "What CD?"

Chapter Twenty-three

Beth heard a phone ringing, but it fit into the context of her dream. It was still ringing when she opened her eyes. Then she remembered that she had slept on the sofa bed in the living room, so the phone was on the cocktail table.

"Hello," she croaked into the receiver.

"Beth?" The male voice at the other end was familiar to her, but the caller was wavering, uncertain himself as to who had picked up the phone.

"Hi, Bob."

"Are you okay?"

"Yeah. I think so. Why?"

"You sound terminal."

"You woke me out of a terrific dream. Where are you?"

"I'm here in New York."

"You're supposed to be in Providence."

"I came back yesterday afternoon. The general manager of WKYN invited me to the Ranger game last night."

"Did you get the job?"

"I'll tell you later. Listen, I need to see you."

"Today?" Her mind was fogged with sleep.

"Yes, of course today."

"Today's Sunday. I can't make it today. My mother's in town. What's the matter?"

"I got a call from Marcie this morning. My apartment in Providence was trashed last night. I think it has something to do with my father's death."

The impact of that revelation cleared her head. "What time is it?" she asked, sitting up and putting her feet down on the Persian rug under the couch.

"It's eight."

"Jesus, Bob. Mom and I stayed up talking and drinking twenty-five-year-old brandy until three thirty a.m."

"Come on. The day's half over."

"Okay, tell you what. Meet me in an hour and a half at La Hosteria over on Sixty-fourth and Third. They open early on weekends. You can meet my mother and buy us breakfast."

"See you at nine thirty."

She hung up the phone and tiptoed into the bedroom, where her mother was still asleep, and kissed her on the cheek. "Morning, Mom," she said in a stage whisper.

"Hi, darling. What's up?" Andi groaned without opening an eye.

"C'mon. Get up. We're going out for breakfast."

"Wrong turkey. You're going out for breakfast. I'm going back to sleep. I didn't get off watch until nearly four a.m."

"Don't be so nautical. Get up. You're going to meet Bob."

That offer got her immediate attention. She sat up in bed, whimpered once pathetically, and put her head back on the pillow. "I can't believe you made me pour that last shot of brandy over the Häagen-Dazs vanilla ice cream."

"Getting drunk and fat at the same time is a nirvana few are privileged to attain. I'm taking a shower."

"Did you make coffee?" Andi asked.

"The pot's on the kitchen counter."

Beth was in and out of the shower in a flash. She continued to think about the break-ins while getting dressed. By nine twenty a.m., she was putting on her parka. Her mother was already dressed and in the living room, browsing through the Sunday *New York Times*.

They left the building and walked briskly over to the restaurant. Bob was there when they arrived, waiting in a corner booth. He got up to greet Andi politely with a smile and an awkward kiss on the cheek, uncertain how to act when meeting her for the first time. His kiss on the lips for Beth was tentative at first, but she responded warmly, and they lingered in each other's embrace, like new lovers everywhere.

It was early, so the neighborhood restaurant was not crowded. Beth sat next to Bob and across from Andi as the waiter poured their coffee. "Look," Bob said after they ordered, "I'm concerned about last night."

"Tell me what happened," Beth said. Bob looked at her, uncertain whether he should talk about it in front of Andi, but Beth reassured him with a nod, adding, "Mom knows all about it."

"I got a call early this morning from Marcie. She went down to feed my cat last night. I have a separate entrance around the back. She said someone had broken in and left a total mess."

"Is anything missing?" Andi asked.

"She didn't hang around to look, just grabbed the cat and ran out. She called the cops when she got back upstairs to her own floor. She said the major pieces are still there, though."

"Did the police do anything?" Beth asked. She paused while the waiter unloaded their food.

"I doubt it," he said, first picking up the salt and then the pepper to season his eggs. "They told her to have me call them when I figure out what's missing."

"You said it had something to do with your father's death. How come?" Beth asked.

"I called Justin at the radio station before I woke you up. You met him, remember?"

"How could I forget him."

"Justin said an insurance investigator stopped by to see me at the station yesterday. When he told the guy I wasn't in, he asked if I still lived over on Atwells Avenue. Justin wouldn't tell him. Then when I called Marcie back, she told me that when her husband came home from bowling last night, he noticed two Chinese dudes parked in a car across the street."

"I guess the rest is simple deduction."

"Exactly. I asked Justin to take a look at the place later this morning when he gets off work. Now why would some insurance company investigators go to such an extreme for a lousy little life insurance case?"

Beth put down her half-eaten bagel and took a sip of coffee, allowing his question to dangle unanswered for the moment, debating with herself over how much to say. Her mother's warning kick under the table was a clear vote in favor of caution, but she decided to go with her feelings for this man. There were some things he had to be told, although the part about the missing bank codes was not on her agenda.

"This doesn't have anything to do with an insurance case," she finally answered with a deep breath, and stopped.

"Don't be enigmatic this early in the morning," Bob broke into her silence. "What are you talking about?"

"My apartment was ransacked last night also, and it wasn't a coincidence."

"What in hell are you talking about?" He was incredulous, and his expression showed it.

"I told you about your father leaving town with Leung's money. I think C.K. is doing all this to find it."

"But aren't the cops looking for the money?"

"C.K. told us not to report it."

"Why didn't they want you to report it?"

"He wasn't into discussing that, but I figure they must have serious issues regarding the source of their funds or maybe even money laundering. All I know now is that Leung thinks you or I have some information."

"So you figure his guys broke into both our places?" he asked Beth, endearing himself to Andi by impulsively spearing the last forkful of home fries from her plate.

"Yes. Last night, the doorman said that when Mom and I were at the opera, two Asian guys came to the building to deliver flowers for me. The flowers were from C.K. His deliverymen must have used the flowers to keep the doorman busy while another goon broke in the back way."

"Did they take anything?"

"Not a thing. But they went through a file I keep at home with some papers on your father's case."

"You're conducting your own private investigation, aren't you? Independent of Leung," he asked.

"I've grown since this mess began. Besides facing total disaster, I know what it feels like to be psychologically roughed up, thanks to C. K. Leung and his fat henchman."

"Not to mention being assaulted by a couple of their hired goons," Andi volunteered.

"I also know now that I can give as good as I get. One of those bastards won't be getting a hard-on for a while."

166 / *Michael Rudolph*

"Beth!"

"Sorry, Mom. . . . So yes, Bob," she continued, "I am looking into this on my own."

"When are you going to the cops about it?" he asked.

"I'm not. I want to find the money before Leung does. I also want to know why he's so insistent on keeping me out of it."

"He probably feels he lost face."

"You're right. That was his excuse, but you know what? So did I. It was only money for him, for me it was my career."

"Look, I know fear and revenge can be compelling, but these are not exactly nice guys you're playing with," he admonished. Andi stopped chewing and nodded emphatically in agreement. "My father never did anyone any good, in life or in death," Bob added regretfully. "You need to be careful here."

"I will be," Beth said.

"Do you have any idea where the money is?" he asked.

"None whatsoever." She shrugged without blinking an eye, the lawyer in her withholding any more of what she knew and what she had found. She probed instead: "Do you?"

"No idea at all."

"Do you have any idea where your father may have been heading? I'm sure it's somewhere down in the Caribbean."

"We were strangers. I didn't even know he'd gone to Puerto Rico until the Coast Guard called about his death."

"Did they say anything about owning a sailboat down in the Caribbean?"

"No. It's the last thing in the world I would have figured him to have. When I was a kid, he hated it when sailboats got in the way of our speedboat. Sailing must have been Erica's idea."

"Are you going back up to Providence now?" Beth asked.

"I told Justin I'd call him before noon. I'll grab a cab over to Grand Central and take the first train I can catch."

"When you check your apartment, pay attention to any-place you keep personal papers. See if they've been taken or look like they've been moved."

"Okay, Counselor. I can see you're not about to let this thing drop. If you're so sure they wanted to find out if I knew any-thing about the missing money, I'll check it all out carefully."

"Now that's being a good client," she said. "Call me if you learn anything."

"I'll call you anyhow. And if you're determined to see this thing through, let me know how I can help."

"I will, and thanks," Beth responded. "When are you com-ing back into town?"

"I'll be back Wednesday. WKYN wants to announce my new radio show to the press on Thursday." He said this with an exaggerated demonstration of casualness.

"You got the job!" she shouted with delight. "I'm so ex-cited. I totally forgot to ask you about it." She reached for his hand and squeezed it. He was beaming.

"I wanted to surprise you with a copy of the press release on Wednesday, if you're free for dinner."

"It's a date. You can join Mom and me." She impulsively threw her arms around his neck, hugging him until he groaned with pleasure. "I'm so proud of you." Then she gave him a kiss, thrilled at having to stretch upward in order to meet his lips.

"We've got a good thing, Beth. I don't want it to stop."

"I hope we can survive this mess."

"We can," he said reassuringly. "I'll see you Wednesday." After putting him in a taxi, Beth and Andi walked back to the apartment.

Chapter Twenty-four

That afternoon, Max was on a plane to New York less than four hours after the phone call from Andi. When she told him about the mugging and the break-in at Beth's apartment the night before, the instincts of father and husband took over and nothing could dissuade him from coming up, especially since Andi also thought it was a good idea.

Red Sky was high and dry on a cradle in the boatyard, so Max packed a bag and left for the Beef Island airport. He hired a twin-engine Cessna 340 at the airport, sharing its expense with an Italian sweater manufacturer living in Barranquilla, Colombia, and flew to San Juan, where he cleared U.S. customs and caught a flight to New York. With only a telephone call from Andi to give him the skeleton details of what had happened, Max could only stare out the plane window and let his imagination complete one wild scenario after another. At first he was worried about Andi and Beth and angry at Leung. Then he was angry at Beth for her stubbornness and angry at Andi for raising her like that. Finally, and most of all, he was angry at himself and felt guilty for sending Beth that reward notice in the first place.

When they landed at LaGuardia, he got a cab, threw his suitcase onto the seat next to him, and gave Beth's address on Sixty-third Street to the driver. "Do you want me to take the tunnel?" the driver asked.

"No. Take the bridge," Max answered. "I want to see the skyline."

"No problem." They got onto the Grand Central Parkway and headed westward.

"Should be able to breeze in tonight," Max observed.

"No problem. Sunday night's easy even on Thanksgiving weekend."

Beth's street was one-way against him, so he got out of the cab at the corner, preferring to walk for a few minutes in the cold night air, enjoying the collective aromas from ethnic restaurants and the sidewalks crowded with pedestrian traffic. He felt like an outsider carrying his suitcase and tan among the holiday shoppers, their fingers looped through the handles of crammed shopping bags. The soul of New York always in fast forward. As ever, the painted lady had its charm for him, and he was glad to be back. Then he arrived at Beth's apartment, hugged and kissed his ladies, and they began the debriefing.

Their conversation had not been going well. Beth could see Max was holding himself tightly in check, and that made her more anxious. He was sitting across from her, on the couch next to her mother. His cup of coffee, cold and untouched, remained on the cocktail table in front of him. His arms were crossed, his legs were crossed, his mind was shutting down, and he could only hear that his wife and daughter were in danger. He was exhausted from the long trip and the drastic change in climate.

"What do you mean, 'may' be alive?" he asked Beth.

"Just what I've been telling you. It all adds up. I think he and Erica, and the money, are down in the Caribbean somewhere. Possibly Guadeloupe, but most probably Antigua."

"Well, that narrows it down. How did you figure that one out?"

"It's all in the documents I showed you, and the computer printouts. I've also been seeing his son and—"

"You've been seeing his *what*?" he shouted compulsively, interrupting her in midsentence.

Andi quickly got up from the couch and went into the kitchen, momentarily distracting Max and Beth with the sound of ice cubes falling into a glass as she poured vodka on the rocks for Max and wine for Beth and herself.

Max continued on as Andi handed him the drink. "Now let me have that one again," he said to Beth after taking a sip of the vodka.

"His son, Max. I've been seeing his son. He's given me a lot of solid information about his father." Her mouth felt dry as she spoke, and she forced herself to bring the wineglass slowly and deliberately up to her lips.

"Are you out of your mind?" He, too, was trying hard to be calm, but his ominous tone betrayed the fatigue.

"What are you so surprised about? You knew I met him in Rhode Island last month."

"Meeting him is not seeing him."

"It's only a matter of degree."

"So is the difference between a summer breeze and a hurricane."

"You might as well know I happen to like him too." She could feel his upset from across the living room.

"Of all the guys in the world. I want you to know I'm just furious." He confirmed the obvious to her.

"Furious at what?" she asked, not easily intimidated. "You asked me to do some investigating, remember? Now will you listen to the rest of it?"

"Okay," he said. "Finish." But he wasn't hearing yet.

"He's a nice young man. I met him this morning," Andi cautioned him firmly, wanting to keep a heated discussion from escalating into a full-scale debacle between the two people she adored.

"I'm worried sick," he mumbled, shaking his head in disapproval. He picked up his drink, finished it with one last gulp, and tilted the empty glass back over his open mouth until one big ice cube fell in.

"I'm going down to Antigua in two weeks," Beth said.

"If your mother doesn't shoot you, I will."

"What do you think about all this, Mom?" Beth asked.

"You're talking to me, not your mother!" Max raged. "And don't be a damn idiot. You're dealing with people here that don't live by our rules. . . . What if, God forbid, you and your mother had come back while they were still here?"

"You're right about that," Beth conceded. "They need those bank codes, and they'll do anything to locate a copy."

"How did you find out you had a copy on that CD?"

"Brian helped me pull it up on the computer."

"How much is in the secret accounts?"

"Nearly a billion U.S. at any one time, maybe more. The banks are mostly down in the Caribbean. Some in the U.S., some in Switzerland. The deposits come from Arab banks."

He whistled in disbelief when he heard the amount, shaking his head in utter amazement as he realized his daughter was in more trouble than even he thought originally. "Where'd you put the CD?" he asked.

"I created a fictitious new client, put the phony name on a red rope folder, and stashed it in the file room along with thousands of other files. No one can ever find it."

"I hesitate to ask, but what did you call it?"

"ProCKtoscopic Research Corporation, named after what Sloane wrote on the CD. He was obviously telling C.K. to stick it up his ass."

"Clever, wasn't he."

"I burned an extra copy of the CD. I want you to take it with you. Hide it someplace on *Red Sky* or at the boatyard so we have a backup copy. . . . It's our safe harbor."

"Don't tell me about safe harbors. Minors are doing contract killings in New York for five hundred dollars or a vial of crack cocaine, and you think Leung will let you stand in his way? . . . What did Clifford say about all this?"

"He doesn't know."

"What do you mean, he doesn't know?" Max was closing in on apoplexy.

"I never told him."

"Let me see if I understand this now: Your mother and I know, Brian knows, and Sloane's son knows, Amy *must* know, so half of New York must know, but your boss, my partner, has no idea that you're standing between Leung and a billion dollars of his very hot money?"

"Well, Clifford okayed my handling the insurance case. I just didn't tell him that the client was Sloane's son. The rest of it developed afterwards. And you know what else? I don't have to apologize for it!" She shouted back at him angrily, "I'm the fucking injured party and I'll handle the fucking problem."

Intent on his own position, Max ignored her outburst and continued his own harangue. "You've been handling that dinky little insurance case in the office without telling Clifford the straight truth, including the part about the CD? He should throw you out on your ass."

Beth could see, feel, and hear her stepfather's rage. The directed force of his anger was a new experience for her, and she was shocked. She tried to defend herself. "But I knew he'd never let me handle it otherwise," she said, uncertain of her position now, her voice dropping momentarily.

"And he would have been right."

"You knew I was going to investigate the son," she said, parrying his attack with unfelt confidence born of desperation. "We talked about it when I first discovered his existence. You can't just nail me to the wall now when you see where it's led. That's sandbagging."

"Don't give me that sandbagging crap. We never discussed your getting involved with the son of a man who, if he's alive, I might add, is guilty of grand larceny, embezzlement, and nearly destroying your career. We only discussed a nice impersonal meeting in a nice impersonal public place. His son could be Jack the Ripper for all you know."

"He's not Jack the Ripper, and I don't believe he was involved in any way with the embezzlement. . . . Besides, Mom likes him."

Max ignored her comment. "So what makes you think that Sloane and the seventy million are down there?" he asked, glancing over at Andi, now absorbed in flicking dust off her slacks.

"Haven't you been listening to me for the last hour? All the documents I got from Antigua. Here, look at them again." She handed the envelope back over to Max.

"It's all pure conjecture," he observed, peering through his bifocals at the deed and other papers. "How do you know Leung didn't tell Sloane to buy that property?" Max asked as he continued to scan the papers.

"Using phony names? Be reasonable," Beth countered. "Sloane had a house there, a car there, a boat there. He bought all of it over the past few years with money he must have si-

phoned off from the Leungs. That's where the two of them decided to go when the Jasco windfall came through. It was a
ready-made escape haven for them. The money's got to be there
also."

"What if they withdrew it in negotiable bonds? How do you
know it didn't drown on the boat with them?"

"Because there's one other thing. . . ."

"Damn it, Beth," he said, his voice rising to a crescendo
again. "Stop making me drag it out of you."

"Well, then stop cross-examining me!" she shouted back.
"I'm not on trial. We're on the same side, remember?"

"Then stop treating me as an adversary."

"That's how you're acting."

"I hate these people every bit as much as you do, and more
so for putting you and your mother in danger last night. . . .
Now tell me what you have." For the first time that night, he
was speaking to her as one lawyer to another, ready to assimi-
late the information.

"Dieter Rheinhartz sent me a card from Venezuela a few
days ago. Take a look at it." She handed it to him and watched
intently as he looked first at the printed side and then turned it
over.

"Did you check it out?"

"Of course I did. I called the bank the minute I saw the note
and verified it was Eric Leonard's."

"Why are you so sure he's Sloane?" Max asked her.

"There was a cash deposit of five hundred thousand in U.S.
dollars made on September first. That's a week or so before
Satin Lady sank and it's the same amount they withdrew in
cash from the bank account Erica set up in Switzerland. . . .
And there's more."

"What?" Max asked, now listening with rapt attention.

"The money was withdrawn from the bank in Caracas on September 25, more than two weeks *after Satin Lady* sank." The admiring gasp from her mother and the satisfied smile on Max's face was enough of a reaction to restore all of Beth's confidence in the conclusions she had reached.

"They must have needed it for pocket money," Max finally replied. "Could the bank in Caracas tell you where it was moved to?"

"No. They said it was taken out in cash. Apparently that's not too unusual down there."

"They're used to laundering millions at a time in those Venezuelan banks. Is that where the money trail ends?"

"So far. That's why I want to follow the document trail down to Antigua. Jesus, Max, you went to San Juan to interview the Coast Guard on less concrete information."

"That was different."

"Sure it was. That involved your hunch. This involves mine."

"Do you know why Rheinhartz is being so good to you?"

"There wasn't any love lost between him and Leung when I met them for lunch. They've been at each other's throats a number of times."

"I'll ask Clifford."

"You can't. He'll want to know why you're asking," she said, and then, seizing the warming trend, continued, "Look, Tortola's only a few days' sail from Antigua. Can't you and Mom sail *Red Sky* over there? You can pick me up a week from next Wednesday."

"If I meet you on Wednesday, it's going to be to have you committed. We're amateurs, Beth. This is a police matter." He said this firmly, but without anger.

"You know the police won't do anything without a complaint from C.K." She gestured futilely. "And then before they get finished trying to figure out which country has jurisdiction, we'll all die of old age."

"That's the point." He grimaced. "At least we'll die of old age."

"Max . . . what are all the speeches about truth and justice supposed to mean if nobody searches for them? I can't just walk away from this. I want Sloane before C.K. gets him. He's alive, Erica's alive, and they're both laughing up their sleeves about me, the jerk lawyer."

"What are we talking about here, Beth? Justice or revenge?"

"A fair dose of each. Jail and reparations sound good to me. Will you deal in?"

"Let me sleep on it tonight."

"Well, before you sleep on it, I'm going to call C.K. and I want you both to listen."

"At this hour?"

"About what?"

"Just listen."

Beth already had the phone to her ear and was dialing.

"C.K., this is Beth Swahn."

"Beth, how are you?"

"I got your messages, so let's skip the civility. Your goons almost killed me and three of my friends last week, they mugged me a few days ago, and last night they frightened my mother."

"I don't know what you're talking about, Beth. Have you been drinking?"

"If you don't know what I'm talking about, then perhaps I should hang up."

"You called me, so do what you have to do, but I agree it might be better if we talked."

"I have the CD."

"What is on it?"

"It has something to do with bank access codes."

"I need it immediately."

"I have two problems with that. Number one, I discovered it in connection with Bob Talcourt's case involving Sloane's life insurance policy, so it's attorney-client privileged. And number two, I suspect the codes relate to Arab accounts that may be listed on federal restricted lists, so if I give you the CD, I could be accused of participating in a money-laundering conspiracy."

"What do you propose?"

"I intend to file the CD in federal court and start an interpleader action. We'll let the court decide who's entitled to possession. I intend to do the same thing when I locate the seventy million."

"That is not acceptable. We need that CD immediately."

"Then get it from Sloane."

"You know that's impossible."

"Come on, C.K., you don't still believe he's dead."

"I told you we had proof."

"Well, I don't buy it. Good night, C.K. See you in court."

Click.

"I believe you just had what they call a 'come to Jesus' meeting with C. K. Leung."

"I love you, Max."

"Yeah, yeah," he said with false gruffness.

"I do. I'm glad you're mine." Beth got up from her chair and crossed over to the couch, leaning down to give him a kiss on the cheek he offered her.

"I know. I love you too."

Andi finished her wine and took a deep breath for the first time since Max had entered the apartment.

Chapter Twenty-five

It was still the tail end of hurricane season, so the midweek flight to Antigua wasn't crowded. With only a carry-on bag, Beth was quickly past immigration and into the intense island heat. She briefly familiarized herself with the left-hand stick and the right-hand wheel in the rental, rolled back its canvas top, and, driving British style on the left-hand side of the road, managed to avoid most of the curbs getting out of the airport.

Red Sky had been ninety miles away from Antigua when she'd called them from JFK. With only four hours to go before *Red Sky* figured to anchor in St. John's harbor, she whipped through the villages of Sutherlands and St. Johnson and entered the city of St. John's from Old Parham Road. In the vacant lots between some of the houses, dense with fertile undergrowth, fierce-looking roosters strutted proudly among the officious hens.

It was less quaint than Beth remembered, a little shabbier and more shopworn. She parked the car on High Street and walked back on the sidewalk to check out the major island banks. When she saw that the banks had closed for the day, she continued instead on her way over to the courthouse on the corner of Temple and High to examine the public land records.

She entered the courthouse, scanned the directory, and

found a long, narrow room without any air-conditioning, but with all the windows wide open and several fans operating in the corners.

"Can I help you?" the young woman behind the counter asked Beth in a courteous tone of voice, tinged with a British accent.

"I hope so," Beth answered. "I have a copy of a deed on some real estate here on the island and I'm trying to learn if the purchasers still own it."

"Well, the place to start is over in the grantee-grantor indexes on that table," the woman said, pointing over to her left. "We're not computerized in Land Records yet, so the books are kept in longhand. It's alphabetized, so if you look up the buyer's name, it will also give you the name of the seller."

"Thanks."

"Over on the table by the near wall are the grantor-grantee indexes, with the seller's name first," the woman continued. "You can check there to see if your party has sold the property to someone else."

"Are mortgage records in this room too?"

"I keep them under the counter here. They're listed by the borrower's name. We don't have enough banks on Antigua to alphabetize the index books by lenders."

"I understand. Thanks for your help."

"If you have any problem, let me know and I will be happy to give you a hand."

"Can I get an address for the property from the index?"

"You talk like you're familiar with our land registration system. Are you a solicitor, by any chance?"

"I'm an attorney from New York."

"I could tell. Are there many woman solicitors in the United States?"

"More now than ever. My class in law school was nearly half female."

"Well, here on Antigua we hardly have any. The men do not allow it."

"They're chauvinists all over."

"Yes, they certainly are that." The clerk nodded in agreement. "Anyhow, our records do not have street addresses, and most of the houses out of town don't bother with street numbers. So when you're ready, let me see the deed and I'll show you the property on the map over there." The clerk pointed over to the big map of Antigua on the wall behind her.

The cumbersome index books were on metal shelves, lying on plastic rollers to aid in their removal. Beth located the volume she wanted, a linen-bound journal with aged red leather binding and the letters *P-Q-R* embossed in gold. She opened it up, releasing a sigh of moldy air from its parchment pages, and found an entry made back on November 17, 2009, when Paramount bought the property from a Nehemiah Throckton.

Next, she went over to the grantor-grantee books, got the volume for *S-T-U,* and found Throckton. The entry disclosed that he had bought the real estate from an outfit called Lenco Importing the day before deeding it over to Paramount. Beth remembered the seller's name from somewhere. Intent on the chase, she opened the file she had brought with her. In one of her computer printouts, she found the connection: on its latest tax return, Paramount Equities had listed a Lenco Importing as sole shareholder!

She continued to follow the paper trail, went back to the grantee-grantor books, and wrestled the massive *J-K-L* volume to the table. In her eagerness, she dropped it with a hollow thud, causing the clerk to glance up sternly from her work.

Starting with the latest entries, she quickly found that Lenco acquired the real estate from an Elliot Andrew MacElliott a week before the sale to Throckton. Back again like a yo-yo to the other side of the room, she learned that MacElliott had owned the property since 1961, so she decided to search no further in that direction. She wrote down MacElliott's last address in case she wanted to get in touch with him.

She now had to determine whether Paramount still owned the property. She had a suspicion they didn't. With all the transfers taking place in such a short period of time, somebody was trying to create a smoke screen. She pulled the grantor-grantee index for *P-Q-R* and saw that on November 26, 2009, Paramount sold the property to an Eric Leonard.

If her theory was right, this Eric Leonard was still the record owner of the property, and the name was an alias for Sloane, who had intended to live happily ever after on Antigua. She crossed back to the *J-K-L* volume of the grantor-grantee index and found no subsequent entry for a sale by Eric Leonard. He was still the owner.

With that in mind, she asked the clerk for the mortgage volumes covering *P* and *L*. She didn't find any mortgage under the name of Eric Leonard, but that didn't surprise her. If Eric Leonard was an alias, Sloane wouldn't want any bank to run the inevitable credit check. In the *P-Q-R* book, however, under the name of Paramount Equities, she did find a mortgage held by the Antigua Commercial Bank. The mortgage had been recorded on the same day Paramount bought the property, so when Paramount transferred title to this Eric Leonard, the bank already had its lien recorded.

She closed the mortgage index book and handed it back to the clerk, who replaced it in the rack underneath the counter. "Did you find what you were looking for?" she asked Beth.

"I think so," Beth answered. "Here's a deed describing the

real estate." She handed the Paramount deed to the clerk. "Can you show me where the property is located?"

"Certainly," the clerk said. "Come over to the map and I'll point it out."

Beth walked through the gate in the middle of the counter and followed the clerk over to the map of Antigua.

"Here," the clerk said, putting her finger on the map down by English Harbour. "The property is right here in the town of Bethesda. It's on Willoughby Bay, see, just east of English Harbour."

"How do I get there?"

"That is no problem," the clerk answered. "I have a whole pad of maps here. We use them to give directions to the tax assessor after a sale."

"Can you mark one for me?" Beth saw it was exactly the same map she had gotten from Avis earlier in the day out at the airport.

"Yes. Certainly." The clerk circled a spot on the map and tore it off the pad, handing it to Beth. "Here," she said, outlining the way with a yellow felt marker from her desk drawer. "All you have to do is follow the coast road north out of English Harbour and then make a left turn when you get here." She made another circle on the map. "And a left turn when you get here. You won't have any trouble."

"You've been very kind."

"Do you have a rental car? If you don't, my sister's husband, Ernest, has several for hire down the block. He can give you a very good price."

"Thanks, but I have a car already. I'll probably take a ride down there tomorrow."

"Well, here is a card with his phone number anyway. If you've no use for it, perhaps you will give it to a friend."

Beth smiled and took the card from the woman. She left the courthouse and walked past the Antigua Commercial Bank again on the way back to her car. She glanced at its hours on the door.

She got into the car and drove down to the docks, settling in with a cold beer to wait for *Red Sky* at a nameless, signless open-air bar. In less than an hour, she spotted her tall mast and blue hull proceeding through St. John's harbor and into the inner Deep Water Harbour. A solid yellow quarantine flag flew from the starboard spreader near the top of her mast to let the authorities know she was seeking permission to land.

Beth waved but was too far away to get any response from Max standing at the wheel or from Andi, who had her hands full of chain on the foredeck, preparing to drop anchor. Beth was anxious to share what she had learned at the courthouse. First thing tomorrow morning, they would visit the banks.

Chapter Twenty-six

Beth spun through the revolving door leading out of the Antigua Commercial Bank and took the marble front steps two at a time, sunglasses swinging wildly on the chain around her neck. "I found Sloane's checking account!" she announced to Max and Andi waiting on the sidewalk. "It was hidden under the name of Eric Leonard."

"Any money in it?" Andi asked.

"Not much. Only enough to cover the monthly payment on their real estate mortgage."

"What about the boat mortgage?" Max asked.

"Paramount owned the boat," Beth answered. "Payments stopped when the boat was stolen."

"Who paid before it was stolen?"

"The bank doesn't know. The mortgage on *Sindicator* was assigned to them by a bank on Barbados. They didn't keep any record of who paid. All they know is that the loan went into default."

"Did they foreclose?" Max asked.

"They didn't have to. An insurance company paid off the loan before it got that far."

"So how do we know it was Leonard Sloane using the name Eric Leonard?" Andi finally asked *the* question.

"We won't know until we see a face behind the name, but I'll tell you something else: the address they have for Eric Leonard is English Harbour. He's at Nelson's Dockyard."

"Does he live on a boat?" Andi asked.

"Do they have the name of the boat?" Max asked.

"That would have been too easy," Beth replied. "That's why we've got to hit the dockyard right away," she insisted. "Let's nail this clown once and for all."

With Beth in full stride two paces ahead, they marched back to the car, got in, and drove out of the downtown area. The day's heat was beginning to boil the stagnant air. Beth turned onto Nevis Street and made a left on Market, taking them past the congested public market at the West Bus Station.

Most of the stalls under the shed were occupied by brightly dressed women fussing over their fruits and vegetables while socializing noisily with one another and their customers. The vivid colors of their papayas, mangoes, yams, and tomatoes tumbled out of wicker baskets or just lay in piles on the dirt floors around them.

The meat and poultry dealers were all men, all wearing blood-soaked aprons. They had their fly-covered goat and chicken carcasses, headless and gutted, hanging on hooks around the stalls for inspection by their customers. The steady buzzing of the hovering flies and yellow jackets added to the manifest horror of thin-lipped tourists exploring the aisles with purses and cameras clutched tightly in their grasps.

Beth slowed behind an old pickup truck and stared at the vendors outside the market, some under makeshift awnings, others with their wares lying on the ground. An impatient horn sounded behind her, breaking the trance. Caribbean poverty with its riot of heat, color, and frantic laughter released her from its compelling fascination. She eased up on the clutch. In a few minutes, they were heading south around Antigua on All Saints Road.

"Do you mind telling me what we're looking for?" Andi asked with her healthy air of skepticism. "Strictly as a matter of curiosity, what does our Eric Leonard look like?"

"Let's assume, for the time being, he looks like Leonard Sloane," Beth answered.

"I agree," Max said.

"I met Leonard Sloane and Erica Crossland once," Andi said. "I don't think I would recognize either one of them today."

"I've never met Erica at all," Beth said.

"Then I think you're daydreaming," Andi said. "They'd have to be pretty dumb to steal their own boat from Guadeloupe and sail it over to Antigua."

"As long as we're going to be there, we might as well have lunch at the Admiral's Inn."

"Stick to basics, huh, Dad?"

"Exactly."

"Good," Beth said. "We'll park at the dockyard, and after lunch, we'll inspect the boats tied up to the dock."

The man in dark sunglasses was staring at Beth. She noticed it when they sat down for lunch on the terrace. A bald-headed guy with a mustache and a Vandyke beard, sitting alone at the Admiral's Inn. And to make it almost absurd, he was watching her through a newspaper. Later, as the waitress was serving their iced tea, she saw him get up and walk quickly out of the inn, leaving his unfinished food, drink, and newspaper on the table.

Afterwards, with their lunch topped off by the English trifle they shared for dessert, the logy threesome staggered down the irregular stone steps leading from the Admiral's Inn and walked over toward Nelson's Dockyard. The quay was crowded with luxurious yachts tied up by the stern to every available slip, an anchor from the bow securing their safety in the harbor.

"After a meal like that, a walk around the dockyard will do us good," Max said.

"Did you see the strange-looking dude sitting by himself over in the corner?" Beth asked.

"No, I guess my back was to him."

"He looked startled when we sat down."

"What'd he look like?"

"Bald, Vandyke."

"Tell me if you see him again," Max said. "In the meantime, it's after three already. Remember what we're here for."

"I know, Captain," Andi answered.

"Right," he said. "So let's wander along the edge of the dock like any tourists after lunch at the Ad."

The bulkheaded dock around the perimeter of the yard jutted out into English Harbour like a small peninsula of land with a hexagonal border of sleek fiberglass sailboats interspersed with the occasional wooden hull of an older boat.

They walked slowly around the dockyard, carefully observing each sailboat, mentally measuring length with experienced eyes, paying particular attention to ketches, and concentrating on the names painted on the transoms.

By the time they reached the last section of dock, they were all uncomfortably hot. "Remember, Sloane's boat was a fifty-one-foot ketch. The name was *Sindicator*," Max droned on aloud, repeating his mantra.

"Yes, I know, Dad."

"You're being obsessive for a change, my love."

"Hey! There's one," Beth announced triumphantly, motioning over to her left. "It looks like about a fifty-foot ketch." They walked together over to the sailboat tied up to the dock. Laundry was hanging out to dry on the guardrails. The sound of a television soap opera rose up from the open hatch leading to the cabin below.

Max leaned over the water's edge to examine the serial numbers on the transom. "She is a fifty-footer," he said. "Your guess was right. Made in 2006. *Serenity.* I like that name."

"Her hailing port is Bar Harbor, Maine. They've traveled a long way."

As they looked over the boat, a plumpish young woman with short, curly red hair climbed up out of the hatch with an infant in one arm and a toddler close behind. A miniature snow-white poodle brought up the rear. When she saw the threesome looking at her boat, she smiled warmly. "Hi, how are you?" she said. "Lovely day, isn't it?"

"Yes, it really is," Andi responded. "We were just admiring your ketch. My husband loves the name."

"Thanks. It's my mother-in-law's name," she said, reaching over to feel the laundry. "Thank God the diapers are dry. I was down to my last one."

"How old is the baby?" Andi asked.

"He'll be eleven months old next Thursday."

"He's beautiful. So is your daughter. She's a redhead just like her mother."

"I know. She hates it."

"She won't when she grows up. Is this your boat?" Beth asked.

"It belongs to my in-laws. My husband sailed it down from Maine last summer with them. We both teach at the university."

"I guess you're off for the midsemester break," Beth surmised.

"You got it." She nodded. "We flew down with the kids last week to spend the recess here."

"We're going to stroll around the dockyard some more. Walk off some of our lunch." Beth was anxious to get on with the search. "Have a good day."

"Same to you," the woman said, putting the infant into a crib on the cockpit seat while she and her daughter folded the clean diapers. Beth continued along the dock as Max and Andi followed behind.

"Scratch one fifty-foot ketch," she heard her father mumble.

"Cute grandchildren," she heard her mother mutter, and ignored the obvious implication.

She picked up the pace. "There's another one about the right size." She pointed to a single-masted sailboat tied up a few boats away. "It's for sale too."

"Too bad it's a sloop," Max said.

"*Atrophy*. What a strange name for a boat," Andi commented.

"Her hatch is locked," Max said. "Nobody's on board."

"What's the difference, anyway?" Beth said. "We're looking for a ketch. This sloop won't do us any good."

"Look where they put that drop-leaf table." Max freely offered his critique. "Bolted to the deck midway between the wheel and the hatch. Strange place. Obstructs the freedom of the whole cockpit area. Just looks wrong," he said, always the nautical purist.

"Let's keep on walking." Beth pushed on, starting to feel discouraged. "We're almost finished. Some boats may be out sailing for the day. Maybe we ought to stick around for a while. See what comes back later."

"No. It's late enough. I want to come back out here early tomorrow morning anyhow," Max said. "With the binoculars this time. We'll look for the real estate first and then check the dock again. We'll be able to take a look at the boats moored in the harbor."

"It's not even four thirty," Beth protested, holding up her wristwatch for effect. "Let's at least go see if we can find the house. See what we can learn there."

"Tomorrow."

"Come on, Dad. It's early."

"No, it'll be getting dark soon and we're not going to deal with driving on Antiguan roads after dark," Max said quietly and calmly.

"But there's still time," she protested. "Let's find out once and for all if we have Len and Erica."

"No. We'll go there tomorrow morning just as we planned." He spoke emphatically, making it clear the debate was over. "If it's Sloane out there today, it'll be Sloane out there tomorrow."

"I guess you're right," she agreed reluctantly. "I'm just disappointed. I really thought after the bank we'd find the boat out here."

"So did I."

"So what do you want to do now?" Andi asked, ignoring the protest.

"I want to go back to *Red Sky*," Max said. "We've been away all day. I want to run the engine for a while to charge the batteries. You guys can come back on board with me or spend some time shopping before dinner. We need a lot of stuff."

They were all disappointed by the lack of progress and worn out by the hot sun and the breezeless air on shore. It showed on the trip back to St. John's. Beth was quiet and concentrated on her driving. She made it back in less than thirty minutes, careening adroitly around the curves with the best of the locals. Max was absorbed in thought and said little except to respond to Andi when she commented on some interesting sight. None of them paid any special attention to the little red Honda that followed them all the way back to St. John's.

Beth parked on a quiet narrow street by the pier, as close to their dinghy as she could manage. The man in the red Honda parked it down the block from them and watched from his car. Max crossed to the pier and climbed into the dinghy while Beth and her mother walked away in the opposite direction, searching for a supermarket.

When he saw Max board *Red Sky,* the man got out of the Honda and strolled casually over to Beth's Suzuki. They must be here on a cruise, he thought, pure coincidence. I'm sure there's nothing to worry about. Then he looked inside the open vehicle and saw the Avis map with the clerk's markings that Beth had left on the dashboard.

He turned to walk away, took a few hesitant steps, and changed his mind. Acting on the impulse, he looked around furtively and saw that no one was in sight. He took out his pocket knife, opened the hood of the car, and cut every wire he could reach. Then he grabbed the map on the dashboard, tore it in half, and drove off, smugly satisfied with his clever little prank.

Chapter Twenty-seven

"They're anchored in St. John's harbor," Len said to Erica, rubbing the ice-filled glass around his neck before taking another drink. "The name of their boat is *Red Sky*. She's a forty-seven-foot sloop. Got a blue hull."

"How many on board?"

"I told you: the three of them."

"How can you be so sure they didn't recognize you?" She repeated the question, her attention still focused on the memory of her delightful afternoon spent with a Dutch couple on their sailboat across the yard.

"I'm sure," he insisted in response to her question, sweat pouring down his forehead. "They had their backs to me." He sat down in the cockpit across from her, the Bimini top sheltering them from the worst of the late afternoon sun.

"What about the kid lawyer, Beth What's-her-name?"

"She saw me, but there's no way she recognized me." He reached into his pocket, pulled out a bottle of pills, and swallowed one, washing it down with a mouthful of rum and Coke.

"You ought to lay off that stuff. It knocks you out, especially with the booze chaser."

"I have a headache."

"Stop it! The doctor told you there's nothing the matter

with you," she vented her disgust at him. "What do you think Beth is doing down here?"

"She must be on a vacation with her parents. They live on that sailboat over in the British Virgins. Running into them at the inn was just a coincidence." He took off his shirt, wiped his face and chest with it, and threw it on the floor of the cockpit.

"Maybe, but let's move up our plans anyway. Instead of flying to Panama on January second, we'll leave tomorrow. No need to take any unnecessary chances."

"I tell you we're both dead as far as they're concerned. Anyhow, they're not coming back tomorrow. I fixed their car."

"You did what?"

"Cut all the wires," he bragged. "So you see, there's no need to change our plans."

"You're wrong," she snapped, annoyed by his act of petty vandalism. "We should have left weeks ago like I wanted. I never should have let you talk me out of it just because you wanted to sell the damn house and this boat. Get out to the airport now and change our reservations."

"I just got back from driving all the way to St. John's," he protested. "I'll go a little later when it's not so damn hot."

"Stop complaining for once in your life and get going," she insisted. "Move the tickets up to tomorrow. We'll pick up the bonds in Panama and be in Auckland by the end of the week."

"Then let's move the boat before I go. In case Beth and her parents find another way to drive back out here. Don't forget her father knows me too."

"They have no reason to notice *Atrophy*, but maybe it's not such a bad idea. Okay, we'll move her out into the harbor and drop a hook. Tomorrow we'll sail over to St. John's and leave her there before we go to the airport. Nobody'll notice an abandoned boat for a month in that harbor."

"After we're gone, it won't make any difference anyhow. Let the guy who buys it worry about it."

"All right. Go raise the anchor while I start the engine. I'll take her out myself while you go to the airport."

He went forward, up to the bow, and began to pull up the anchor she had insisted they drop for extra holding power. The exertion caused his heart to pound and his eyes to burn from sweat. He was thoroughly uncomfortable. As soon as the stern lines were brought in, the boat was ready to move out of its slip. He got their passports and tickets, put his shirt back on, and left her on board while he drove out to the airport. He turned on the car's air-conditioning system and pointed it full blast at his face. Driving from one end of the island to the other took an hour.

When he drove up the circular entrance to the airport, he saw four Chinese men in black suits and ties coming out of the terminal, walking quickly toward a waiting taxi. There was not a piece of luggage among them. As he watched, two of them got into the taxi and drove off while the other two walked back into the terminal. Despite the throbbing in his head, he recognized one of the two who stayed behind. It was Andrew Leung, C.K.'s brother.

The paralysis that forged into his brain didn't prevent him from driving instinctively. He continued around the airport, past the entrance, without stopping, covering his nose and mouth protectively with his free hand, praying not to be seen. Somehow he made his way out of the airport, although he later had no recollection of driving back to English Harbour.

The dinghy was waiting for him, tied up at the dock where he had left it. Erica was in the cockpit when he climbed back on the boat. He grabbed immediately for the warm remains of his rum and Coke still hanging in the drink holder and finished it in one breathless gulp.

"Any trouble getting us on tomorrow's flight?" she asked, looking up at him. Even with her lack of sensitivity, it would have been hard to miss the desperation stretched across his face. "Christ, what's the matter? You look awful."

"I saw one of C.K.'s brothers at the airport." He stared at her, searching for some reaction, some indication of shared upset.

"You saw who?"

"Andrew Leung. I met him last year in Taiwan."

"Did he see you?" Her face remained impassive.

"If he saw me, do you think I'd be back here?" He searched wildly around the cockpit, dumping the contents of the portside lazaret out on the cockpit seat. "Where's my Xanax?" He frantically opened up eyeglass cases and binocular cases. "I put the bottle here yesterday, in one of these empty cases."

"Never mind that. Did you get the new tickets at least?" If nothing else, she was focused.

"I told you! He was waiting at the airport. He had three other guys with him. Two left in a cab."

"He couldn't have recognized you."

"Look, he's here to get us. They have the airport covered. If we show up there, it's all over. It's too small an airport. There are only a few flights to watch."

"Calm down. This is no time to lose your cool."

"*You* calm down!" he shrieked. "I nearly got caught twice today."

"I told you we should have left weeks ago. We gave them too much time to figure it out. Now we're going to have to sail to Panama. Go get Vincent and bring him here."

"I don't like that kid. What do you want him for?"

"Do as I say. If we're going to sail across the Caribbean, we'll need an extra hand on board."

"How can we sail all the way to Panama?"

"It beats swimming," she answered glibly. "I want us to be ready to sail over to St. John's in an hour. There'll be plenty of moonlight. We'll get the radar mount repaired first thing tomorrow morning and be on our way by noon. Let's use whatever lead time we have left."

"*Red Sky* is in St. John's. We're looking for trouble by going there."

"If it comes, I'll be ready for it." She got up, walked over to the hatchway, and stuck her hand down inside, reaching under the first rung of the ladder. When she brought her hand back up, it was clutching a nasty-looking Glock 9mm pistol. She dropped out the clip and checked to make certain it was full before reinserting it into the grip. Without a flicker of emotion, she pulled back the slide expertly and released it to chamber a round.

"Christ, what are you doing that for?" He blanched, looked around nervously to see if anyone was watching, and sat down heavily in the cockpit.

"Listen, Leonard . . . ," she said in a determined tone of voice that left no doubt of her intentions. "If that lawyer of yours or any of Leung's guys come within range of this boat, I'm going to blow their friggin' heads off." She pointed the gun at him, shaking it like a fist for emphasis before putting it down on the bench next to her. "Nobody is getting between us and that money."

"Do you really think it'll come down to that?" He was shocked back to relative calm by the sight of the gun in her hand.

"No, of course not." She softened her tone, recognizing the need to reassure him. "As long as you and I stick together, we can pull this thing off. Now, go pick up Vincent."

"We don't need him."

"Just get him, will you, and stop wasting time. Tell his mother he'll be back in five or six days."

"How're you planning to arrange that?"

"We'll send him home on a plane when we get to Panama." Again her tone softened. "Now get moving so you can hurry back to me." She was talking to him now like a naughty boy. He moved quickly in conditioned response to the stimulus.

Chapter Twenty-eight

When the tiny Suzuki refused to start at seven fifteen a.m. the following morning, Beth opened the hood and saw the tangle of severed cables. Max and Andi joined her around the engine, staring somberly at the destruction. Their first reaction was that it was malicious mischief by local teenagers, except that none of the other cars parked nearby appeared damaged. Then, when Beth noticed her torn map, she knew there had to be more involved.

Beth called the police on her cellphone to report the vandalism and then called Avis, hoping to obtain a replacement car. The police responded, but Avis was a dead end. Their answering machine cheerfully advised Beth that they did not open for business until ten a.m.

Beth did not intend to wait. Digging around in her bag, she located the card given her by the clerk in Land Records. She called the number on the card, and within ten minutes, Ernest, the clerk's brother-in-law, arrived in a vintage yellow Chevy belching thick black smoke from its exhaust, with the hand-lettered word *Taxi* and an irregular black-and-white checkerboard painted on both sides.

Although Ernest apologized profusely for having no rental car available, he was able to splice the cables on the Suzuki with a big roll of electrical tape and a few feet of baling wire he found in his trunk. By eight thirty, they were on their way.

After leaving St. John's, they drove around for nearly an hour, half of which was spent getting lost and unlost, until they passed a familiar palm tree in English Harbour for the third time. It was at a point where the road turned north up toward where they hoped the Eric Leonard property was located, somewhere between Bethesda and Willoughby Bay.

"Okay, navigator," Beth said to Max, "the easy part's over. Where do we go now?"

"I have no idea," Max answered confidently, looking for some hint of an answer on the detail-free map he held.

"I know," Andi offered gratuitously from the backseat, "let's ask somebody."

"I don't even know what to ask," Max said. "There are no street numbers and no street names. Only an 'X' mark on this ridiculous map."

Beth drove on aimlessly for another five minutes before pulling off the road next to a shirtless young man in tight cutoff shorts and long dreadlocks, working on the rear engine of a battered Volkswagen Beetle.

"Excuse me," Max said to the man, who stood up from his engine repairs and ambled easily over to the passenger side of the car. "Can you help us?"

"I'll be happy to help you, sir."

"Could you please take a look at this map and tell us how to get to this spot over here with the 'X' on it?" Max held up the map for him to see, wondering if everybody on Antigua was really as polite and cooperative as they all seemed to be.

"I know the area well," the man said in a lilting West Indian English, ultrasolicitous and anxious to accommodate the carload of tourists. He examined the map carefully. "Ah, yes," he finally said, a big smile extending across his face. "You are not far from there now."

"Good," Andi said, relieved at the news.

"You must follow this road that you are now on," the man said, indicating to Max with his finger on the map. "Past the fork here, going left and then bearing right until you reach its intersection with Barrow's Bull Road, where you must make a right turn. Stay on that road until you reach Fair Crossing Road and Cobb's House Road, where you must make another right turn. The property you seek is on that road."

"How far away is it?" Max asked, confusion setting in.

"Oh, it is not too far," the Antiguan responded. "Less than a kilometer away from here."

"Thank you very much," Max said. "We appreciate your help."

"It is my pleasure, sir," the man said, waiting respectfully by the side of the road until Beth pulled the car away from him. He then returned to his own ministrations, tending to his car.

Beth continued on in the same direction, driving slowly on the left-hand side of the narrow road, passing fewer and fewer houses, two forks, and no pedestrians. The road became more remote and the potholes larger and more frequent. She stopped the car at the first intersection she reached, a five-corner conflu- ence of confusing choices.

There were no street signs to mark any of the roads, two of which were nothing more than dirt lanes. There was a small grocery store nestled between two stunted palm trees on one of the corners, its shutters down, its door closed, its shabby walls with more paint peeled off than remaining. A faded red metal sign hung above the door, half of it rusted away, identifying the premises as the Red Lion Supermarket.

"It's almost nine thirty," Beth said, looking down at the car's digital clock glued onto the dashboard. "If that stand was ever going to open today, it would be open already."

"Let me see that deed," Max said. "Maybe I can figure something out from the metes and bounds description of the property. It has to name some starting place."

Beth reached behind her into the backseat for the blue canvas bag with the Columbia logo lying on the seat next to Andi. She wedged it against the steering wheel, unzipped it, hunted around briefly inside, and pulled out her photocopy of the legal-sized piece of paper. "Here," she said, passing it over to Max, "I couldn't make any sense out of it."

"Didn't they teach you to read a deed in law school?"

"Yes," she said defensively, "but where I come from, they all have civilized references to street names, street numbers, and lot and block designations."

"Bah! Humbug!" He took his eyeglasses out of their case, dropped the case back on the dashboard shelf, and began examining the deed. The front seat was barely wide enough for the two of them, so Beth had no trouble reading over his shoulder.

"Here we go. Look," Max announced, jabbing his finger midway down the front page of the deed. He began to quote: "Beginning at a point on the northerly side of Cobb's House Road at a distance eight hundred and seventy-six feet, seven inches from the southwesterly side of the intersection formed with Fair Crossing Road . . . See? It's easy. All we have to do is get out of the car and pace it off."

"Yes, but I hate to state the obvious fact that none of these roads are marked."

"Thank you, Andi," Max said, somewhat less than appreciative. "We can narrow it down a little. We need an east–west road for it to have a north side."

"That eliminates the road we're on and only leaves us with three other choices," Beth said, adding, "two of which are nothing more than dirt paths barely wide enough for this car."

"Assuming this is even the right intersection to start with," Andi said, looking around at the various options. "Can I see the map for a second?" She reached into the front seat for it as Max handed it to her.

"I feel like we're playing *Sword and Sorcery* on the computer," Beth declared.

"Come on, you naysayers," Max said. "It'll take us two minutes to check them all out. We'll use the car first and then we'll pace out any likely-looking house."

"You don't have to try them all," Andi said with complete authority, looking up from the map. "Take the blacktop road." She pointed over to her right.

Without objection, Beth made a right turn and proceeded slowly in an easterly direction along the single-lane road, avoiding only a fraction of the potholes that pockmarked the surface, exposing the underlying coral base. "This four-wheel drive is sure coming in handy," she commented. The car proceeded slowly, serpentine fashion, its chassis and passengers bouncing up and down, swaying from left to right.

The road quickly deteriorated and closed in on both sides of the car, becoming overgrown with tropical growth. Beth recognized the familiar yucca plants and the occasional manchineel tree with its poisonous potential, but not the more exotic, spiny-looking bushes with their bright red and white flowers or the ones with yellow leaves and dark brown fruit.

"This road doesn't look like such a good choice," Beth volunteered the obvious conclusion, and in return received icy glares from the front and backseat passengers.

They passed a derelict automobile body, abandoned off on

the right, partially hidden in the underbrush, its usable parts long since scavenged, only the rusting hulk remaining. A small green lizard scurried over its engineless hood and jumped into the brush as their car invaded his private sanctuary.

As they approached what appeared to be a clearing on the left, the north side of the road, about fifty or seventy-five yards away, Beth felt her heart begin to pound. She continued to inch the car along the road at less than five miles per hour. "Something's coming up on our left," she said. "How far since we turned?"

"Feels like a long way," Andi said.

"Let's see what's there first," Max responded.

Beth slowed the car down even more as the heavy growth on the left thinned out, became sparse, and then opened up on the remnants of what must have once been a lawn. The yard sloped down in the rear, providing an unobstructed view of the water a few hundred yards beyond where the crashing waves and turbulence announced that they were on the Atlantic Ocean side of the island. The property fronted the road for a few hundred feet before giving itself back into dense brush.

The remnants of a two-story house stood in the middle of the property, its faded pink stucco walls standing, half its roof missing to expose it to the sky, revealing the charred remnants of a disastrous fire. Its doorless portico was protected by a wrought-iron gate hanging ajar on one remaining hinge. The same style of grillwork covered all the entire first-floor window frames, with jagged shards of broken glass still embedded in several of the panes.

Beth felt her anticipation ebb as the destruction became apparent. The weeds climbing for light out of one of the first-floor windows made it abundantly clear that the house had been in this condition for some time. "Nobody's lived here for

a while," she said, commenting on the obvious, slowly steering
the car off the road onto the shoulder. She turned off the igni-
tion and the three of them got out. "Dad, why don't you pace
out the distance back to the intersection? At least we'll know
then if this could be the right property. In the meantime, I'll
look around with Mom."

"Okay, might as well." Max walked over to the spot where
the clearing started and began pacing westward, back toward
the main road, counting to himself as he took his long, measured strides.

Beth and Andi strolled toward the back of the property, circling aimlessly around the house and peering through windows
at its gutted interior. Finally, they sat down on a conveniently
placed coral outcrop to await Max's return. Free from the
sound of the car engine, they could hear the roar of the Atlantic surf pounding up against the rock-strewn coastline.

In about ten minutes, they saw Max walking up the road,
one deliberate step at a time. His lips moved silently as he
marked off the distance. When he saw them, he crossed over the
property and sat beside them. "Well, I'll tell you," he said. "It
could be the right property. I measured two hundred and eighty-
six paces going and two hundred and ninety-three coming. At a
one-yard pace, that would be about right."

"It's a dead end anyhow," Andi said, her voice tinged with
dejection. "Might as well go."

Beth nodded sympathetically and looked around for a final
moment. Her curiosity was piqued by the sight of several lizards sunning themselves on a long, narrow bundle lying on the
ground on the far side of the property. It was covered by a faded
green tarpaulin held down by several large stones, a pile of
empty paint cans, and discarded chicken wire. "Why don't you

two head for the car?" she suggested. "I want to take a look at that pile over there for a second."

"Okay," Andi said, standing up next to Max. "Don't stick your hands in any strange places. You might get bit."

"I'll be back in a second." She turned away from Max and Andi and strode over to the mound.

Their backs were to Beth as they walked to the car, so they didn't see her kicking the stones away from the tarp with her sneakered right foot. They also didn't see her bend over the pile to peel back the tarp with her left hand after she chased the lizards away. They did hear her shout, however. They certainly heard that. Andi froze, absolutely certain that her beloved daughter had been fatally bitten by a snake.

Max reacted instantly. He spun around and started running to Beth as fast as he could. Andi wheeled and followed right behind. As soon as she saw the animated way Beth was gesturing, jumping up, and pointing at the ground, she slowed to a fast walk and then stopped halfway.

"Jesus, Beth," Max exclaimed, reaching his stepdaughter. "You scared the shit out of us. What's the matter?"

"It's the mast!" she shouted. "It's the fucking mast!"

"What in hell are you yelling about?" Then he looked down at the ground and saw that Beth had partially uncovered a sailboat's aluminum mast, its rigging and halyards attached. It was resting on the ground next to a faded yellow canvas sail bag.

"So it's a mast. Big deal." Max was unimpressed. "It's a small one," he estimated. "No more than forty feet tops, so it must be from a small sailboat, maybe twenty-five feet long. What's that got to do with us? We're looking for a fifty-footer."

"It's a mizzenmast from a ketch!" Beth said, still shouting excitedly. "That's why it's so short. Look at the name marked on the base, *Atrophy*. Remember? That's the name of the sloop with the 'For Sale' sign we saw at Nelson's Dockyard yesterday. Only it wasn't really a single-masted sloop, it was a converted two-masted ketch."

"Come on, that's nuts."

"No, it's not!" she insisted. "The mizzenmast on a fifty-foot ketch would be just about this size. They took down the mizzen to make it look like a sloop. Remember that funny-looking table in the cockpit? That was covering up the hole in the deck from the missing mast."

"Let me see what's inside the sail bag." Max knelt next to the bag, coaxed the knot apart, and opened it up. He pulled out the sail that had been stuffed inside, and Beth helped him stretch it out on the ground.

She noticed a plastic identification tag attached to a grommet through the clew of the sail, reached over to look at it, and started to shriek all over again: "*Sindicator!* It says *Sindicator*! This sail came off of *Sindicator*! I cannot believe it!" She jumped up and grabbed her mother by the shoulders. "We have the slimy bastard!"

"We still have to find him." Max tried to calm her and himself.

"We have to get down to Nelson's Dockyard right away."

"It can wait for five minutes," Max said. "I saw a lady opening that grocery stand when I was walking back along the road. Let's talk to her first."

The three of them piled back into the Suzuki. Beth started up the car and drove back out to the five-cornered intersection. An elderly woman sitting in a beaten-up wooden ladder-back chair outside the grocery stand stood up and smiled broadly, revealing a gap of several teeth, as Beth pulled the car to a stop in front of her.

"Good morning, young lady," the woman said to Beth. "And good morning to you too, sir, and to the lovely lady in the backseat. How may I assist you on a beautiful day such as it is?"

"We were trying to find a house out here," Beth said. "Is that Cobb's House Road over there?" she asked, pointing to the road they'd just come out of.

"That certainly is. You are quite right. But nobody is living on it."

"We saw an old dilapidated house down the road a bit," Max said. "Is that the only house on the road?"

"That's the only one, you can be sure. Its roof is blown off by the big hurricane year before last, and some scurrilous vandals set it afire before the family could repair it. Teenagers, they were. Godless and shiftless. Smoking their filthy ganja." The woman hawked and spit noisily into the dirt, shaking her finger in the air as if admonishing some invisible child who had misbehaved.

"Do you know who lived there?" Beth asked.

"Of course I do. I've lived here since coming over from Barbuda as a girl half your age. Owned this supermarket by myself for more than six years and ran it with my dear husband for thirty-two years before that, God rest his soul. I cannot get anybody to help run it. That is why I open it up so late in the morning. I cannot do it all myself."

"It's important to take care of your own health," Andi said sympathetically.

"It certainly is. At seventy-two, it certainly is," the woman repeated, nodding in agreement.

"Do you remember who lived there?" Max prompted.

"Yes, of course. Lord and Lady Cobb never came back to Antigua after the war. Their children only came here long enough to sell the property thirty years ago to old Andy MacElliott, manager of the Antigua Commercial Bank in St. John's. Andy and his wife, Emma, lived there until the roof blew off during that devil hurricane in September of 2009. They never rebuilt it."

"Do they still own it?" Beth asked.

"Oh, my goodness, no! They didn't need such a big house after their three children all married and moved off the island, so they sold it right after the storm to Americans. Not nice people."

"You've met them?" Max asked, surprised by her comment.

"Oh my, yes. They stop by the supermarket. I believe they are living down in the harbor."

"Do you know their names?"

"No. They are always too busy to chat."

"Could you tell us what they look like?" Beth asked, mentally kicking herself for not asking Bob if he had a photograph of his father.

"They're white folks, like yourselves. The man is bald, not tall. He got a funny little beard and a mustache. His wife is taller. But not at all friendly, you know."

Beth barely managed to stifle a gasp when she heard the man described. "And they told you they were living in English Harbour?" she asked.

"The man once said to me that they had to live there on a boat until the house had been restored. That was before the fire last summer finished what the hurricane had started."

"Have they come by recently?"

"The lady stopped by my supermarket about two, maybe three weeks ago but did not buy anything. She said they planned to rebuild the house as soon as their insurance company stopped fighting with them about what damage was caused by the hurricane before they bought the house and what damage was caused by the fire after they bought the house."

"Well, I guess that's about it," Beth said, satisfied she had heard enough. "I'm sorry we've taken up so much of your time. Do you have any cold soda?" she asked.

"Of course," the woman said with a pleased expression covering her face. "What may I get for you?"

"Whatever is sugar-free. Diet Coke, Diet Pepsi. As long as it's cold. Can we have three cans, please?"

The woman went inside her store and returned in a moment with three cans of a generic diet cola. "I am sorry," she said apologetically, "but that is all I seem to have at the moment. They are a dollar each."

"That will be just fine," Max said, smiling warmly at her. He reached into his pocket and handed her a five-dollar bill. "Have a very nice day."

"I'll be back with your change in a moment." She turned to head back into the store.

"Please don't bother," Max said, stopping the woman with his upraised hand. "You've been kind enough to let us take up your time. Enjoy the day."

"And the very same to you, sir, and to you two ladies also. . . ." The woman walked back inside her store as Beth drove the car onto the road to English Harbour.

"She was a delight," Andi said.

"You know who she described, don't you?" Beth asked, shifting the small Suzuki through its gears.

"No, who?" Andi asked.

"That guy who was staring at me yesterday at the Ad. He fits the description that old lady gave us."

"You figure it's Len Sloane?" Max asked.

"I'm sure. Connecting *Sindicator* to *Atrophy* with that mizzen clinches it," Beth said. "Sloane wore a hairpiece. I never saw him without it. He could have taken it off now, and anybody can grow a beard and mustache." She downshifted smoothly around a sharp curve in the road, avoided an oncoming truck partially over on her side of the road, and accelerated into the straightaway.

"Take it easy, will you, please?" The plea came from Andi in the backseat, wiping soda off her chin.

"Sorry, Mom." Nevertheless, Beth accelerated the Suzuki adroitly all the way back into English Harbour. She was absorbed in strategizing the showdown if she came face-to-face with Leonard Sloane. She finally decided she'd punch him out first and worry about it later. Max would know what to do anyhow. She looked over at him and saw a look of cold determination fixed on his face. It relaxed her enough to laugh and shake her fist triumphantly at the next driver she cut off.

Chapter Twenty-nine

They were flying high on optimism when they got into English Harbour at ten thirty a.m. The elation turned to disappointment when they got to Nelson's Dockyard and found *Atrophy*'s empty slip. The sailboat was nowhere to be seen.

They questioned everyone they saw. One of the workers told them he had seen *Atrophy* leave her slip late yesterday afternoon to anchor out in the harbor. Another remembered he had seen them in the moonlight sailing out of the harbor around nine o'clock but didn't pay any attention to their heading.

They went over to the supply store across the yard. Except for apparel and souvenirs, the merchandise in the store was sparse, limited to essential marine parts displayed in a few widely dispersed areas.

"Good morning," said the man behind the counter. "What can I do for you?"

"We're looking for friends of ours, the Leonards," Beth said. "They live on board *Atrophy*. Do you know them?"

"Sure. Mrs. Leonard was my last customer last night. She came in to buy chart CDs."

"We're going to be cruising with them. What charts did they buy?"

"So you're going through the Canal with them too, huh?"

"Yes," Max said, expanding on Beth's lie. "We're going to spend the year cruising the Pacific."

"What charts did she buy?" Beth repeated.

"From here to Aruba, naturally. Large and small scale. And from Aruba to the Canal."

"Did they buy charts for the direct route from here to the Canal?"

"They did. It's a rough sail too. A beat to windward the whole way."

"Yeah, you're right," Max said. "Anyhow, better give us the same charts in CDs and paper copies." He knew without looking that the muttering he heard came from Andi standing behind him.

"Just to be safe, Dad, get some large-scale charts covering the whole area."

"Be my pleasure," the clerk responded. "Are you going to meet them over in St. John's this morning?"

"Actually we were supposed to meet them here for breakfast."

"I'm surprised. They sailed over to St. John's last night. They need a part for their radar antenna mount and I didn't have it here. They're going to pick it up in St. John's this morning and leave for Aruba from there."

"Just as well. Our boat's in St. John's anyhow. We'll drive back and meet them there."

Max deferred to Andi as she came over to examine the charts. "Do you have a small-scale chart that gives a good close-up of the approaches to the Canal?" she asked. "Better yet, give me the Imray catalog. I want to see all the available charts. I don't want to get too close to the coast of Colombia."

"Yes, ma'am," the clerk said respectfully, handing her the catalog.

Andi scrutinized the catalog herself this time and asked the clerk for several additional charts not available on CD. When he returned with them, he handed them directly to her. She looked them over, nodded affirmatively, and handed them back to the clerk. "We'll take these," she said to him.

"Yes, ma'am," he repeated. He rolled up the charts and slid them into a narrow tube, which he handed to Andi.

"Do you take credit cards?" Max asked, relieved to see Andi assuming her role as navigator.

On the first mile or so of the trip back to St. John's, the only sound heard in the open car was the wind. When Andi's explosion finally came, its vehemence was not exactly unanticipated. "You two are out of your respective God-given minds!" she exclaimed loudly from the backseat.

Behind the wheel, Beth was tempted to make a comment about not being able to hear her mother over the wind, but she wisely thought better of it.

"What do you think this is?" Andi continued. "Some sailboat race where if you get fouled, you can complain to some committee dressed in white ducks and blue blazers?"

The silence from the driver and passenger in front was deafening. As a result, Andi became even more irate.

"We are not sailing *Red Sky* to the Panama Canal!" she raged.

The silence up front continued.

"One of you two better say something."

"Look, I know you don't want to hear it," Max finally offered, "but I agree with Beth. I want to find those two."

"And then what? Heave to and prepare to board? Cutlass in your teeth while you swing over on a halyard?"

"No, but the idea has appeal," he gibed.

214 / Michael Rudolph

"Don't you realize they have seventy million dollars to gain and nothing to lose?"

"Look, there isn't going to be any confrontation. When we catch up with them, we'll call the Coast Guard and let them handle the arrest."

"Good! Then call the Coast Guard right now."

"Mom, it would be days before they sort it all out and a week before they start a search. By then, all our efforts would be lost in the Pacific Ocean."

"You two are certifiable!" It was all she could say.

Andi was still fuming when they got back on board *Red Sky*. Even Marylebone rubbing against her leg got ignored. "And suppose you don't catch up with them?" she continued her tirade. "They have a bigger boat and probably a seven- or eight-hour lead at least. It's a big ocean out there."

"In the first place, Mom," Beth started, "the three of us can sail circles around them."

"And in the second place . . ." Max paused for effect. "We can track them."

"Hold on just a second. What are you talking about?"

"They don't know it, but they have a GPS homing beacon on board. The guy at Gold Coast Charters told me they install one on every boat to keep track of their fleet."

"How come Sloane doesn't know about it?"

"Because they put it in after he chartered the boat."

"Why didn't they use it to recover the boat themselves?"

"They didn't even know they had a missing boat for over two weeks. Sloane chartered it under a phony name and then simply didn't return it. By then, it was too far away for the thing to work."

"So what do we use from our end?"

"A GPS tracker. It's already built into our GPS. Gold Coast gave me the code. That's what we look for."

"That's all there is to it?"

"As long as we're within its range."

"Well, I suppose I might as well start working on the charts," Andi said reluctantly. "Give me the damn things and I'll go below. It'll take me a while to program the GPS."

"Don't forget to back it up with the satnav."

"I know the drill. Now let me go below and navigate. And, in case you're interested, *yes,* I'm still pissed." Andi climbed down the companionway ladder.

"Hey, Mom," Beth said, treading softly. "Do you think you'd better also chart the direct course to the Canal?"

"They wouldn't go that way this time of the year," Andi replied. "The northeast trade winds are too strong. Everybody goes to the Canal via Aruba."

"But Beth may be right," Max interjected. "We should be ready for that contingency."

"We'll be ready."

"Let me know as soon as you chart the opening course for Aruba."

"I'll let you know."

"It's five hundred and fifty miles from here to Aruba," Andi announced as Max came down through the hatch twenty minutes later, unable to resist standing over her at the chart table. "After we leave St. John's harbor, we can either head 249 degrees between Nevis and Montserrat straight to Aruba, or we can sail 192 degrees over to the Guadeloupe Passage between Montserrat and Guadeloupe and then set a course of 252 degrees for Aruba."

"Do you have a preference?"

"Besides divorcing you and that child of mine, my inclination is the direct way. I want to check the prevailing winds for this time of year against the weather reports."

"Let me know what you decide."

"If we take the direct route, the first waypoint will be Redonda." She put her finger down on a speck of land on the chart. "It's a tiny islet about fifteen miles southeast of Nevis. After that, it's a straight downhill run to Aruba."

"Any problems between here and Redonda?"

"No. It looks like there's plenty of water all the way. There's some shoaling on the south side of Redonda, so we'll pass it to the north."

"Any other land between that and Aruba?"

"Not if you want the quickest way to get there. We could follow the Windward Islands to Grenada, but somehow I don't think you have the scenic way in mind. Now go away and let me finish."

"I'm glad you're my navigator."

"I love you too, Max. Now go!"

Max left and continued preparing *Red Sky* for sea. Beth was busy examining all the rigging to make certain that every turn bolt, shackle, and cotter pin was secure. "I've checked the bow, Dad, and I'm almost finished with the mast."

"Better check the lifeline stanchions. I noticed the base by the portside gate is loose. One of the screws may be stripped."

"It's next on my list."

"If you can't tighten it, use some epoxy filler."

"Don't worry."

"I'm going to check the oil and batteries and mess around with the gearbox. I heard a funny noise in reverse yesterday. As soon as your mother's finished charting the course, we'll take *Red Sky* into the dock and top off the fuel and water tanks."

Max turned and climbed back down into the cabin, getting his toolbox out from the storage compartment. He lifted the companionway ladder from its hinges, exposing the engine. After checking the oil level, he opened the Volvo manual to a diagram of the gear system. He cleaned and reconnected several wires and tightened a few related bolts before putting the ladder back on its hinges. He then climbed back up into the cockpit.

"Any luck?" Beth asked, sitting with her legs crossed in front of one of the lifeline stanchions, pliers in one hand and a shackle key in the other.

"I hope so. I gave it my best shot. Your mother's a better mechanic than I am. I'd hate to lose our reverse gear."

"We'll get them. With you and me doing the sailing and Mom navigating, we'll take them in no time at all." She was silent for a moment before adding, "I wish Bob were here too."

"I didn't realize you felt that way."

"I miss him."

"Did you tell him why you were coming down here?"

"It would have been too complicated. I just told him I was coming down to spend some time with you and Mom. That's all I told Clifford too. I've done a lot of lying to people that I care a great deal about."

"There's going to be payback, you know."

"Tell me about it," she agreed, reaching over to the idle winch behind her shoulder and spinning it with her hand for emphasis.

"I want you to know this little adventure of ours doesn't thrill me."

"You worried about what happens when we catch them?"

"That's what I do, worry. I figure our twelve-gauge shotgun is maybe good for seventy-five or a hundred yards."

"It won't come to that."

"What if they have a heavy-caliber rifle that can shoot ten times that far?"

"We'll stay out of range and let the Coast Guard handle it."

"What if they get too close? A sailboat's clumsy in close quarters."

"Can't worry about it, Dad."

"Worry is the best shield we have."

"We'll sail *Red Sky* and do whatever has to be done when we get where we're going. The rest is all crap."

"Okay, coach!"

"Before we go to the gas dock," Beth said, "let's take a slow run around the harbor to make sure *Atrophy* isn't anchored somewhere out here."

"Good idea. Take the wheel while I start her up."

Max reached over to the engine controls. The diesel caught immediately. He looked back over the transom to assure himself there was a good flow of water coming out of the exhaust pipe. No more time to worry, he urged himself. His crew was lionhearted, killers all.

Beth steered *Red Sky* under power in a slow pass around the harbor while she and Max kept a lookout. She maneuvered carefully, weaving her way through the fishing boats and the dozen or so sailboats anchored about. No *Atrophy* was seen.

She finally pulled *Red Sky* into the dock as Max threw a stern line to the attendant. Andi jumped gracefully onto the dock with the bow line and made it fast to a forward cleat on the dock. She sat on a rusty folding chair on the dock to wait while Max unscrewed the fuel cap and took the hose from the attendant.

Max started pumping and then stopped when he heard the fuel gurgling to the top of the tank. He squeezed in a last few drops and handed the hose back to the attendant. He screwed the fuel cap back down tight and turned on the blower to ventilate any fumes out of the engine compartment.

"Busy today?" Beth asked the attendant.

"No. Mostly local fishermen."

"Did you see a sailboat, about fifty feet?" she asked.

"Yes, miss. There was one. Five, maybe six hours ago. They came into the dock too fast, in a real hurry."

"Couple on board?" Max asked.

"Yes, sir. Man and woman. Arguing about something. They had a deckhand too. A local boy."

"Sounds like friends of ours. Did you get the name of their boat?"

"No, sir. My boss only tells me to write the name down when the people pay by credit card. They paid cash." He walked over to the transom and carefully wrote *"Red Sky"* down on the slip.

"Did they say where they were going?" Beth asked.

"No, miss. But they sure in a hurry to get there. When their mate had trouble untying one of the dock lines, the man, he yelled at him, and then the woman, she be yelling at the man for yelling at the mate."

Max looked at his watch and shut off the engine blower. "It's five o'clock now. You figure they left about noon?"

"Twelve thirty, maybe one o'clock. They left here so fast, they nearly run down Berris Christopher rowing out to his fishing boat. Poor Berris did not know whether to be bailing or rowing, but he sure be cursing them all the while."

Beth restarted the engine. "Well, we're going to try to catch up with them. Will you throw off the stern line for me?"

"Yes, miss." He bent down to grab the line.

"Ready the bow line, Mom."

As soon as the stern started to pull away from the dock, Andi slipped the line off the cleat and climbed back over the lifelines onto the deck. Beth backed *Red Sky* away from the dock, shifted into forward, and slowly pulled out into the harbor. Max walked aft, coiling the bow line he was carrying, and stowed it in one of the cockpit storage lockers, together with the stern line that Andi handed him and the big blue air-filled fenders. He sat across from Andi while Beth, at the wheel, motored out of the harbor.

"Dad, we should be taking the direct route to the Canal. It's the only way we can make up for the lead *Atrophy* has."

"Forget it," Andi replied emphatically, answering for him. "It's too dangerous."

"But they have a five-hour head start and a bigger boat than ours," Beth insisted. "We'll never catch them otherwise."

"Look, Beth," her mother continued, "I'm willing to try to nail them, but I'm not willing to die in the effort."

"They're running scared now, Mom. Suppose they decide to head straight for the Canal. We'll lose them."

"They're not heading straight for the Canal and we're not going to lose them. The route through Aruba isn't much longer. The prevailing winds are more favorable and there's less likelihood of a bad storm."

"I want Sloane so badly I can taste it."

"Then let's get started," Max interjected. "All the waypoints programmed?" he asked Andi.

"All done. The GPS and the autopilot are all set."

"What's the first course?" Beth asked.

"Take the Sandy Island Channel out of the harbor." She pointed over to her left. "The first marker buoy is right there. See the flashing red light?"

"I got it." She turned *Red Sky* toward the buoy, a half mile or so away.

"When you clear the Sandy Island light, head 249 degrees until we reach Redonda. As soon as we raise the sails and you're happy with their set, we can turn on the autopilot."

"If you want to take the wheel, Dad, I'll raise the main. We can unfurl the genny after we clear the harbor."

Max steered while Beth grabbed a winch handle and climbed on top of the cabin. She took the sail ties off the mainsail and stuffed them in the pocket of her shorts. Then she unhooked the main halyard shackle from the lifeline stanchion and attached it to the eye in the headboard of the mainsail before taking several turns with it around the starboard winch attached to the mast. "All ready," she announced to Max.

"Okay. Haul her up."

Beth began vigorously cranking the winch handle, and the mainsail climbed rapidly up the mast, exposing the builder's logo and the boat's racing numbers. Beth watched the sail reach the top of the mast, gave the winch one extra tug for good measure, and then secured the halyard to the cleat below the winch. The main filled with air, adding its powerful thrust to the auxiliary power of the diesel engine.

Max hesitated for a moment, then looked straight at Andi, his expression serious, his face suddenly creased with doubt. "Andi?" he asked.

She saw his concern. "What is it, Max? What's the matter?"

"Am I being a total idiot, risking us all this way?"

"Yes, Max."

"Is that a vote of confidence?"

"It is. It's enough for me that you're trying to make things right for Beth. I'll absolutely back you."

"Thanks, Andi. I needed to hear that." He pressed her hand between his and got up. "Take the wheel, will you, Beth? I'm going below to turn the GPS on and see if I can pick up that signal from *Atrophy*."

Beth jumped down into the cockpit. "Want me to unfurl the genny?" she asked.

"Wait until I'm back. We'll be in the lee of the land for another ten minutes anyway, so there's not much wind. Let's stay under power until we clear that buoy out there. I'll be back up before then."

He went down into the cabin, turned on the GPS tracker, and adjusted its tuning dials for a few minutes, looking for a signal, any signal, without success. "Nobody said it was going to be easy," he muttered. He turned the VHF onto one of the weather channels, listened to a local report, and turned it back to channel 16.

He went back up the ladder into the cockpit, sat next to Andi by the big self-tailing primary winch on the port side of the boat, and took a deep breath of air.

"What's the weather look like?" Beth asked.

"Not bad. Winds from the northeast at seventeen to twenty-two knots. I checked the weatherfax. There's a nasty-looking low developing to the northwest, but we're far enough south to avoid most of it."

"There's that channel marker, Dad. Let's raise the jib."

"Okay."

He uncleated the sheet, gave it a few turns around the winch, and began unfurling the sail. He then trimmed it in until satisfied and sat back down next to Andi. Beth turned off the diesel and *Red Sky* charged ahead, propelled only by the silent thrust of the wind's power.

Chapter Thirty

It should have been a beautiful sunset to honor the noble chase they had undertaken, but it wasn't. The sky should have been filled with stars, but it wasn't. It should have been a peaceful watch for Andi, but it was not going to be. Something is wrong with this picture, she thought as she sat behind the steering wheel.

She stepped up onto the cockpit seat to increase the visibility, and then, looking around the horizon one last time, she called down to her husband through the open hatch, "If you're not sleeping, Maximilian, come up topside, will you?"

While Beth was fast asleep in the forward cabin, Max was lying on a berth in the aft cabin, working on a chapter of his *Guide for Antique Camera Collectors*. "Coming right up," he answered as he put down his manuscript and got off the bunk. He climbed the gangway ladder into the cockpit of the sloop.

"What's up?" he said. The question became rhetorical as he took a look around. Clouds that had been pure and innocent when they left Antigua that afternoon had become nasty and dark gray. Waves that had been a comfortable height were building up. The once steady wind was now gusting, and he saw lightning off in the western sky.

"Looks like fun and games tonight," she said.

"I'm glad you called me. We'll roll up the genny and take a reef in the main."

"Okay. I'll wake Beth up."

"Yes, better get her up here. The sailing's been too calm to suit her today anyhow. Turn off the autopilot and I'll take the wheel."

Andi went below and returned in a minute followed by Beth, still wearing the women's varsity lacrosse sweatshirt she'd put on over her tank top that afternoon. Stimulated by the prospect of rough weather, Beth climbed the gangway ladder two steps at a time and jumped into the cockpit.

"It's about time we had some excitement. Nothing like a little wind to get back some of that head start we spotted Sloane."

Max was paying close attention to the approaching front. "Andi, take the wheel, please." His voice was all business.

"You're not going to shorten sail, are you?" Beth protested mildly, more from force of habit, well aware of her stepfather's cautious nature. "With this wind, we'll catch *Atrophy* in no time."

"I don't want to meet this squall with all our sails up. Head her up into the wind, Andi."

"You got it."

"Beth, give me a hand. We'll roll up the genny first and then reef the main." He exchanged places with Andi as she stepped around him.

"I'm with you, Dad."

Andi turned the teak steering wheel to port. *Red Sky* quickly pointed toward the west and stopped dead in her tracks as her two sails lost the wind's support and started flapping wildly. Beth untied the furling line and, with Max's help, pulled on it smoothly, hand over hand, causing the genoa sail to wind itself up onto the forestay. Then she cleated down the line.

As soon as Beth had the genny securely wrapped up, she and Max went over to the mast and began reefing the mainsail. When it had been shortened to their satisfaction, they returned to the cockpit. Andi then turned *Red Sky* back onto her northerly course. They were nearly ready.

"Dad, I'll go check the anchor locker and the forward hatches if you'll handle the kitty."

"That's some trade-off."

Beth climbed out of the cockpit and walked confidently out to the bow again, followed closely by her mother's watchful eyes.

"Hold on tight, Elisabeth."

"Yes, Mom."

"I guess I might as well go down into the cabin and wrestle Marylebone into his life preserver." Max was not enthusiastic.

"Good luck!"

"Pray for me."

Reluctantly, he went down into the main salon. After he finally cornered the big Persian under the oven and strapped him into the vest, he checked the last weatherfax and the radar and then rechecked all three cabins to make sure that everything was secured or stowed away. He then went up the ladder and closed the hatch behind him.

Beth opened the locker underneath the portside cockpit seat and pulled out their bright yellow foul-weather jackets with the built-in personal flotation devices. She tossed the extra-large to Max, handed the small to her mother, and put on her medium.

"Might as well let me take over the wheel now, Andi," Max said. "It'll give me a chance to get into the spirit of things before the real fun starts."

"Okay, love," she said, moving away from the wheel. She pretended not to hear the tension in his voice or the little cough that exposed his concern. His kind of person succeeded despite fear, not without fear, and that was a trait she admired.

As Max got behind the pedestal, he hooked the line from his safety harness onto the base of the column and continued to scan the horizon. Andi and Beth each hooked their tethers onto one of the guardrails that surrounded the deck and sat down under the Bimini.

"Let me know when you want me to take over," Beth said hopefully.

"We'll see if it gets bad enough for you," he said, both proud and envious of her confidence.

Now they were ready, and the storm was still at least twenty minutes away to the west. Plenty of time for each of them to be alone with thoughts of their own mortality. The wind and the waves continued their preparation.

"I took a look at the radar and the weatherfax when I was below," Max said. "This is going to be a bad one, but it looks localized. We shouldn't be in it for long."

There was no comment from his passengers.

The storm continued to build as it approached from their port side. Boiling clouds were closer. The anemometer dial on the bulkhead wall showed the wind speeding up to 35 mph. It was raining hard.

Max thought of his father's admonition never to take a storm at sea personally, because the ocean applied all its laws equally and indiscriminately to those who imposed themselves upon it. It was incapable of compromise. Let your concentration lapse or wander for one moment and know with absolute certainty that the shit will hit the fan.

His glasses were becoming hopelessly caked with salt.

"These are useless, Andi," he said as he handed them over to her. "Get rid of them for me, will you?" Involved with the task of controlling *Red Sky,* he made the request an order and talked without looking directly at Andi. In the early days, this had intimidated Beth, then a teenager not used to having a father. She knew now that it was only a sign of his total absorption.

"You okay, Dad?"

"I'm fine, puss."

"I'm ready to drive whenever you say."

"You can take her, if you want."

"The wheel's mine." Beth changed places with Max and got behind the wheel. She felt the adrenaline pumping, all her senses acute, as she maneuvered the sixteen tons of tossing sailboat through the mountainous waves while trying to maintain some semblance of their original course. The wind and waves slashed at her from opposite directions. All of nature's forces were ganging up in an effort to broach *Red Sky* or knock her flat down into the water. She had no time to worry about yesterday's unsolved problems or tomorrow's anticipated headaches. The storm required total concentration, and that's what she gave it.

She felt water working its way under her jacket collar, down her neck, and through her sweatshirt. The waves had crests of white foam being blown off by the force of the wind. She continued to steer through the sea, surfing down the biggest waves, fighting to stay on course through the others.

The storm created an emotional anomaly for her between the terror and the exhilaration. She was singularly responsible for placing her family and *Red Sky* in the situation. Now that she was here, all she wanted to do was swear to all concerned that if they survived this storm, she'd park the boat on the beach and never sail again. But she knew they'd survive this one and another one and another one after that, and it would never become routine or second nature. Each storm was different, new and intoxicating, so she just kept on sailing.

As the time passed, the weather continued its intimidating efforts. Beth now needed two hands to control the boat. The wind was blowing needles of cold salt water into her face. She could barely make out the soft red glow of the dials on the bulk-head only ten feet away. The wind was gusting close to 50 mph. It felt like more. It was dark. She was getting cold. She was wet. She was, at the same time, up for the storm and anxious about what it would do next.

"Better let out the main a little bit, Dad."

"Okay." He reached over and uncleated the mainsheet, al-lowing the sail to spill some of the wind. *Red Sky* straightened up momentarily as he eased the sail out and then heeled over again as he recleated the line.

"Thanks, Dad." She kept her eyes on the situation in front of her.

Even with the shortened main and no jib, *Red Sky* was soon heeled over at an uncomfortable angle. The full power of the storm must be upon them, Beth thought. The bow and leeward railings were buried with each passing wave. *Red Sky* was a heavy boat, designed for cruising, and managed to push on steadily through the confused water. Beth was able to maintain control; the rudder was still responsive to her touch. Andi took a deep breath and relaxed her grip on the stanchion.

"How're we doing, Beth?" Andi asked from under the Bim-ini cover, where she and Max were trying unsuccessfully to avoid some of the weather.

"We've been through worse," she confidently answered her mother, sitting a few feet away.

The sea heard her and replied without hesitation. A man-eating wave climbed over the bow and destroyed her visibility, threatening to drown her as it smashed its way back toward the stern. Blinded, coughing, and spitting salt water out of her mouth, Beth screamed back in anger at the sea. The sea, more than her equal, was not impressed. With a resigned shrug of her shoulders, she looked over at Max, ready for another turn at the wheel, and motioned for him to take over.

Chapter Thirty-one

Leonard was unhappy with the decision. "The direct route to the Canal is too dangerous this time of year," he argued with Erica. "If we have to go, let's at least go by Aruba." The thought of sailing directly across the Caribbean in the middle of December frightened him.

"It'll work out fine." She was a pragmatist and a good sailor. The first step was to empty the safe-deposit box waiting for them in Panama. She'd decide then what to do next and whom to do it with.

Len was sitting in *Atrophy*'s cockpit, laptop on the bench, charts on his lap, making notes of the waypoints he needed to program the GPS and autopilot. He put his sunglasses on, looked at his watch, and noted the time on the chart.

He glanced at her in her flowery orange bikini, standing calmly behind the wheel, one foot up on the windward cockpit seat, steering the heavy boat, plodding slowly along at only 6.8 knots. Because of her missing mizzenmast and sail, the 15-knot breeze couldn't push the unbalanced and ponderous boat any faster. "I'm telling you we should go to Aruba first. We can leave the boat there and catch a plane to the Canal."

"No. Aruba's even smaller than Antigua. They'll have it watched. Look, I tell you there's nothing to worry about. We save two days or more this way, and a little spray won't hurt.

Once we get finished with the bank in Panama, we're home-free."

"But we didn't have time to get ready," he argued. "The radar's not working properly and the weatherfax is completely down. All I get out of it is blank paper."

"So use the weather channels on the VHF."

"That's local only. It doesn't tell us what's doing a hundred miles out to sea. The direct route to the Canal is tough enough, close-hauled all the way. The last thing we need is to run into a tropical storm on top of it."

"Stop worrying so much. Just plot the course and I'll get us there. Vincent will give us the extra hand we need if things get sloppy." She motioned with her head toward the husky youth sitting placidly up in the bow of the boat, legs dangling over the bowsprit, his face pointed directly into the wind, nose up in the air like a sculptured ebony figurehead on an old three-masted schooner.

"He doesn't know squat about sailing. All he knows how to do is clean the boat badly and spill drinks. He's lazy and he's got an attitude like all the rest of them down here."

"He's okay," she defended him. "He's a good kid and we need him, so stop riding him so hard." The jib started to flap wildly as *Atrophy* rounded up into the wind. Erica instinctively dropped her raised foot to the deck and turned the wheel to port a few degrees, letting the boat fall back off. The knot meter reflected the boat's response as it heeled over and accelerated briefly to 7 knots before settling back at 6.7.

"See, she's got a weather helm already," he complained. "I told you we should have put that mizzen back up before we left."

"She doesn't have a weather helm. I just took my mind off steering for a moment so she headed up a little, that's all. We're doing fine, so stop worrying and finish with those charts." She put her right foot back up on the seat for balance, knowing it would attract his attention to the narrow crotch of her bikini. It had the desired result.

He bit hungrily: "Want me to put some more of that sunscreen on your back before I go below to program the autopilot?"

"No," she replied. "I had Vincent put some on me before when you were below fiddling with the radar." There was no humor in her voice, only a continuation of the increasing friction between them.

He reacted with as much bravado as he could muster, but his face was beet red as he turned from her and walked over to the hatchway. He felt humiliated, whether she was telling the truth or not. He could feel his ears burning with her laughter as he climbed down the ladder into the cabin.

Chapter Thirty-two

Beth came up out of the cabin on *Red Sky,* a chocolate-chip cookie in one hand, and saw Max sitting in the cockpit, the GPS on his lap, patiently hoping to come up with a signal from the homing device on *Atrophy.*

"Any luck, Dad?"

"Nada."

"It's been two days. Do you want half of my cookie?"

"I didn't know we had any left."

"It's the last one." She extended her hand to him, cookie in the leather palm of her fingerless sailing glove.

"I'm moved, truly." He took the offering.

"Marylebone only nibbled it a little after I dropped it on the floor of the cabin."

"Thank you for sharing that information with me." He popped it gratefully into his mouth. "What's your mother doing?"

"Reading. She said to tell you we did over sixty-five miles on autopilot last night. We averaged nearly eight knots with one reef in the main."

"Not bad. The new wind vane steerer is working well. I wonder how Sloane did."

"I just checked the radar. There's nothing on the screen."

"Who knows where *Atrophy* is. Maybe they're heading straight for Panama?"

"If they are, they're in for one hell of a winter storm. Here's the weatherfax Mom just got." She handed him the weather map. "Check out that low."

He took the piece of paper she handed him and looked at it carefully. "That's the low I saw developing when we left Antigua two days ago. We should still miss most of it."

"If Sloane's north of us, he'll be in for a pounding."

"That's a bit of an understatement," he said, still examining the map. "Winds at the center are gusting to over sixty-five knots. If Sloane is taking the direct route to the Canal, we might not have to bother catching him and Erica."

"Do you think we'll find them?"

"Who knows. Losing the mizzen should slow them down."

"Suppose they put it back before leaving?"

"I'm figuring they left unexpectedly and didn't do it."

"I hope you're right."

"We've maximized our speed pretty well since leaving Antigua. We're out forty-one hours and we've logged three hundred and twelve miles. That's better than 7.5 knots. They can't beat that."

"What's our distance to Aruba?" Beth asked.

"Two hundred and forty-six miles, according to the GPS."

"We're more than halfway there. If they're taking the same route, we have a chance."

"Your guess is as good as mine."

Chapter Thirty-three

Len looked at the barometer, tapped it, and looked again before checking the wind indicator. The only weather report he was able to pick up on VHF came from Caracas and was in Spanish, crackling with static. He couldn't follow it, and he couldn't find any station broadcasting in English. The weatherfax was still turning out blank paper, and he had given up on it. When he finally located Aruba Radio on the AM band, the weather report was in English, but it sounded like a travelogue: "Warm, mostly sunny, possibility of a brief shower or two later in the day."

According to his calculations, *Atrophy* was 110 miles north of Aruba, heading on a direct southwesterly course for the Panama Canal. A weather report from some disk jockey in Aruba wasn't reliable, and anyhow, the barometer was telling him a different story, painting the only picture he needed to see. It had been falling at an increasing rate since midnight, dropping from 30.04 inches to where it now stood at 29.81. In the last hour alone, it had dropped an alarming 0.05 inch.

A glimpse out the porthole over his left shoulder disclosed a cloudless southern sky. No problem if that was the only sky to check. Unfortunately, it wasn't. He got up from the navigation station and crossed the cabin over to the starboard side, bending slightly to look out one of its portholes. Clouds were developing ominously in the northeast. They were in for a storm, probably before noon.

Erica had taken over the watch at three a.m. and was still up in the cockpit. He had spent his watch dozing on and off behind the wheel, sporadically checking the horizon for cargo ships. They were satisfied to let the autopilot do most of the work as *Atrophy* continued to sail close-hauled for Panama, constantly heeled over ten to fifteen degrees or more.

Vincent had spent the night up on the deck, sleeping under a blanket on one of the cockpit seats. He hadn't stirred during Len's watch, preferring to be awake when Erica was at the helm. Now that she was up there, he could hear her talking softly to Vincent. Vincent was giggling like a little boy in response.

Len stretched out on one of the berths in the main salon of the cabin and closed his eyes in an effort to get some sleep before going back up to relieve Erica on watch. He was able to close his mind off from worry about the impending storm, but he couldn't stop thinking about the disintegration of his relationship with her. She had changed since they came down to the Caribbean, and not for the better.

All his carefully conceived plans for the future were being rendered meaningless by her efforts to humiliate him. He was finding it all difficult to handle without the reassuring love she had shown him back in New York. Submitting to her domination when it was tempered with affection turned him on. After all, she deserved the respect. It was another thing to accept hateful maliciousness. He didn't deserve it.

They'd have to talk. He had no intention of going to Australia by boat or by plane with a nasty, foul-tempered bitch. That's not what he'd planned this whole thing for. That's not what it was all about. If she couldn't straighten out, he'd split in Panama with the bonds but without her.

After trying for an hour, he gave up on his efforts to sleep and got up to go to the aft head. The silence from the cockpit attracted him, so he took a step up on the ladder and stuck his head out to see what was doing. Erica was sitting down behind the wheel, her face and torso hidden from his sight by the pedestal that held the steering wheel and the binnacle on top of it.

He could see Vincent, wearing short cutoff jeans, lying down on the other seat along the length of the cockpit, gazing at her adoringly, his long legs hanging easily over the transom.

Len climbed silently back down into the cabin and continued to the head, allowing his fury at her to abate without a confrontation. He then went into the cabin, put on a pair of trunks and a clean T-shirt, and alerted her to his presence by shouting topside to ask if he could bring her up a cup of coffee.

This time he went all the way up the ladder and into the cockpit, handing her the cup of coffee and keeping one for himself. She looked at him without any trace of concern for what had just transpired, while Vincent kept his back to the two of them and walked out to his private sanctuary on the bow of the boat.

Len sat on the seat across from her after taking a look at the instruments on the pedestal. The knot meter showed a speed of 6.2 knots, while the wind indicator showed a 19-knot wind coming in from the northeast. The northeastern sky was not perceptibly cloudier than when he had looked earlier from below. "We're in for a storm within the next couple of hours," he declared authoritatively.

"I see it," she responded, looking to her right. "It's going to hit us right on the nose."

"The barometer's dropped fast since last night."

"Too bad that weatherfax isn't working. It'd be nice to know what to expect."

"I told you that would be a problem. Come on, let's change course for Aruba," he said. "I have all the waypoints programmed into the GPS. It'll get us out of the way of the storm. A beam reach will be easier than getting our brains beat out like we've been doing close-hauled for the last three days."

"We'll be all right. *Atrophy* is a heavy boat."

"But her balance is off without the mizzen. The radar is acting up. The weatherfax is out. We're not in condition for a storm."

"It'll probably just be a short squall, and we're halfway to the Canal already. I don't want to lose time detouring to Aruba, especially if Leung or Beth Swahn is there."

"Then shorten the main."

"We can shorten it later. Those clouds don't look so bad and they're a long way off." She looked at her wristwatch and then at him. "It's nearly five. Take the watch so I can go below for some sleep while it's still dark." She stood up from behind the wheel and moved toward the hatch opening. She noticed Vincent looking at her from the bow and silently motioned for him to come below. He got up and began wending his way aft.

"Did you show Vincent the leather jewelry in the forward cabin?" Len asked.

"No, but he did something very vulgar before. I'm going to talk to him about it now."

Chapter Thirty-four

Beth was slouched down behind the wheel, lazily steering *Red Sky* with her feet. Max was stretched out on the windward side of the cockpit, his head propped up against a red cushion, making revisions to his book. Off in the distance, a container ship was passing on its way south.

Andi came up out of the hatch carrying a tray loaded with food. Three sets of eyes, triggered by insatiable appetites, homed in on her, carefully following her progress toward the stern. Only Marylebone moved, wanting to be closer to the action. Beth automatically reached her foot through the steering wheel and, with her toes, released the folding teak table that was attached to the front of the pedestal.

Red Sky was heeled over smartly on a starboard tack with the knot log reading a steady 9.2 knots, close to hull speed for a forty-seven-foot sloop confined by the inexorable laws of nature governing displacement vessels. The arrow on the wind indicator dial was pointing to the northeast, with the LCD readout showing a wind speed of 22 knots. The waves looked to be about four or five feet high. A fair number of them had whitecaps cresting off their tops.

"What a glorious day for a sail, huh, Mom?"

"A beam reach all the way," Andi said, putting the tray of

food down on the table. "Why don't you turn on the autopilot and we'll have lunch."

"I'd rather stay at the wheel. Make better speed than on auto." In deference to lunch, however, she sat up, replacing her feet at the wheel with her hands.

"What's on the radar, Andi?" Max asked.

"I just checked. There's that tanker you can see passing ahead of us now and a couple of other big ships crossing our stern about fifteen miles away, barely on the screen."

"No sailboats, I take it?"

"No sailboats. Who but us would be crazy enough to sail across the Caribbean this time of year?"

"Len Sloane," Beth volunteered.

"He's not on the radar screen."

"We'll get him."

"I know, but better have a sandwich first." She handed Beth a plate with a tuna-salad sandwich and potato chips, gave one to Max, and then sat down herself, reaching over to the table for her plate.

"Did you check the weather?" Beth asked between mouthfuls.

"The storm is still off to the northeast. About a hundred miles away on a parallel course. No real trouble."

"Good thing we didn't head straight for the Canal."

"We may get winds up to thirty-five knots later this afternoon, but not much worse."

"With this beam reach we're on, it'll be a sleigh ride to Aruba." Beth was excited by the prospect.

"The wind's at twenty-three knots now," Max said. "As soon as we're finished eating, I want us to take a reef in the main and get the umbilical cords on. Harnesses for everyone on deck."

"Oh, c'mon," Beth protested, skillfully steering *Red Sky* along on her rhumb line to Aruba. "We're flying. We just hit ten knots a minute ago and almost fifteen knots surfing down the backside of that last wave. Let's not slow down now." She was eating with one hand and steering with the other as the bow dug its nose confidently into each wave and then lifted up, causing spray to blow back, deflected by the dodger.

"We are going to reef," Max said, popping the last olive into his mouth, "and when she hits twenty-five knots, we'll roll the genny up a little. No sense in pushing the rig too hard."

Chapter Thirty-five

When the full darkness of night closed in, enveloping *Atro-phy* within its frightening confines of blindness and loss of depth perception, Leonard could no longer see the waves smashing into them. His daylong anxiety became terror.

Since leaving Antigua, they had been beating to windward, as near to the wind as possible, for three days of wet, jarring, and miserable sailing, with their lee rail in the water much of the time. Len had been unable to relax, being whiplashed by the ceaseless pounding of the ocean against the boat. Then, when the storm hit around three p.m. with heavy sheeting rain, ten-foot seas, and gale-force winds gusting to 45 knots, it became intolerable for him.

Vincent was useless around the deck, and the more Len screamed at him, the more useless he became and the more Erica defended him. Vincent had lived his entire life on Antigua, and while he had seen mountainous waves and felt the force of hurricanes, it had been from the relative safety of shore. He was unprepared for a storm at sea, so the teenager spent most of the time huddled pathetically in a fetal position on one of the berths below. Erica's ministrations, clandestine or overt, erotic or otherwise, did little to enlist his help.

It was now slightly after nine o'clock, and the red glow from the wind meter reflected a velocity of 43 knots, gusting to 48, 49. Then it suddenly zoomed past 50 to 54 knots, before settling back again to 45. They didn't have a heavyweight storm sail on board and had long since furled up the genoa. Erica decided it was time to take the third reef in the mainsail.

She steered *Atrophy* up into the wind and tightened down the boom. The deafening sound of the wind combined with the wildly flapping sail unnerved Len. The deck under him was a gyrating, erratic platform, moving up as the boat climbed waves and dropping down precipitously as the boat fell off.

He and Erica climbed up on the cabin roof, trying to maintain their balance. They had the tethers from their safety harnesses hooked into the base of the mast and were desperately holding on to the boom with one hand while trying to shorten the sail with the other.

Len uncleated the main halyard and struggled to lower the sail until the grommet that marked the third set of reef points was next to the tack hook on the boom. After catching the grommet on the hook, he raised the halyard back up the mast until the shortened sail had been pulled tight, and then he recleated it. Erica used the small winch at the end of the boom to pull in the reefing line.

After ten minutes of intense effort, they had the job completed. Erica climbed down off the cabin top, returned to the steering wheel, and hooked her safety line to the pedestal. As soon as she had *Atrophy* back on course, she turned on the autopilot, but it stubbornly refused to engage.

Len, making his way back from the roof of the cabin, lost his footing and fell heavily into the cockpit, landing on his back just as a wave flooded in. He lay in a heap on the floor of the cockpit, trying to catch his breath.

"You clumsy idiot!" Erica berated him reflexively, and then, concerned he might really be injured, she asked, "Are you okay?"

"I think so," he gasped, pushing himself up to a sitting position. "Look, we've got to get out of this," he pleaded. "We've made no progress in the last five hours and been blown God knows how far off course. We're heading right into the storm and getting beaten to death. Let's head for Aruba. It's only about eighty-five miles south of us."

"You jerk!" she screamed again, demanding to be heard over the shrieking wind. "The only thing waiting for us in Aruba is Leung."

"Anything's better than this."

"This storm won't last long and we'll be back on course. You might as well go below and dry off while I wrestle with the autopilot. Check on Vincent and I'll be down in a second."

He picked himself up from the cockpit floor just in time to be flattened again as a wave hit them broadside, causing *Atrophy* to round up abruptly, threatening to broach. Suddenly, three more waves hit them in rapid succession. The last one rolled the boat over so far that the mast scooped into the water before she finally righted itself. Erica was smashed down onto the seat against her shoulder but grabbed on to her shortened safety line and pulled herself painfully back up to the wheel, where she continued to work on the autopilot controls.

"Are *you* okay?" he asked her.

Stunned by the pain, she looked up to see him staring at her, horror in his face. "Yes, now go below," she ordered, out of what little patience she had. "You're not helping up here." She continued to struggle with the autopilot, trying to get it back in operation.

Without another word, Len opened the hatch and made his

way down into the cabin, closing the hatch behind him, leaving
Erica tethered to the pedestal, alone on deck.

He saw Vincent lying faceup on the leeward berth in the
forward cabin. The seasick kid was practically unconscious, secured to the bunk by Erica's leather bracelets. Len thought of
moving him into the main salon but decided against it when he
saw the remains of Vincent's pitiful retching covering the front
of his shirt. He decided that no purpose would be served by
moving him.

He thought to settle his own stomach with a Coke from the
refrigerator but poured only enough to flavor the rum used to
wash down the pill he swallowed.

He unzipped the front of his red flotation jacket and reached
inside to reassure himself that the waterproof envelope was sitting securely in the inside pocket, then sat at the navigation
table. He looked at the GPS and made a note of the time, latitude, and longitude on the chart. The storm had blown them
far off course, and he could see they were now on a heading
midway between Aruba and Panama. *They were actually farther away from Panama now than they were six hours ago
when the storm hit.*

He turned on the VHF, hoping for a weather report that
might tell him how long the storm was supposed to last or
where it was heading. It was no use, though. The VHF was
programmed for four weather station channels and he couldn't
raise any of them.

Disconsolate, he turned the radio back to channel 16, inad-
vertently following normal maritime practice this time by leaving it on. There was nothing to be heard except for static, but
he was too groggy to adjust the squelch control, too seasick to
monitor any of the other channels.

He took a deep swallow of rum and put his head down on

the table, covering his ears with his hands to block out the roar of the wind. He just sat there, anticipating that every monstrous wave slamming into the boat would be the one to turn them over for good or send tons of water cascading in through the hatch. He waited for the roll that would start and not end, broaching them on their side or pitchpoling them down by the bow. Either way, they were finished.

The head-splitting crash he heard up on the deck instantaneously forced him out of his self-commiseration. The entire cabin shook with the force of the blow. It was followed by the sounds of the diesel engine cranking over and over and then starting and stopping. He quickly closed up his jacket and scrambled across the cabin to the companionway ladder.

He clambered up to the top of the companionway and reached for the hatch cover to slide it back but couldn't budge it. It was jammed shut. He tried to force it open but wasn't strong enough. It was hopeless. He was trapped. He panicked and started shouting for Erica through the closed hatch. Then he realized that she couldn't possibly hear him on deck.

He skidded back down the ladder, went over to the galley, and reached up to unbolt the small hatch cover on the cabin roof above the sink. He pulled himself up, stuck his head out the open hatch, and saw what had happened. The gale force of the wind had shredded the mainsail into a hundred independent strips of Dacron, all of which were flapping wildly in the air. The heavy aluminum boom, no longer supported by the sail, had fallen on the cabin roof. Its full weight was now lying on the hatch cover, jamming it in its closed position. Erica was behind the wheel, trying to get the diesel started, desperate for some auxiliary power to get the boat under control.

"I'm stuck below!" he shouted to her. "Can you move the boom off the hatch?"

"I'm trying to start the engine!" she screamed back at him.

He climbed on top of the sink and tried to boost himself out of the small ventilation hatch, but the opening was too narrow for his body. He was able to get his head out of the hatch and his arms up to his elbows, but that was all. He got stuck at the shoulders and had to withdraw back down into the cabin, trying to close the hatch cover as he did.

Just as he began to pull it shut, another mountainous wave hit *Atrophy* broadside, crashing down with full force on its deck, pouring water through the open hatch into the cabin below. It buried Len under a torrent of water and left him sitting, choking and coughing, on the galley countertop. The force of the wave lifted the boom and moved it three feet across the cabin roof, where it came to rest atop the hatch he had just vacated with his head.

There was nearly a foot of water on the floor of the cabin, but fortunately the bilge pump had turned itself on automatically. He was able to close the hatch and prayed the pump would be able to handle the water.

He climbed down from the countertop and went back over to the companionway, climbing up the ladder. This time, thanks to the force of the last wave, the hatch opened easily with the weight of the boom removed. He clambered up to the cockpit and closed the hatch behind him.

The night around him was black—blacker still because his eyes were not adjusted to it. The shrieking wind made concentration impossible for him. The violence of wave after wave hitting the sail-less, engineless boat was enough to shatter whatever composure he had left.

When he was finally able to see, at least to the end of the cockpit, he was able to make Erica out, still behind the wheel, still trying to get the engine started. He hooked his safety line to a handy block on the now useless track formerly used by the mainsheet traveler and made his way over to her.

"We're sinking!" he yelled.

"We're not sinking," she replied calmly enough. "We'll be okay as soon as I can get this engine started."

"Should I send out a Mayday?"

"And let everybody know who and where we are? I'll get the diesel working in a second and we'll be able to make our way under power. Now go below and let me work."

"We're going to sink," he repeated.

"You impotent little prick!" she exploded violently at him, ignoring any pretense of self-control. "I can't stand any more of your goddamn whining!"

He just stared at her, speechless, paralyzed by her vehemence as wave after wave battered them about. She was staring at him, her face frozen with cold fury. "Get below and leave me alone," she repeated.

He finally turned away from her, more eager to escape the immediate force of her anger than the storm. He scrambled back to the hatch, slid it open quickly, and climbed down into the cabin again, closing it behind him. At least in the safety of the cabin, the sound of the wind wouldn't be so loud and maybe he could figure out something to do. He glanced over at the wind indicator, but when he saw it hit 65 knots, reasoning became impossible. They were practically in a hurricane, he thought, or maybe they were.

He staggered over to the settee and threw himself down wearily, putting his feet up, not bothering to open his parka, satisfied just to take off the hood, grateful to be out of the storm. *Atrophy* pitched and rolled violently, totally out of control. Then it climbed heavily up the side of a wave and paused. Len closed his eyes, his body shuddering out of control.

The roar got louder and louder, and when he didn't think it could get any louder, it got still louder. The wave hit the boat in a head-on collision, tossing him hard up against the side of the hull, where he stayed, pinned. The boat continued to roll over. He felt or heard a thud on the deck and then thought he heard her shouting at him again. He was tossed violently up onto the ceiling, except that it was now the floor.

The plastic rum bottle he had put in the sink for safekeeping came flying out and hit him in the head, causing no real damage, but the toaster and electric wok that fell out of the storage locker did. One or both of the appliances opened a wide gash on his forehead, but by that time, he was unconscious. Everything was tossed around in the cabin like so much trash until *Atrophy* slowly righted herself.

For a few brief moments, the storm abated, and when he regained his senses, things were quiet, relatively speaking. He felt intense pain in his elbow and knew it must be broken. He touched his forehead and saw blood on his hand. He got up slowly, stumbled over to the companionway, and, using his good arm, made his way up the ladder and out into the cockpit.

When his eyes adjusted to the dark this time, he knew instantly that she was gone. She wasn't behind the wheel. She wasn't up on the foredeck. She was simply gone. Overboard gone. The bitch had deserted him. He became hysterical, screaming for her. He shouted at her and he shouted for her. He looked for her in the water, but it was too dark.

Then the wind returned.

He skidded down the ladder into the cabin and slogged over to the VHF radio. Someone had to help him. In a distant corner of his addled brain, he heard Vincent screaming to be released, but he was too preoccupied to respond. The kid wasn't his problem. Grabbing frantically, he snatched the mike off its hook. "Mayday, Mayday, Mayday!" he called, wondering if the sea remembered distress calls. "Mayday, Mayday, Mayday!" he screamed.

Chapter Thirty-six

Beth opened her eyes, concentrated, and heard it again. This time she focused her attention on the radio. There was definitely a Mayday call coming in. It was garbled and there was a lot of static caused by the storm to the north, but the operative word *Mayday* came through clearly enough.

She got off the bunk, went to the radio, and grabbed the mike, firmly keying the transmit switch as she replied, "This is the yacht *Red Sky* responding to the Mayday call. Over." She repeated the message and then released the switch, listening for a reply. She waited a painfully long minute and tried again, but no reply was forthcoming.

She put the microphone back on its clip, noted the call in the log, and climbed up into the cockpit, where Max and her mother were sharing the evening watch, content to let the autopilot steer toward Aruba on the deserted ocean.

"We just had a Mayday call," Beth announced dramatically to the idlers, who were instantly all ears. "But I didn't get any details. I was half-asleep."

"Too far away?" Andi asked.

"It must have been," she answered. "I heard the call, went over to the radio, and answered it, but they never came back to me. Some other boat must have responded."

"That's exciting," Andi said.

"I think I'll go back below and monitor channel sixteen for a while." Beth went over to the hatchway and bounded down the ladder, two rungs at a time, into the cabin.

"Well, I'm going to sleep," Andi replied. "What about you?" she asked Max as she got up to follow Beth.

"You two go ahead. I'm going to stay up top for a little while longer. I'll be down soon."

"Okay, love. How're we doing otherwise?"

"We're making incredible time. The wind is averaging twenty-six to twenty-eight knots now and we're doing close to nine knots under a reefed main with the genny almost half furled up."

"Do you think we ought to put a second reef in the main before we turn in? Take some of the pressure off the autopilot."

"I've been thinking about that. Let's see what happens in the next half hour or so."

"I'd rather do it now than in my bra and panties during the middle of the night, getting buried in spray."

"What did the last weather report say?"

"The worst of the storm has passed to the northeast of us. The barometer should start rising before morning."

"We're staying fairly dry and comfortable on board. Maybe I'll roll up the genny a little more. That'll depower her enough for the night."

"Whatever you say."

"Give me a hand with the sheet." He reached for the furling line that controlled the size of the genoa.

"You got it." She uncleated the genoa sheet and held it loosely in her hand as Max grabbed the furling line.

As soon as they had the genoa shortened enough, Andi re-cleated the sheet and went below. Max stayed behind up in the cockpit to see if the autopilot needed any adjustment as a result of shortening the sail. While he was waiting, however, Andi came partway back up the ladder to tell him that she and Beth had just heard another Mayday call. Max went below immediately.

Beth was seated by the radio. "This is *Red Sky, Red Sky, Red Sky,* calling that vessel making the Mayday call. Over." She released the key and stood by.

There was no response. Then a moment later, the Mayday call was repeated and this time they were able to hear the voice pleading on the other end: "This is *Atrophy* calling. We're sinking. A woman has been washed overboard. We need help. Over."

"Jesus, it's *Atrophy*!" Max exclaimed excitedly, jumping up and unintentionally pounding Andi on her back. "Quick, get their position. . . . Jesus, how about that!"

Beth didn't need to be urged on. She keyed the mike again. "*Atrophy,* this is *Red Sky*. We copy your message. Give us your position. Over."

Again, there was no response, only a trancelike repetition of the original call.

"We're not reaching them." Beth finally suggested, "Let's see if I can raise the Venezuelan Coast Guard. I can relay the Mayday to them."

"See if you can track them on the GPS."

"Good idea, Mom."

"While you're doing that," Max said, "I'm going to try the radio direction finder. If that homing device is working on *Atrophy,* maybe I can pick it up on the RDF." He opened the storage locker under the navigation table and pulled out the RDF, turned it on, and started rotating the antenna. The first several turns of the dial proved fruitless, but suddenly the unmistakable sound of a Morse code transmission was clearly heard: "——· —·—· —·—·."

"That's it," he announced. "G - C - C. Gold Coast Charters. I got it!" He continued to fine-tune the antenna until he got a bearing on *Atrophy*. In the meantime, Beth was trying to reach Aruba or Venezuela on the single-sideband radio while Andi monitored the VHF and GPS in case they received another transmission from *Atrophy*.

"I'm not having any luck," Beth announced.

"Keep trying," Max said. "Somebody'll wake up and respond sooner or later. In the meantime, I have a bearing on *Atrophy*. They're on a line ten degrees northeast of us. All we have to do is sail along that course and we'll find them."

"They could be anywhere on that line," Andi interjected.

"Not quite," he responded. "They're not on the radar screen, so they're more than fifteen miles away from us. And the range of the homing device is fifty miles maximum. I figure we'll be there in anywhere from two to five hours."

"You're going to sail us right into that storm?"

"Look, I'm not any more interested in sailing into a storm than Beth or you. But that was a Mayday call they sent out, remember. This isn't only a matter of catching the bad guys anymore. This is a matter of responding to a distress call. I hate to moralize, but we have an obligation to respond."

"Even if it means putting us in danger?"

"I have no intention of putting us in danger. The worst of the storm will be over by the time we get there."

"What's left may be bad enough."

"If it gets too bad, we'll turn around. Beth, how do you feel about it?"

"As far as I'm concerned, the two of them could drown in boiling water before I'd lift a hand to help them. . . ."

"I know what you mean."

"But you know what also, Dad?" she continued. "I've been tilting at windmills since October. Now it's for real. I need to see it through to the end, and if we have to save Sloane to catch Sloane, then so be it."

Andi looked at Beth, and Beth looked at Andi. Finally, without a spoken word passing between them, Andi nodded and reached over to the GPS receiver mounted on the wall. "Might as well program in the course to *Atrophy*."

"Let me know when you're ready to interface the GPS with the autopilot."

"It'll just take a second or two."

"Come up topside with me in the meantime," he said to Beth. "We're going to have to come about as soon as your mother's finished programming the GPS."

"Give us a shout when you're ready, Mom."

The farther they proceeded toward *Atrophy,* the closer they came toward the remnants of the storm that had disabled her. *Red Sky* was on a port tack, sailing under a double-reefed main and a genoa furled to less than half its maximum area. With the wind at 35 knots, she was under control, making good headway despite being pounded by the confused and heavy seas, accentuated by twelve- to fifteen-foot waves. The night sky was overcast, with temperatures in the low sixties.

There had been no radio transmissions from *Atrophy* since *Red Sky* had changed course two and a half hours ago. Their GPS was not picking up any signal, either. Beth had no idea whether it was even Sloane on board or, if it was him, whether he knew help was on the way. The absence of any communication from *Atrophy* indicated her radio was dead, or worse.

Andi was in the cabin below, monitoring the radio for any

sign of *Atrophy*. Every fifteen minutes she repeated her calls to *Atrophy* and to the Coast Guard, all without success.

At eleven fifteen p.m., she checked the radar screen and for the first time saw a blip at the outer edge of the sixteen-mile screen, indicating a vessel located directly in front of them. She went to the companionway and stuck her head up out of the hatch.

"I have something on the radar," she announced to Max and Beth. "It's right in front of us, about fifteen miles."

"Any luck raising them on the radio?" Beth asked.

"No. I haven't raised any Coast Guard either."

"I guess we'll know the answer in two hours or so."

"How're we going to be able to spot anything in this weather? It's pitch black out here."

"Maybe they'll have their running lights on."

"Somehow I don't think they will. If they're still afloat but not transmitting, it's because their batteries must be dead. I'll get the spotlight out."

"Right, Beth."

"I'd better get the flare gun out of the cabin also. A white parachute flare might come in handy when we get closer to their position."

"I already thought of that. I'll go below in a second and get it."

Chapter Thirty-seven

The sight was ghostly, bizarre, painted by a surrealist in monochromatic shades of black and white. They could do nothing but stare at the yacht, hypnotized by the stroboscopic effect of the brilliant white light from the parachute flare flickering a thousand feet overhead.

Beth stood in the cockpit, the flare pistol still in her hand, Andi by her side, Max at the wheel. In the aftermath of the storm, the sky was pitch black, covered by clouds, and moonless. The wind had calmed down to 20 knots, but the waves, slower to react, were still cresting at nearly six feet. Beth was the first to break out of her mesmerized state. She stuck the flare pistol in the pocket of her yellow parka and took out the small camera she carried around. She brought it up to her eyes and quickly snapped off several frames as her mother picked up the binoculars she had hung over the binnacle.

The vessel was about half a mile away, dark and invisible in the night except for the flare's reflected light. She was a single-masted sailboat, but the mast looked like it had been snapped in two by some monstrous wave. Like a broken matchstick, the top half was lying in a tangle of stainless-steel cable on the deck. From this distance through the binoculars, nobody could be seen topside. By the time the flare went out, Andi had the spotlight on, its powerful beam reaching out through the darkness to illuminate the boat.

"I want to approach them under power," Max said, "so let's start up the engine and furl the genoa up the rest of the way. We'll leave the main up. It'll help keep us steady."

Beth reached down to the engine controls by her left leg and started the engine, shifting into forward gear. "Mom, did you ever raise anybody on the radio?"

"Nobody," Andi replied as she rolled up the rest of the genoa around the forestay, using the winch to crank in the furling line. "I tried *Atrophy*. I tried calling her *Sindicator*. I tried the Coast Guard. I tried any damn boat that would answer my call. . . . Raising the dead would be easier."

"Their batteries are probably dead," Beth said. "That homing device stopped beeping an hour ago."

"I also saw another blip on the radar screen," Andi said.

"Besides *Atrophy*? I didn't notice anything."

"It was smaller. South, southwest of us. I entered the latitude and longitude in the log. It's not moving at all."

"We'll run it down after we're finished with *Atrophy*," Max said. "Where did you put the flare pistol, Beth?"

"It's in my pocket."

She opened the Velcro flap and handed the gun to him. He took it and loaded a white star shell into the chamber. "Tell you what I'd like to do. Let's get the portable loud-hailer out. We're going to circle them first a few times from about a hundred and fifty yards out. Identify the boat, take a safe look around, and see if anybody comes up on deck in response to our call."

Beth turned off the autopilot and began to manually steer *Red Sky* the rest of the way toward the other vessel. When she approached to within a quarter mile, she started a slow circle.

Andi kept the spotlight fixed on the boat, all three of them looking for any sign of life on board.

When they passed by the stern of the boat, Max pointed the flare gun in the air over his head and fired. The shell arced high into the air, hesitated at its apogee, and then burst, illuminating the boat below. Looking through the glasses, Beth was finally able to see that the name on the transom was indeed *Atrophy*. She handed the binoculars to her mother while Max used the hailer for the first time. Its strident amplification shattered the night air. "Ahoy there on *Atrophy*. Is anybody on board?"

There was no response, nor was any forthcoming as *Red Sky* continued to slowly circle the boat. Beth took more photographs of the eerie hulk, thinking to establish salvage rights. Max hailed her repeatedly, but to no avail. Apprehensive as to what he would do if anybody answered, he was relieved by the lack of response and felt some of the accumulated tension ease out of his body.

Atrophy was incapable of making any progress under sail. Her boom had been bent like a pretzel and was now shaped like an inverted V, with its top half protruding off the deck like a bowsprit. Beth could see now where one of the spreaders on the broken mast had smashed a hole through the hull on its way down, although the hole appeared to be above the waterline.

"She's very low in the water," Andi observed, her eyes pressed into the binoculars. "Her cabin must be flooded. What do we do now? Prepare to board?"

"Not as long as it's dark out," Max answered. "We're not going to risk it in this rough water. Too dangerous for us and the boat."

"What if someone on board is hurt?" Beth asked. "The wait could kill them."

"That someone is Sloane and Erica Crossland, and yes, I'm putting our safety before theirs. If they're on board, they might decide we're not welcome. We're not going to deal with that on a night like this."

"He's right, Beth. It's two o'clock already. Whatever happened on board has already happened. On top of it all, they really could be dangerous. They're crooks, remember: bad guys."

"I know," she replied, "but we have another three hours until it's light. We need to board her now!"

"No. We'll stay in the area, keep our eyes open for survivors, and if the Coast Guard doesn't show up by dawn, then we'll board."

"Dad, listen to me," she insisted. "We're here now. They're here now. We need to handle it now. We can't let this opportunity pass." She looked at her stepfather imploringly and reached out to touch him on the arm. She saw the indecision etched on his face. "Dad, I know it would be easier to wait for daylight, but we can't postpone this confrontation."

Max stared at her for the longest time and then simply nodded. "Okay, baby," he finally said, "let's beard the damn lion and be done with it. You and I will go over to *Atrophy* in the dinghy and I'll board her. Andi, you'll stay on *Red Sky* and keep circling around."

"Max," Andi asked, "are you sure we shouldn't just hang around until the Coast Guard shows up? They're better prepared to handle these kinds of things."

"Look, there's no sign we ever reached the Coast Guard on the radio. No, Beth is right. This is our problem and we're going to handle it, now."

"We're alone out here, Mom."

Together, they unfastened the dinghy from on top of the

cabin and wrestled it over the double lifeline railing and into the water, still connected to *Red Sky* by her painter.

"Hold on a second, Dad. I'll be right back," Beth said, having made another decision. "There's something else we need from the cabin." She went below and reappeared a minute later carrying the 12-gauge shotgun in one hand and a handful of shells in the other. She didn't know the rules of this new game yet, but she knew how to shoot straight and fast.

As she loaded the shells into the magazine, there was no sound or protest from Max or Andi, only the same unspoken resolve they all shared. Max, waiting for her by the transom, nodded in resigned agreement. "We're a team, Dad," she said. "I'm going to board with you. You'll cover me with the shotgun."

Max dropped the swim ladder and climbed down into the dinghy. Beth detached the small outboard engine from its mount on the transom and handed it down to him. He attached it to the dinghy and gave three tentative pulls to the starter cord. Nothing, followed by three more pulls, then an adjustment to the choke, three more pulls, and still nothing. He looked up at Beth. "Better do your magic before she really floods."

She handed the shotgun down to him and got into the small boat. As usual, the outboard started right up for her. Max pumped the shotgun once to chamber a round and put on the safety. Andi untied the line and threw it into the dinghy as Beth advanced the throttle and shifted into gear.

The water was choppy, making the crossing treacherous. Beth had her hands full. She skillfully brought the dinghy up to *Atrophy*'s stern and held it firmly against the swim ladder while Max waited for a break in the wave action and then climbed on board.

Beth handed him the shotgun, tied the dinghy to the ladder,

262 / *Michael Rudolph*

and scrambled up behind him. She went over to the hatch and looked down into the flooded main cabin, following the flashlight beam with her eyes, but saw nothing in it except for a floating clutter of personal effects, oily towels, and plastic bottles.

Max walked around the deck with the shotgun cradled in his arm, pausing only to examine the open canister that had once contained *Atrophy*'s emergency life raft.

Beth climbed down the companionway ladder and sloshed her way into the aft cabin, but it was also empty. Suddenly the boat rolled into a deep trough, and she heard a loud thud come from up forward. Lulled into complacency at finding the first two cabins empty, she was startled by the sound from the third cabin. She went back into the main salon and stood by the galley, sensing the presence of her stepfather right above her, watching from the cockpit, shotgun in a ready position. Its safety was now off.

"Who's there?" he challenged, pointing the shotgun at the closed door to the forward cabin, certain he would pull the trigger if Beth's life was endangered.

"Whoever's in there, this is the Coast Guard. Come out now with your hands up!" Beth's demand sounded hollow to her ears. There was no response from the cabin, only another thud as the boat continued to roll precipitously.

Beth walked back across the main salon and over to the forward cabin. Max stood off to one side, aiming the shotgun at the cabin door. She opened the door slowly, her heart pounding, and looked inside. Then she saw Vincent. The moan started low in her throat and reached a crescendo of pure horror in the second it took Max to reach her. When he saw the teenager's gimballed body swinging naked in leather shackles over the bunk, he turned Beth away, took her into his arms, and silently held her there until she regained control of herself. Then he brought her back over to the hatch and made her wait for him in the cockpit. There was no protest from Beth.

It was obvious the boy had drowned, imprisoned by the heavy leather bracelets binding his wrists and ankles to the massive steel chain plates bolted to the hull. In his last desperation, perhaps, he had managed to kick out the bunk he had been strapped to, but the futility of the effort had left him swinging helplessly in space. In death, his youthful face was frozen in terror; he had been abandoned by Sloane and Erica, unable to affect his fate.

Max, outraged by the tragedy, was determined to photograph the entire scene for the police in Aruba. He took out his camera and took pictures until nausea overwhelmed him. Then he and Beth returned to *Red Sky*.

"The life raft has to be that blip we saw on the radar a couple of hours ago," Andi said.

"Can you give us a course for it?" Beth asked.

"I can try."

"Any luck with the Coast Guard?" Max asked.

"No, but I did raise a Dutch oil tanker heading out from the Panama Canal. I gave them *Atrophy*'s location and asked them to pass it on to the Venezuelan Coast Guard. They promised they would."

"Let's locate the blip you and your mother noticed."

"I'll go get a course from the GPS," Andi said. "Be right back." She went below and sat down at the navigation table, punched a few numbers into the GPS, and brought up the original location of the blip she had entered earlier. She then punched in a drift factor based upon the current flow outlined on a chart of the area. The GPS was constantly updating their

264 / Michael Rudolph

own position, so with a few additional entries, it gave her a projected course toward the present location of the blip.

"Steer southwest, 217 degrees," Andi said on her return to the cockpit. "It should be twelve, maybe fifteen miles."

"You got it. Southwest, 217 degrees," Beth repeated.

"The weather's improving. Let's shake the reef out of the main, unfurl the genoa, and sail her," Max said. "Head her up into the wind."

With Beth behind the wheel, he reached up to the boom and untied the wraps they had used to secure the shortened mainsail. After raising the sail back up to its full height on the mast, he unfurled the genoa and winched it in until satisfied with the trim. Beth steered *Red Sky* onto the desired course and turned off the engine. Sail power took over, and the rushing wind and waves filled the void.

For the first forty-five minutes on the course, they saw nothing, despite the appearance of the sun now rising behind them in a mostly cloudy sky. Then, when Max went below, he noticed a small blip on the radar screen. "Andi," he shouted up to the deck, "can you come down here a second? There's something on the radar screen—"

Andi was down the ladder and in the cabin beside him before he finished the sentence. She started plotting the information from the screen. "It could be a raft," she suggested. "It's small enough and hardly moving at all."

"What's its relative bearing from us?"

"Southeast, about 125 degrees."

"How far?"

"Maybe six, eight miles."

"Come around to 125 degrees," he said up to Beth, who was watching them from outside, sitting on top of the cabin.

"We'll have to jibe," she said.

"I know. We're coming right up."

Beth went back to the steering wheel and turned off the autopilot, while Andi and Max climbed the ladder. Andi went to the leeward side of the boat and uncleated the genoa sheet so that she could release it when the boat jibed. Max uncleated the mainsheet and hauled in the boom until it was taut along the center line of the boat. While the genoa would swing harmlessly over to the other side of the boat during the jibe, the massive boom would cross like an aluminum scythe, giving instant headache or worse to anybody unfortunate enough to be in its path.

"Everybody set?" Beth asked.

"All set," Andi responded.

"Heads down and let her rip," Max said.

"Prepare to jibe," Beth announced, followed immediately by, "Jibe ho!" as she turned the steering wheel to the left, taking the boat's stern through the eye of the wind, putting *Red Sky* on her new heading.

With the jibe, the boom slammed violently over their heads to its new tack. As soon as it did, Max released the mainsheet partway, permitting the boom to swing out safely over the boat. Andi released the genoa sheet, crossed to the other side of the cockpit, and cranked in the genoa. The big sail ballooned with air as *Red Sky* settled down on her new course.

It wasn't long before Beth shouted and pointed excitedly off the port bow. "I see something in the water at ten o'clock."

Andi was closest to the binoculars and grabbed them before Max could. She peered out over the water in the direction Beth had indicated. "I can't see anything," she complained.

"I can't see it anymore either," Beth said.

Andi relinquished the glasses to Max's grabbing hands. He quickly had them up to his eyes, adjusting the focus. "There it is!" he said, pointing with one hand while keeping the glasses glued to his eyes with the other hand. "Over there. . . . A raft. It's got a canopy on top. Steer a little more to the left."

Beth turned the wheel slightly to port.

"A little more," Max said. *Red Sky* reacted perceptibly to the adjustment. "There, that's fine now," he said. "Stay right on that course."

In a minute, Beth spotted the raft again with her naked eye, and soon it was readily visible to all of them. She wanted to approach under power, so while Max furled up the genoa, she started the engine, throttling up to 2,500 rpm. Andi lifted the port seat in the cockpit, dug into the lazaret, and brought out two twenty-foot lines for use if needed.

Max then opened the starboard lazaret, took out the shotgun, and handed it to Beth. "It's still loaded and the safety is on. If Sloane or anybody else is alive on that raft, they may be troublesome after abandoning that kid. Let's be ready."

Beth nodded in assent. She put the shotgun down on the seat behind her while she continued steering *Red Sky* toward the raft. As the distance narrowed, her anticipation of the confrontation increased. One way or the other, the chase was about to be over. The conclusion was unknown, but its revelation wasn't more than a few hundred yards away and closing.

She dropped the throttle down to 1,500 rpm so the wake from *Red Sky* wouldn't create additional problems for any survivors on the life raft. *Red Sky* slowed to 5 knots, approaching the raft from the rear. Beth made a pass around to the front and shifted into neutral, but the entrance in the front of the canopy had been zippered shut. "Ahoy on board the raft!" she shouted through her cupped hands. "Is anybody there?"

There was no answer, but the entrance to the canopy opened slowly when Beth repeated the call a third time. Max grabbed the shotgun as a hand appeared first from inside the raft, followed by the bearded countenance, bald head, and upper torso of Leonard Sloane, a laceration on his forehead caked with blood, his other arm dangling uselessly at his side. He stared silently at them, passively, without any sign of recognition.

Hardly a formidable adversary, Beth thought as she stared back at him, trying to visualize the man who had nearly destroyed her. Where was the satisfaction she had been seeking, the payback for the wrongs? The elements had cut Sloane down to a pitiful wretch. Beth had had nothing to do with it.

Chapter Thirty-eight

Beth replaced her jacket with a life vest, secured herself with a safety line, and jumped into the water. Andi threw her another line, which she tied to the raft before climbing on to help Sloane. He was unable to help himself and too beaten to talk. Max rigged a block and tackle from the boom, attached a sling, and swung it out over the water. Beth grabbed the sling and managed to get it around Sloane. Then, with Max using the winch, they hoisted Sloane's dead weight out of the raft and into the cockpit of the sailboat, where he collapsed from exhaustion on the seat, a yellow canvas bag clutched in his grasp.

Andi brought the medical kit up from the cabin. Sloane's right arm was obviously broken, and he had to be in intense pain. It was hard for her to manifest much overt support for the anger she still felt toward him. Despite what he had done to Beth, he presented no immediate threat and she couldn't let him sit around in the cockpit without doing something to help. She made a sling to relieve some of the pressure and gently eased it over his neck while putting his arm through it. The head wound wasn't bleeding, so she decided to leave it alone.

While Andi was ministering to Sloane, Max swung the boom back out over the raft and used the line Beth attached to winch the cumbersome platform out of the water. As it hung suspended over the deck, he and Beth opened its air valves and deflated it. Finally, they folded it up and stuffed it into the big lazaret under the captain's seat.

"No point in hanging around here," Max said quietly to Beth and Andi. "We should be fairly close to Aruba by now. I want to drop Sloane off with the police there."

"We ought to tie him up or lock him up in the meantime," Beth said, her free hand resting easily on the shotgun. "He's facing some heavy time back home."

"I know," he started to agree, wondering at the same time if Beth didn't look a little too comfortable with the firearm under her hand. "But he doesn't look particularly troublesome." He nodded in the direction of the survivor huddled under the canvas dodger for protection, propped up against the cabin bulkhead for support.

"If we're going to lock him up, we ought to do it before he starts to look troublesome."

"I know."

"Mom, can you give me a course and distance to Aruba?"

"I'll go below and figure it out for you. In the meantime, sail south, that's the general direction."

"You got it. Want me to stay at the wheel?" she asked Max.

"No, I'll take it now. Why don't you unfurl the genny and then I'll turn off the engine."

Beth switched seats with Max and opened the genoa. After receiving the exact heading to Aruba from Andi, Max turned on the autopilot and turned off the diesel. He continued to sit at the wheel, though, still thinking about locking up Sloane, feeling little in the way of comfort from the rigid form of the shotgun resting within easy reach on the seat behind him, its barrel pointed toward Sloane. Beth was right, though. As long as Sloane was sitting in the cockpit, they'd have to keep one eye on him.

He got up, motioned for Beth to get back behind the wheel, and went over to sit beside Sloane. "How are you feeling?"

Sloane looked at him wearily, still without any sign of recognition. "Better, thanks to you."

"Leonard, do you remember me? I'm Max Swahn."

Sloane looked at him, stared at Beth, and finally recognized them. "My eyes are so blurred from the salt and the glare that I've been having trouble focusing."

"Leonard, who was on the boat with you?" Beth asked.

"Some native kid and a woman."

"What were their names?"

"Vincent was the kid's name. The woman was Erica Crossland. I think he drowned with Erica."

"Erica drowned? When?"

Numbed by the shock of remembering, Sloane continued on in his disjointed fashion: "Overboard. She went overboard during the storm last night. I couldn't look for her."

"Why not?" Max asked.

"No engine . . . couldn't start the engine . . . mast collapsed after the boat turned over. We were sinking."

"But the boat didn't sink. Why did you leave it?"

"It was sinking. I had to save myself." His responses were rambling. Unable or unwilling to make eye contact, he was gazing out into nowhere, seeing nothing.

"Why did you leave Vincent behind?"

"I don't know. . . . Maybe he drowned with Erica. I must have forgotten Vincent was there. . . . Beth, what are you doing here?"

"We were sailing to Aruba when we heard your Mayday call. Didn't you hear our response?"

"I never heard any response. . . . When Erica went overboard, I figured it was all over."

"You must be very tired," Max said. "Come below with me, now. I'm going to put you in a cabin for a while. Get some of your strength back."

"My arm hurts."

"I can get you a couple of aspirins," Max offered.

"No, I have pills, but I could use some water."

Max helped Sloane up and assisted him on his way down into the main salon, where Andi was still working at the navigation table. Max led him to the small cabin on the port side and opened the door. Sloane went inside, still clutching his yellow bag, and lay down on the bunk.

By the time Max returned with the water, Sloane was asleep, so Max used the opportunity to get a piece of rope out of an overhead locker and tie Sloane's good arm to a grab rail. Then he closed the cabin door again, but for additional security, he jammed a bulky sail bag between the door and the head. Sloane would never get the door open. The narrow cabin had no hatch leading up to the deck, so their guest would not be coming up without assistance. By the time Sloane woke up, they'd be in Aruba.

"Why don't you take a nap for a while?" Beth suggested to Max when he appeared topside. "I can take care of things up here."

"Thanks, sweetie, but I'm too keyed up. I'll stay up here. You can go below, though, if you want. Keep your mother company. I'd feel more comfortable if you were down there with her."

"No, I'm too hyper also. She'll be okay. I'll stay up here with you."

"Feeling a little drained?"

"No. Disappointed. I thought I'd feel more satisfaction after catching up with Sloane." She shrugged. "He looks like such a zero. . . . Abandoning ship while that kid was still on board. His girlfriend dead, the kid dead." She shook her head slowly. "I don't feel any sympathy for him, but I don't feel any righteous gratification either, just disgust."

"It's like you don't remember what got you so mad in the first place."

"The chase was great, though, wasn't it?"

"It sure was. We'd have made a great team of detectives, you, your mother, and me, tracking them to Antigua the way we did."

"Not to mention sailing circles around them for the last four days. We'd have caught them even without the help of the storm."

"Damn right!"

"I love you, Max. I'm glad me and Mom picked you." She suddenly reached across to him with her arm, picked up his hand, and kissed it, holding it against her cheek before letting go.

"I love you too, baby," he responded hoarsely, leaning over to kiss her softly on the forehead. All he could do after that was sniff and blow his nose. He abruptly went up forward to the mast and busied himself recoiling the halyards to his left-handed satisfaction.

A few minutes later, Andi stuck her head up out of the hatch, saw him standing by the mast, and asked him to come below. He went down the ladder and stood behind her at the navigation station. "What's up?" he asked.

"See that blip?" She pointed to the radar screen.

"Isn't that *Atrophy*?"

"No," she replied, moving her finger to another blip. "That's *Atrophy*. This is a new blip, very fast moving. Forty knots or more."

"Who do you think it is?"

"It's probably the Venezuelan Coast Guard finally heading out to *Atrophy*. That tanker must have forwarded on our message."

"Maybe we can get rid of our passenger. Did you raise them on the radio?"

"No luck."

"How can it be the Coast Guard if they're not monitoring channel sixteen?" He stared at the radar screen, half expecting an identifying label to appear magically next to the blip.

"I guess you're right."

"How long before they reach *Atrophy*?"

"The way they're moving? Say twenty minutes, a half hour at most."

"Where are you going to be?"

"I'm going to stay down here and read for a while."

"With Sloane? I'm not thrilled by that."

"He can't open his door with that sail bag wedged in. Anyhow, I'm comfortable stretched out on the settee. If his cabin door moves, I promise I'll yell."

"Keep an eye on the radar screen too. Let me know when that boat reaches *Atrophy* and what direction they take after they leave her."

"I'll watch them as long as they stay on the screen. *Atrophy* is almost off it already. We're too far away."

"If that boat is heading for *Atrophy* and then comes looking for us, how long before they get to us?"

"Hang on a second." Andi turned to her laptop and made a series of calculations before turning back to Max. "Figuring their average speed at forty knots and ours at 8.5 knots, I'd say we have at least an hour and a half. That's without counting any time they spend nosing around *Atrophy*."

"Okay. You stay down here and relax, then. Sloane is fast asleep and I tied up his good arm. I'm going back up topside with Beth."

The brilliant sunlight streaming through the disappearing clouds signaled the final exit of the storm. Max stretched out on the cockpit bench across from Beth, who had already assumed a similar position, complete with eyes shut tight. "You sleeping?" he asked, doubling over one of Andi's sweatshirts into a comfortable pillow behind his head.

"No. I'm thinking."

"About what?"

"Whether or not I have any future with Bob."

"Well, if you want to pursue the relationship, honesty is certainly the risk you're going to have to take. It's going to be even tougher if you have to testify against his father in a criminal prosecution."

"I know. I guess there's nothing I can do about it but tell him the truth and accept his decision."

"You're going to have to deal with Clifford also."

"I know that too."

"Was catching Sloane worth it?"

"Absolutely!" she replied emphatically. "I'd have risked anything to get him, but now that we've caught him, I'm feeling a letdown. How did such a pitiful creature engineer this whole thing? Did you speak to him about the money?"

"No. He was nearly incoherent when I took him below. Anyhow, that's a problem for the police."

"I know, but let's ask him anyway."

"Works for me."

"If I've learned anything from all this, it's that rules and fairness don't count for squat in the real world."

"I'm not sure I agree with that, and I don't think you really do either. I think the rules were there. They were just different rules you hadn't learned yet."

"You mean if I'd been more experienced, I'd have seen through Len's scam?"

There was no response from Max other than the sound of his heavy, peaceful breathing. Beth didn't hear him start snoring because by that time she had also dropped off to sleep. The sun, their lack of sleep, and the easy sailing motion of the broad reach had achieved its effect.

Chapter Thirty-nine

Andi found them asleep on deck when she stopped reading and came topside an hour later. "Max, are you awake?" she asked, shaking him gently. "That blip on the screen. It's heading our way."

"I'm awake," he said. "I was just resting my eyes for a minute. Is it the same boat as before?"

"I think so, but it's moving faster than before. Almost fifty knots."

"How soon before it gets here?" Beth asked, rubbing her eyes and sitting up.

"I figure about twenty minutes."

"What's their relative bearing?"

"They'll be coming in right behind us, slightly off to starboard. You should be able to see them soon."

"I'm going to go below, Dad." She stood up and walked over to the hatch. "I want to talk to Sloane before we turn him over to the Coast Guard."

"I'll go with you," he replied, following her down into the cabin. Beth took the small microcassette recorder out of the plastic bag in the liquor locker, turned it on, and stuck it into the pocket of her shorts.

Max removed the sail bag he had stuffed into the passageway and opened the door to Sloane's cabin. Sloane was lying on his back, his eyes wide open, staring at the small patch of sky visible out the porthole. "Do you feel better?" Max asked him, untying his arm so he could take some water.

"It doesn't make any difference," he answered. "I heard what you were talking about up on the deck. The Coast Guard will be here in a few minutes."

"What happened to the money?" Beth asked him.

For the first time since his rescue, a look of total comprehension crossed his face. "I guess seeing you at the Admiral's Inn last week wasn't such a coincidence."

"You could have had me disbarred with that scam."

"We had planned it for years. We were only waiting for the opportunity. If it wasn't Jasco, it would have been something else."

"How did you move the money?"

"With Erica's connections, we had it wired in and out of eight banks around the world so fast it was totally untraceable and converted into triple-A bearer bonds within four days."

"Where is it now?"

Len was silent for a moment, reluctant to give up the last vestige of his scheme. "That could be a problem," he finally answered.

"How so?" Beth asked.

"It's in a bank safe-deposit box, but it takes three keys to open it and Erica had one of them on her when she fell overboard. The president of the bank has a key and I have the third one here." He reached up and removed the necklace from around his neck and handed it to Beth. "Here. You keep it. The chain is eighteen-karat gold."

"I'll turn it over to the Coast Guard." She put the chain into her pocket.

"Don't be silly. Turn over the key but keep the chain. It cost me over twelve thousand dollars. Consider it a gift for saving my life."

Beth ignored the gesture and continued, "Did you convert it all into bearer bonds?"

"The whole seventy million except for five hundred thousand in cash we kept for living expenses. Erica had that in a money belt she was wearing."

"So where's the bank?"

"Forget it. I'm saving that one for plea bargaining."

"Where were you guys planning to live happily ever after?"

"New Zealand. A couple of years ago, I bought a house in Auckland with money I *borrowed* from Leung. Erica and I planned to live there. We bribed a clerk on Antigua to issue us phony passports."

"You took other money from Leung before Jasco?"

"He never missed it."

"Tell me something. If you were headed for New Zealand, why not just fly there?"

"I planned to, but then things started going bad between me and Erica, so I kept postponing the flight in case I decided to break up with her."

"Did she know that?"

"No. I just told her we had to sell the boat and the house on Antigua first. When I saw you at the inn last week, we had just taken a deposit to sell both to a French doctor. Then I spotted one of Leung's brothers out at the airport, so Erica insisted we sail to Panama and fly to Auckland from there."

"You saw one of Leung's brothers out at the airport? Which one?"

"I forget his name."

"What was he doing there?"

"Same thing as you, I guess."

"What about that phony Mayday you pulled in Puerto Rico?" Max asked.

"It was the perfect way to fake our disappearance." Whether from simple fatigue or complex amorality, he showed no remorse at all.

"How did you do it?"

Sloane, proud of the achievement and feeling more alert, was eager to provide the details. "On paper it was easy. Doing it was the tricky part."

"I know you chartered *Sindicator* under a phony name and chartered *Satin Lady* under your real name. What happened then?"

"After a few days on *Satin Lady*, I sabotaged her engines, and while she was laid up for repairs, Erica and I flew to Guadeloupe, picked up *Sindicator*, and sailed her to St. Croix. Then we went back to *Satin Lady*, got rid of the captain, and headed for St. Croix."

"And scuttled *Satin Lady*?"

"Exactly, and broadcast the Mayday from *Sindicator*."

"What then? You changed her name to *Atrophy* and removed her mizzen to disguise her as a sloop?"

"Right!"

"But why did you store the mast at your house? That's what finally led us to you."

"Son of a bitch!" he exclaimed. "Erica couldn't bear to dump the damn mast overboard. Figured one day she'd restore the ketch. . . . And then she started screwing around with Vincent."

"Who was Vincent?" Beth interrupted.

"Some kid she hired to work on the boat."

"Did you chain him up?"

"Erica did it to punish him."

"But how could you abandon ship and leave him on board? He's dead, you know, and you're responsible for his death."

"We were sinking. I had to get off. I didn't know he was in the forward cabin. I thought he washed overboard with Erica."

Their conversation was interrupted by Andi's presence at the cabin door. "Max, Beth . . . ," she said, "I need you. Can you come topside?"

Without another word, they quickly left Sloane in the cabin, closing the door behind him. Beth jammed the bulky sail bag back in place and followed Max and Andi up the ladder, re-membering to turn off the tape recorder still running in her pocket. Andi handed Max the binoculars and pointed off in the distance. Although still too far away to identify, the wake of a fast-moving speedboat pounding through the heavy seas was unmistakable.

"I can't identify it," Beth said. "It's heading toward us bow on. I can't see any markings."

"It's too fast and too low for a Coast Guard boat," Max said, his eyes glued to the glasses.

"I should go below and keep trying to raise the Coast Guard," Andi suggested, moving to the companionway.

"Good idea." He reached for the throttle control on the pedestal, pumped it once, and then leaned down to turn the key for the diesel. As soon as the engine started and was running smoothly, he moved the throttle back to its idling position, leav-ing the transmission in neutral. "We'll continue sailing on our course," he said to Beth, "but I want the engine warm and run-ning."

"What about the autopilot?"

"Leave it on. I want all our hands free until I see what devel-ops." He put the binoculars back up to his eyes. Every horror story he had heard about pirates and drug smugglers in the Caribbean flooded through his mind in graphic detail. "Hey, Andi," he shouted into the cabin below, "any luck with the radio yet?"

"I finally reached the Venezuelan Coast Guard," Andi replied, sticking her head up out of the cabin.

"Glad to hear they're awake."

"I gave them our position, told them about *Atrophy,* and asked them if they had a boat approaching us now. They said they didn't, so that boat over there isn't theirs."

"Are they sending anybody out?"

"Yes. Their closest boat is refueling now in Aruba. It should be here within ninety minutes."

"Tell them we don't have that long. Maybe they can send out a chopper." His eyes remained fixed to the binoculars, tracking the incoming speedboat. "Beth, bring up that twenty-gauge double-barrel shotgun we use for skeet and all the ammo you can find. I want both shotguns ready."

"I'm on it, Dad."

The approaching boat started to bear off from *Red Sky* and passed her starboard beam at a distance of about a mile and a half. Max, following them through the glasses, breathed an audible sigh of relief as they passed. While he couldn't make out any faces, he saw at least three people on board. One of them, wearing a broad-brimmed canvas hat, was staring back at them through binoculars. He recognized the familiar Cigarette logo on its jet-black hull, probably a forty-five-footer, and figured it was some oil-rich Venezuelans out for the day in their million-dollar toy.

The speedboat, now well in front of them, suddenly twisted into a tight, high-speed turn, crossed their bow a good distance ahead, and came back for another pass, port side to port side, this time barely two hundred yards away and considerably slower.

Following along, with the binoculars still at his eyes, Max volunteered a salutary wave at the other boat with his free hand, but there was no response. He could see the man with the binoculars, his face hidden under the shade of the hat, hand them to someone else and then disappear into the cabin.

The speedboat passed astern of them, went into another turn, slower and closer, approaching *Red Sky* this time from the rear on her starboard side. "Max . . . ," he heard Andi calling him insistently from the cabin below. "They're calling us on channel sixteen."

He went below immediately, getting down the ladder in one long step and a quick jump. Andi was sitting at the navigation station, the microphone in her hand, her face ashen. "What's the matter?" He put his hand on her arm, concerned about the way she looked.

"Max, they asked for Beth by name." She was shaken.

"Did you tell them she was on board?"

"I haven't answered the call yet. But how do they know who's on board?"

"I think it's Leung, but let me get at the microphone and we'll know for sure." Andi put down the microphone, got up from the table, and went up the ladder into the cockpit. She waited by the hatch opening to hear the conversation, motioning for Beth to come over and join her.

Max reached over to the radio and pulled the microphone off its clip. He thought for a moment, put the mike to his mouth, and depressed the transmit button: "This is *Red Sky* switching to channel fifty-two and standing by. Over." He released the key, changed channels, and waited for the response.

"*Red Sky,* this is the vessel off your starboard bow," announced a heavily accented Spanish voice. "Is the señorita Beth Swahn on board?"

"Identify yourself, please."

"Standby, señor," the voice said.

Max heard another party talking in the background over the open key. Then that other voice came on the radio with a totally different but unmistakably familiar accent: "Mr. Swahn, this is C. K. Leung. We must talk." Max tried to respond, but the transmit key on the other boat was still depressed. In the background, he heard someone telling Leung to release the transmit button after he finished talking.

"Mr. Leung, this is Max Swahn. Over."

"Mr. Swahn. How are you?"

"What is it that you want?" He looked out the nearest porthole on the starboard side, anxious to keep an eye on the position of the other boat.

"I was merely exchanging pleasantries, Mr. Swahn."

"There's no need for that, Mr. Leung. I'm real angry about the way you and your henchman treated my daughter last month. Now say what you have to say and let's conclude this conversation. Over."

"Mr. Swahn, let me first say that my associate Mr. Rheinhartz far exceeded his authority at that meeting and I apologize deeply for any discomfort caused to Beth. I can assure you that no disrespect was intended."

"Well, then perhaps you need to exercise a greater degree of control over your associates."

"Yes, your observation is well taken."

"Mr. Leung, I'll ask you again: What is the point of your threatening behavior?"

"I need to locate Leonard Sloane and Erica Crossland. We found their abandoned vessel a short while ago with the body of a young black on board. My captain advises that his radar indicated your arrival at that same vessel several hours before us. Do you have them on board?"

"I can assure you, Mr. Leung," he replied with affected righteousness, "that I do not have *them* on board." Technically the truth, he thought to himself.

"Mr. Swahn, my captain monitored a recent radio message from your vessel to the Coast Guard advising that you did have a survivor on board."

"Your captain is correct. We did send out such a message." (Got me on that one, C.K.!)

"Who was the survivor?"

"Like you, we found only the boy's body when we boarded. Several hours later we rescued a survivor off a life raft. That was Leonard Sloane."

"And did you also rescue Miss Crossland?"

"We didn't search for her, but Leonard says she drowned during the storm last night."

"Would you be kind enough, then, to ask Leonard if he would join us on board my vessel? There are several matters I would like to discuss with him."

"Mr. Leung, I am responsible for the safety of my passengers, including those we rescue at sea. That is an elementary rule of admiralty law. Sloane will be turned in to the proper authorities." He hoped he sounded more confident than he felt about that one.

"Leonard Sloane abused the great trust placed in him by my family. It is essential that he be turned over to us."

"Let me remind you, Mr. Leung, that he caused an equally serious outrage to my family."

"That is not my concern." The voice coming out of the radio was icy cold, devoid of any emotion.

Max felt his own tension turning to fury at Leung's arrogance. He pressed the transmit key. "I will turn Sloane over to the Coast Guard when it gets here and he will ultimately be called on to answer for his crimes."

"That will not be a satisfactory resolution of the problem."

"Why not? You'll get your money back and Sloane will go to jail. End of problem."

"Not entirely. There are more important matters we need to discuss with Leonard."

"You can resolve them through the legal system. Sloane will have to stay on board."

As soon as Leung pressed the transmit switch again on his radio, Max was able to hear at least two angry voices talking between themselves in Chinese over the open channel. "Please stand by the radio for a moment, Mr. Swahn," Leung finally said to Max in English. "My brother wishes to discuss something with me."

Max used the opportunity to look through the porthole. Leung's boat was circling slowly around *Red Sky*. The rocking motion caused by the broadside action of the waves against her hull must have been considerable. The Cigarette was totally out of its environment, wallowing around inefficiently in the water, doing about 5 knots. He could see two men in ridiculous black suits standing in the cockpit, staring intently over at *Red Sky*, holding on to the gunnels with both hands, and looking quite seasick.

Max looked behind him and realized with a start that Leonard Sloane had squeezed his way out of his cabin during the radio conversation with Leung. He was sitting on the opposite side of the main salon, supporting his head with his good left arm.

"It seems our guest is up," Beth observed casually from

above. Max looked up at the hatchway and saw her sitting there at the top of the ladder, the 12-gauge shotgun pointed directly at Sloane.

"Do you know what's going on here, Len?" Beth asked him.

"I saw Leung on the speedboat through the porthole in the cabin and then I heard your father talking to him on the radio. That's why I came out here. I want you to let me go over to his boat."

"The only boat you're going to is the Coast Guard boat when it gets here." She wasn't in the mood to debate the issue with Sloane or anybody else.

"Look, the game is over," Sloane protested. "I lost it years ago but never realized it." He sounded convinced of his failure, his stamina beaten down beyond the fatigue caused by the storm.

It was hard for Beth to accept. How could this man be so resigned to his fate? It was unbelievable. She finally decided it must be Sloane's exhaustion talking. "And what do you think Leung is going to do to you if he gets you on board? Pat you on the back for stealing his money?"

"C.K. is not going to let you turn me over to the Coast Guard. There's a lot more at stake besides the Jasco money. He needs me, and the bank codes on a CD in my bag, to access all the Arab money he's laundered."

"Is that the only copy of the CD?" Beth asked.

"Why do you want to know?"

"I'd be surprised if you didn't leave a backup copy behind just in case."

"As a matter of fact, I did. There's a copy of the CD back in my condo."

"Somehow I figured."

"So let me go over to C.K. He's desperate and won't hurt me."

"I tend to doubt that," Beth said. "You go over to C.K. and you're dead."

"Counselor, listen to me, will you?" he yelled with what strength remained. "This is not a courtroom you're in now. There are no guards standing around to protect you. No 911 emergency number to call. Before Leung is finished, the only evidence left of this boat will be a few sharks swimming around with big fat grins on their faces."

"Come on, will you?" Beth replied, exasperated by all this melodrama. "Stop the crap!"

"You don't understand his rules. Let me go over there with his bank codes and you've got nothing to worry about. He doesn't care about you and I don't care about me. That's why I can handle him. It's between him and me."

"I'm not so sure I agree, and anyhow, you seem to have forgotten the little matter of the Coast Guard."

"You think I give a damn about that? I'll never do a single day's time." Though dead tired, he sounded confident about his position.

"What makes you so sure of that?"

"None of your business, but take my word for it. C.K. and Erica took care of my future a long time ago."

"I have no idea what you're talking about."

"It doesn't matter."

"Nothing matters to you, but my reputation matters to me, so I'm afraid you're going to have to stay on board *Red Sky* for a while longer."

"I'm too worn out to fight. Do what you want." Still exhausted from the storm, his right arm throbbing painfully and his head aching, Leonard got up from the settee and crossed over to the galley. He reached into his pocket for the bottle of pills he kept there, looked at the label as though he were just seeing it for the first time, and put two codeine capsules into his mouth, then washed them down with a glass of water. Swallowing was getting to be a problem for him. He staggered and reeled like a punch-drunk fighter back to his cabin, closing the door behind him. Beth went back up to the steering wheel.

Max got tired of waiting by the radio for the call from Leung and decided to go up on deck. He turned up the volume on the radio and adjusted the squelch. Then he went over to the galley to pour himself some soda.

"Dad, get up here!" Beth suddenly called from above as he opened the two-liter bottle.

"Coming right up," he responded, his mind still focused on Sloane's erratic behavior. "Want a Coke?"

"No. Get up here, will you!"

He heard her insistence but kept on pouring. There was a sense of urgency in her voice, too, but he was too preoccupied to hear it.

"Be right there—," he started to answer.

"*Now,* Dad!"

Then he heard the shotgun go off on deck, and that got his attention. The explosive report of a 12-gauge magnum load was a heart-stopper for him. He dropped the soda into the sink and made it up the companionway ladder in two giant steps and one painfully cracked shin.

Beth was standing in the cockpit, the shotgun up against her shoulder, smoke coming out of its barrel. She aimed, fired again at her moving target, pumped the action to chamber a fresh shell, and then fired again before lowering the gun. Andi was standing next to her, reloading the smoking flare pistol in her hand. About fifty yards away now, the object of their disaffection, a twelve-foot rubber dinghy, its outboard engine revved up and screaming in protest, was heading at full speed back toward the Cigarette. The two men in black suits were flattened in the bottom of the dinghy, cowering in terror, while a third, wearing a green bathing suit, was sitting up at the tiller only high enough to see where he was steering.

"You both okay?" was Max's first question as he checked out the situation.

"We are now," Beth responded, nodding. "Those bastards tried to sneak up on us. While Mom and I were watching the speedboat circling around us, they moved their dinghy in on our blind spot. Those two goons were on it. One of them is Scarface, an old 'friend' of mine. If he'd been a little closer, I could have put a few holes in his butt."

"Sloane is right, then," Max said, realization flooding in. "Leung has no intention of walking away from this. Andi, see if you can get the Coast Guard on the radio again."

"Okay, call me if you need me," she said.

"I will."

"I'll leave you the flare gun." She slowly released the hammer on the pistol, easing it down into a safe position, and tried to hand it to Max.

"No. Take it below with you in case Sloane gets cute. If you screw in that .410 shotgun barrel I bought, it will discourage him if he gets in your way. Now go ahead, take a crack at the radio."

"Better make it a Mayday, Mom, and tell them we're being attacked by pirates."

"Pirates?"

"She's right, pirates," Max said. "Let's not quibble. If Leung is monitoring channel sixteen, it may cause him to back off."

Faced with actual violence for the first time, he no longer felt the uncertainty that had plagued him when he had boarded *Atrophy*. He looked over at Beth and saw only the determined look on her face.

"What do you want me to do now, Dad?" she asked.

"Well, first off, let me have that pump shotgun. I've had more experience with it than you, and my two-hundred-pound body will be better able to handle its kick if we have to fire it again."

"I'll be okay," she said, handing him the shotgun.

"I'm not worried about you. Get the twenty-gauge and check on Sloane."

"I'll be right back." Beth went below and came back with the double-barrel. "Mom says she didn't have any luck getting the Coast Guard on the radio."

"I guess we're responsible for ourselves. Maybe that's the way it's supposed to be." He took a box of 12-gauge shells from Beth, ejected the spent one from the chamber, pumped in a new round, and added an extra one to the magazine. Beth opened the 20-gauge and inserted a shell into each barrel.

"Beth!" Andi interrupted from the base of the ladder. "They're calling you on the radio again."

"Coming." She got up and handed the 20-gauge to Max. "Keep your eyes on our blind spot."

"I will."

Beth went below and picked up the microphone again. "This is *Red Sky*," she announced.

It was C.K.: "Beth, I want to apologize for that unpleasant incident a few minutes ago. Unfortunately, my brother Andrew took it upon himself to send our tender over to pick up Leonard. I am sorry that it frightened you."

"It didn't frighten me, C.K., but it did piss me off. *Red Sky* is our home and we deeply resented the effort to enter it without our permission. I trust that no one on the dinghy was injured." Beth was in her milieu. She could obfuscate with anyone.

"Beth, my brother and I are due back in Panama in a few hours. We must resolve this difficulty without any further delay so that we can each go back about our business."

"Then I strongly urge you to head for the Canal now."

"I intend to do that, but I must have Leonard Sloane on board. Our business depends on it."

"C.K., you're making me repeat myself. We'll turn Leonard over to the proper authorities."

"Beth, we are the injured party. You must allow us to pick up Leonard now."

"The answer is no. Now is there anything else you would like to discuss? Over."

"Why don't you and your family take a few minutes to consider the consequences of your decision while I talk with my brother?"

Beth replaced the microphone on its clip and looked at her mother sitting at the table.

"Are we going to be okay?" Andi asked her.

"A piece of cake, Mom," she responded, running her hand through her mother's short curly hair for good luck and bending down to kiss her on the cheek.

Chapter Forty

ed Sky continued under both sail and power, heading for Aruba. Max watched the knot meter and throttled the diesel up to 3,100 rpm, intent on maintaining maximum hull speed, slightly better than 9 knots. The speedboat kept circling them from a safe distance as if undecided, ignoring the sailboat's relatively slow forward progress.

Beth walked over to her mother at the navigation table and put a hand on her shoulder. "How far are we from Aruba now?"

"At our present speed and course, still two hours and twenty-five minutes."

"It'll be dark by then. Can we approach at night?"

"I have the GPS programmed for a lighthouse on the northwest point of the island. After we round the lighthouse, it should be a short sail west to Oranjestad. I don't see any reefs or wrecks on the charts, and the entrance looks pretty straightforward and well marked. There's going to be plenty of moonlight. The answer to your question is yes."

"Good. Now would you please come up topside with Dad and me? I don't like leaving you down here with Leonard, no matter how beat he is. The action is going to be topside anyhow, and we may need an extra set of hands. We'll leave the hatch open so we can hear the radio."

"Okay, I'm right behind you."

They joined Max, who was sitting behind the wheel, shot-gun by his side, his attention on the circling speedboat. Andi sat down on the port side of the cockpit, putting the flare pistol, barrel first, into the drink holder on the pedestal.

"What should I load the flare pistol with?" she asked him. "I have red meteors, white meteors, and three of the red para-chutes."

"Use a red meteor. Put one in their dinghy and it'll burn a big hole."

Andi took one of the big 25 mm shells from the bag, in-serted it in the barrel of the flare pistol, and snapped it shut. "We don't have any white parachutes left."

"Hey, look at the speedboat," Max said. The Cigarette sud-denly increased its speed and began to head away from *Red Sky* at a right angle to her beam.

"Do you think they're leaving?" Andi asked hopefully.

"Not a chance," Beth replied.

Max stood up from behind the wheel and moved over toward Andi. "Take the wheel for a while, will you, Beth."

"Sure, Dad." She moved behind the wheel and stood there comfortably, one leg up on the seat for balance, binoculars dan-gling from her neck. The speedboat continued to head away from *Red Sky* until it was about three-quarters of a mile off her starboard side. It then slowly turned 180 degrees around until its bow was facing *Red Sky* broadside and stopped dead in the water, rolling from side to side in the trough of a wave.

On board *Red Sky,* they suddenly heard the staccato sound of an automatic weapon firing. Before the three of them had a chance to duck, bullets began dropping into the water a hun-dred yards short of *Red Sky*.

Beth watched the developing war through the binoculars. "They look like they're going to try to ram us."

"I think you're right," Max agreed.

"Pull in the mainsheet as tight as you can, Dad. We may have to jibe suddenly and I don't want the boom flying around."

"They're just trying to give us a scare. Want me to take the wheel back?"

"No!" she replied confidently, angling *Red Sky* over toward the speedboat.

With that, as if on cue, the Cigarette roared to life, reared back on its haunches with both massive engines at full throttle, and headed straight for *Red Sky* like a dragster, its speed quickly accelerating to 60 mph.

Beth reacted instantly. "Prepare to jibe," she ordered.

Max and Andi were at their positions in a second, ready to jibe, Andi handling the genoa sheets and Max the main.

"Jibe ho!" Beth ordered, quickly turning *Red Sky* onto the reciprocal of the incoming speedboat's course. At the same time, she shoved the throttle as far forward as it would go, bouncing the tachometer needle into the red, the tiny 42 hp Volvo diesel groaning at maximum output. The two boats were now on a collision course, head-on to each other.

"Now at least we're facing them bow to bow," Beth said as the distance between the two boats rapidly decreased. "And we can maneuver better close up at nine knots than they can at fifty knots. Leung made a mistake with this move."

Beth kept *Red Sky* on a collision course, headed straight for the oncoming speedboat. When it veered off slightly to starboard, she refused to accept the concession and instead steered closer toward it.

"Way to go, Beth!" Max screamed. He pounded the cockpit seat repeatedly with his fist, caught up in the challenge of the moment. Andi just sat there next to him, rigid with fear, knuckles white from the death grip she had on his knee.

At the very last moment, Beth ended the confrontation by steering *Red Sky* to starboard, permitting the two vessels to finally clear, port side to port side. As the Cigarette sped by, no more than twenty yards away, she couldn't miss the smile on the scarred face of Eddie Huang sitting next to C. K. Leung.

Before she had a chance to congratulate herself, the first of the huge waves generated by the Cigarette's wake hit *Red Sky* broadside. Beth had her hands full trying to prevent a broach. The boats had passed so close to each other that there was no time for *Red Sky* to recover between waves or steer into the wake. She fought desperately to round up into the wind, her sails flapping helplessly, her small engine insufficient to give Beth control.

As the wake diminished, Beth regained full control. She looked behind herself to locate the speedboat and saw it circling around, getting ready for another pass. This time, Andi was watching them through the binoculars.

"Those two clowns in the black suits have got AK-47s in their hands," she reported.

"Quick, Dad," Beth said. "See if you can furl up the genoa. It'll be one less thing to worry about."

Max put the 12-gauge shotgun on safety and laid it down on the seat next to the 20-gauge. He uncleated the furling line, locked a winch handle into the winch, and furiously cranked in the sail with both his hands. The genoa got smaller and smaller as it turned around the forestay until it was completely rolled up. He then stood opposite Andi and waited for the Cigarette to commit itself.

"We're going to come about again so we can show them our bow," Beth said, "but I can tack her this time, so the boom won't be a problem."

They heard the engines on the Cigarette roar into life again and saw her bow leap forward toward them. "Prepare to come about," Beth ordered. "Let her rip." She spun the wheel around, while Andi released one sheet and Max cranked in the other. *Red Sky* answered the helm responsively and did a 180-degree turn. She was once again facing the Cigarette head-on.

As before, the two vessels headed for each other on a collision course, except this time it was the captain of the Cigarette who kept bearing over toward *Red Sky*. "They're better at it this time," Beth observed, intent on handling the maneuver. "If there's any room after they pass, I'm going to turn into their wake and meet it bow first."

Just before the two vessels were about to occupy the same space at the same time, the Cigarette veered sharply and cut directly across the bow of *Red Sky*. To avoid the collision, Beth reflexively jammed the wheel over to the left, throwing *Red Sky* into a hard turn away from the speedboat. Unprepared for the maneuver, Andi was thrown violently off the seat onto the deck. Max reacted quickly, grabbing her protectively around the shoulders before her head could slam into the deck. The boat rolled, nearly broaching. Water poured in over her gunnels as the wake again hit them broadside. The laughter coming from the two armed goons on board the speedboat was unmistakable and unrestrained as they gleefully pointed their AK-47s toward *Red Sky* and enjoyed watching Beth struggle to regain control.

"You okay, Mom?" Beth asked, her attention still concentrated on handling the boat.

"I'm fine," Andi replied, rubbing her elbow as she sat on the bench again. "I wasn't holding on. Don't worry. I'm just pissed at myself for being careless. . . . Where are they?"

"Over to the left, behind you," Max answered, tracking the

other boat's progress through the binoculars. The Cigarette was once again crawling slowly ahead, this time idling about five hundred yards off their port side.

Through the binoculars, Max saw C. K. Leung staring back at them, his face frozen into an expressionless mask. He also saw the AK-47 being aimed at him, but before he had a chance to duck, he heard the gunshot and felt a massive hammer blow on the right side of his head. His head slammed back against a winch.

He sensed the sticky dampness of warm blood running down his neck and calmly laid the binoculars back down on the seat. Though he felt no pain, he knew he had been shot. Maybe being shot didn't hurt so much, he figured, or maybe he was in shock. He made a mental note to tell Andi where his last will and testament was, except he couldn't seem to remember its location. His eyesight became blurred and he felt very dizzy.

Andi was on him before he had a chance to pass out. She saw her life shatter before her eyes while she struggled to apply her emergency training. Despite her tears, ingrained reflexes took over and she continued to function.

She made Max lie down on the cockpit seat, grabbed a nearby towel, and immediately applied pressure to the right side of his head. Blood was pouring out of a deep scalp wound and a badly lacerated right ear. The profuse bleeding had to be stopped.

"I'm fine," Max kept protesting. "It doesn't hurt."

"Hold this towel tight against your scalp and let me look at you."

Beth was distraught, aimlessly steering *Red Sky* in a huge circle while she stared at the only father she had known and the growing circle of his blood on the deck. Like her mother, she ignored her tears while remaining in control of *Red Sky,* one hand on the wheel, one hand on the shotgun. "Mom, what can I do to help?" she asked.

"Pass me the medical kit from under your seat," Andi replied.

"And just keep steering south, sweetheart," Max added in a weak voice, fighting to control his reaction to the increasing pain. "I'll be up to help you as soon as your mother's done with me."

"Quiet! Lie still!" Andi ordered while she poked and probed his body, looking for other injuries, holding her breath for fear of finding one. "Do you want a shot of morphine for the pain?"

"No. I need to stay alert."

"I can't find any other injury. See if you can sit up so I can bandage you."

He tried, and then nausea overwhelmed him. He lay back down, eyes closed. Behind the wheel, Beth paled at the sight of her prostrate idol.

"Open your eyes, Max," Andi commanded. After a few seconds that lasted forever, Max obeyed. "Follow my finger," she continued, moving her index finger across his line of sight and then back again. "Still dizzy?"

"Yes," he said.

"Probably a concussion."

Max sat up with an assist from Andi's arm. When she finished bandaging his head, he resumed watching the Cigarette through his binoculars. She was still idling off to port. Then suddenly, reacting to some sixth sense or maybe because of his peripheral vision, he dropped the glasses and spun toward the hatch opening.

When Max saw Sloane coming out of the hatch wearing a life preserver, with a Glock pistol clutched in his good hand and the yellow bag hanging over his neck, his first impulse was to grab the shotgun. Beth's reflexes were faster, however. She already had it pointed directly at Sloane's chest, finger on the trigger. Sloane looked straight at her, but his pistol was pointed at Andi. Mentally blaming himself for the tragedy about to take place, Max yanked the winch handle out from the winch next to him and with one motion threw it at Sloane. At the same time, he jumped up to interpose himself as a shield between Andi and Sloane's gun.

Seeing their frantic reactions, Sloane quickly dropped the gun into the bag now serving as the sling for his broken arm and raised his good hand into the air. "Jesus Christ, don't shoot!" he shouted. "Calm down, you two. I was only checking to make sure it was loaded before I leave."

"What are you talking about?" Max asked, breathing heavily, trying to regain a semblance of self-control despite his painful head wound.

"I called C.K. on the radio."

"You what?" Beth was astonished and at the same time even angrier at herself for not checking the contents of the yellow bag when Sloane first brought it on board, kicking herself for not keeping a better eye on him.

"I told him to send the dinghy over for me."

"You think you two are just going to kiss and make up?"

"You still don't get it. Leung needs me and the access codes on this CD. That's why I can deal with him."

"But I'm the one shot," Max interjected.

"Listen to me, Counselor. Leung is toying with you because that's how he amuses himself. As soon as he gets tired of this cat-and-mouse game, he'll come at you for real with the dinghy on one side and that speedboat of his on the other. He's got you way outgunned."

"Oh, Max . . ." On hearing Sloane's pronouncement, Andi gasped.

Sloane continued, holding on now to the teak handrail for support. "One way or the other, he won't stop until he's got me. Your only chance is to let me go over to him now."

"Let him go, Max," Andi said. "He's not worth it."

"She's right, Dad. We caught him. We saved him. I don't want you and Mom to die for him."

"Forget it!" Max said, his voice filled with rage. "This is my family and my home. That son of a bitch is not going to harm them or it!"

Smirking at the outburst, Sloane reached over to the seat as if to sit down. Instead, he suddenly took one of the buoyant seat cushions and threw it overboard. Clutching his yellow bag, he stepped over the lifeline and jumped into the water, paddling with his good arm over to the cushion.

As Sloane floated off behind them, Beth jerked *Red Sky* into an emergency turn while Max reached over to unclip the horseshoe buoy. Watching all of this through his binoculars, Leung signaled the captain, and the Cigarette headed toward Sloane.

Max cocked his arm back, preparing to heave the life preserver after Sloane, when he felt Beth's arm firmly restraining him. He took his eyes off Sloane and looked at her. "Let him go, Dad," she said quietly. "It's over and we won. It's time we get back about our lives. Sloane and Leung aren't worth another thought."

Max instinctively tensed but then relaxed his arm, allowing the life preserver to fall to the deck. He again located Sloane in the water, holding on to the white cockpit cushion, kicking with his bare feet. The speedboat approached him slowly and a line was thrown. He missed it the first time but managed to grab it when it was thrown again. He was pulled slowly over to the stern of the speedboat, where the captain helped him climb on board. The cushion from *Red Sky* was left floating in the water, bobbing around in the swells.

Beth didn't need binoculars to see C.K. facing Sloane in the cockpit. They were talking quite animatedly while another man standing in the cockpit, probably Andrew Leung, was gesticulating angrily with his hands, pointing an assault rifle at *Red Sky*.

Their conversation continued for some time, and then suddenly Beth knew it *was* over. No fanfare, no crescendo. She watched as Sloane and Leung apparently reached some kind of accord because each seemed to relax and Andrew Leung put down his rifle. Then the three of them went down into the cabin below. The Cigarette turned slowly away from *Red Sky* before accelerating to full speed and heading off toward the southwest. In minutes, it was a speck on the horizon.

"It's over," Beth said with complete finality. "Let's retrieve the damn cushion and get back on course for Aruba."

Max went back down to the galley and reached into the sink for the bottle of Coke still lying there. It wasn't until he tried to uncap it and pour himself a drink that he realized how badly his hands were trembling. His head hurt, and dizziness was overwhelming him. He made it over to the couch in time to lie down and close his eyes.

A short time later, the radio beeped again, followed by, "*Red Sky*, *Red Sky*. This is the Venezuelan Coast Guard vessel *Simón Bolívar* approaching from your port quarter, over."

"You're a day late and a dollar short," Beth muttered before picking up the microphone to respond. "This is *Red Sky,* over."

"*Red Sky,* we are sorry we were delayed. Are you and your passengers safe?"

"This is *Red Sky.* One of our passengers was taken off against his will, kidnapped by pirates about twenty minutes ago."

"Can you describe the other vessel?"

"It was a forty-five-foot Cigarette speedboat with a black hull. They're heading for Panama and they're heavily armed. They shot our captain too."

"We will alert our helicopter unit stationed on Caracas and also the Colombian coastal patrol. They will intercept the perpetrators before they reach the Canal. Do you require any medical assistance? We have a corpsman on board."

"No, we're okay now. The captain's wound has been stabilized. He's sleeping now. We'll get him further treatment as soon as we land in Aruba."

"Understood."

"Also, there's a badly damaged sailboat with a possible homicide victim on board to the northeast of us. I have the exact location for you here in our log." Beth opened the log and read them the latitude and longitude. "If you need us, you can reach us at Oranjestad for the next few days."

"Very well, *Red Sky. Buena suerte.*"

"Thank you, Coast Guard. This is *Red Sky* out."

Epilogue

Max came back to *Red Sky* and dropped his document case onto the cockpit bench before unhooking the gate and stepping on board. "Okay, that's done," he said. "They extended our visa, and the doctor at the clinic said my wounds are healing nicely and promised me the scars will be very macho."

"What about the stitches?" Andi asked.

"He'll take them out Monday or Tuesday."

"Did you speak to the police?" Beth asked.

"They're still tracking down Vincent's mother on Antigua."

"And C.K.?"

"His extradition hearing starts tomorrow in Panama City. I told the prosecutor there that if our affidavits weren't enough, we'd fly over to testify."

"That would be a pleasure. What about Sloane?"

"C.K. told the police in Panama that Sloane got off their boat in Colón and headed straight to the airport."

"I guess if it's true, he's alive and gone, and if it's not true, he's dead and gone."

"Either way, he's gone."

"Did they locate his bank?"

"It was also in Colón. They traced it from the key you gave them and it's been sealed until someone gets a court order to open it. I see you decided to keep his gold chain."

"It's a war trophy. I couldn't very well scalp him."

"It wouldn't have been a bad idea if he had any hair."

"Hey, take a look at what I found tucked underneath the mattress in the forward cabin." Beth handed him an envelope.

"Sloane left it behind?"

"Or forgot it."

Max opened the envelope and removed a small packet of papers held together by a rubber band. "It's a paid-up life insurance policy," he observed.

"Some offshore carrier located in the Bahamas."

"It's for two million dollars. Bob Talcourt is the beneficiary. I guess Sloane was trying to make it up to him."

"I suppose."

Max put the papers back in the envelope. "I also included that CD you gave me." He handed the envelope back over to Beth.

"Sloane had no idea I have the CD he left for Bob. I'm turning it over to the U.S. attorney when I get back to the city."

"How can you? It's attorney-client privileged."

"Not a problem. Bob is the client. I got it from him in connection with his case, not Paramount's."

"C.K. will find payback a bitch."

"Let him explain those offshore accounts filled with untaxed U.S. income from Arab investors," she agreed, and then without another word, she got up from the bench, stepped onto it, and climbed over to the dock.

"Where are you going?"

"I have to make a call."

"To Bob?"

"Yes."

"You're going to tell him about his father over the *phone*?"

"I don't know. I'll see how the conversation goes."

"Then how about calling Clifford too. He's waiting to hear from you."

"Clifford knows we're here?"

"You should have trusted him with the truth."

"I should have done a lot of things better."

"There's a phone booth at the end of the dock if your cell-phone doesn't work."

"I know. I'll be back in a bit."

Acknowledgments

Thanks to Mel Berger, my superlative literary agent at WME: Mel, you made it happen. It couldn't have been easy for you, and I am most appreciative.

Thanks to Kara Cesare, my great editor at Random House: Kara, you gave me a chance, and for that I am grateful.

Thanks to Elizabeth Rudolph, my real-life navigator. To the extent that the many nautical waypoints described in the sailing scenes are spot-on, she deserves all the credit for her skill and hard work. To the extent that they are incorrect, it is totally my fault for not listening to her.

Thanks to my son, Lawrence C. Rudolph. Larry, you have so many of the good characteristics I wanted for my fictional good guy. You always make me proud, just as you did when we put the evil captain ashore on our sail around the BVI that time. All my love.

Thanks to my daughter Elisabeth R. Marcus. Buffi, you provided the positive traits that inspired my heroine to press on, try hard, and face reality. Thank you for being you. All my love.

Thanks to our good friend Nicki Brown: When she was our neighbor and a bank president, she was generous in answering questions about technical banking procedures.

Thanks to my daughter CDR Monica L. Flynn, USCGR (Ret.), for her valued assistance regarding Coast Guard procedures for nautical emergencies and for being my model step-daughter, sailor, and attorney. All my love and appreciation.

And finally to my daughter Jennifer R. Walsh, literary agent most extraordinaire at WME: You were in on this from the beginning, and it never would have happened without your encouragement. To you, I send all my love and thanks.

About the Author

MICHAEL RUDOLPH is a retired Park Avenue attorney, an ex–New Yorker, and an ex–Connecticut Dodger. His idea of nirvana is to sail off into a Caribbean sunset with his wife, Elizabeth, their golden retriever, and a handful of grandchildren. He sailed his own sailboat on Long Island Sound for many years and chartered other sailboats for extended cruising in the Caribbean. He polished his sailing techniques and blue-water skills with many classes in navigation and seamanship. *Noble Chase* is his first novel.

About the Type

This book was set in Sabon, a typeface designed by the well-known German typographer Jan Tschichold (1902–74). Sabon's design is based upon the original letter forms of sixteenth-century French type designer Claude Garamond and was created specifically to be used for three sources: foundry type for hand composition, Linotype, and Monotype. Tschichold named his typeface for the famous Frankfurt typefounder Jacques Sabon (c. 1520–80).